ABOUT THE AUTHOR

M. A. Anderson has always loved things that go 'bump in the night', and that's why she writes dark fantasy.

Having a love of books and reading from an early age led to an imaginative mind, which produced a love of creating stories for herself. From the age of eight she wrote short stories and song lyrics and progressed to playwriting in her teens.

She is an Australian author who writes Urban fantasy, Supernatural crime thrillers, Young Adult thrillers and Contemporary and Paranormal Romance. Books One, Two and Three in the Dark Legacy series are available on amazon.com, smashwords and other online retailers.

You can find out more about M. A. and her books on her website: http://www.m-anderson.com.au or join her on popular social media sites.

SOUL CHASER

ഓഇരു

M. A. ANDERSON

Bella Luna Books
Australia

Copyright © 2016 M. A. Anderson
Brisbane, Australia

This edition published 2018
Bella Luna Books, Australia

Cover photos from canstockphoto.com
Cover design by Maggie Anderson

National Library of Australia
Cataloguing-in-Publication entry

M. A. Anderson (author)

Soul Chaser

ISBN: 9780992513948 (paperback)

Series: Anderson, M. A. Dark Legacy Bk 3

Urban fantasy/Fantasy fiction

A823.4

For Merlin
2003 - 2014

"Hell is empty
And all the devils are here."

~ *William Shakespeare*
The Tempest, Act 1, scene 2

CHAPTER ONE

Three days after Reece proposed he and Charlotte were at LAX waiting for their flight to Las Vegas. Charlotte was excited as she'd never been to Sin City before. It would be a wonderful vacation—honeymoon, and she couldn't wait to arrive at their hotel. Eloping had been a perfect idea. It would be just them, something intimate and personal only the two of them would share.

Their flight would be boarding in twenty minutes, enough time for her to pop to the restroom and freshen up. "Reece, I'm just going to the bathroom before we board. Won't be long." She picked up her flight bag and headed to the ramp leading to a selection of takeaway stores, vending machines and public conveniences.

No one knew about their plans. Only Tommy and Mrs. Jenkins knew the truth. Reece told Andre after everything they'd been through he and Charlotte needed to get away for a while. If anything urgent came up, he could be contacted on his cell phone.

While Reece waited, he gave Tommy a quick call. He felt guilty for leaving him behind, but this trip was their honeymoon, and you couldn't have a honeymoon with your kids around, could you? "Hey, buddy, how's things?"

"Hi, Reece, everything's good. Mrs. J is making pancakes again. I *looove* pancakes."

Reece laughed. "I think you love food in general."

"Yeah, I think I do," Tommy agreed. "Where's mom?"

"She went to the bathroom. When our flight lands I'll get her to give you a call. Ok?"

"Sure. Tell her I love her."

"I will. We'll bring you back a special surprise from Vegas."

"Gee, thanks. Now I'm excited."

Reece checked the time on his cell phone. "Hey, buddy, I better go hustle your mom up. Our flight's almost ready to board."

"Ok. Have fun. Take lots of photos. See you when you get back."

"We will. Love from mom… and me."

He stood up and gazed around the waiting area to see if Charlotte was on her way back. She wasn't. She said she wouldn't be long and it had been fifteen minutes since she'd left. He pressed speed dial. The phone rang for a few seconds then her voicemail kicked in. He left a message. "Hey, hon, where are you? Our flight will be boarding in five."

Reece collected his flight bag, Charlotte's purse and jacket and followed the direction she had taken. When he reached the ladies restroom, he waited outside contemplating whether or not to go in. His gut tightened. He tried her number again. As he did, he heard the musical ring of her cell phone getting closer and thought she was on her way out. Instead, a woman came out of the restroom with Charlotte's things.

"Excuse me, those belong to my fiancée," he said, pointing to the bag and phone in the woman's hand.

"Oh? Here you go." She handed them to him. "They were sitting on the vanity. I was going to hand them to security because I thought someone must have left them by mistake."

Reece frowned at her, then at the bag and phone. "No one was with them or near them?"

The woman shook her head. "Sorry, no."

"Ok, thanks."

The woman smiled. "I hope you find her before your flight."

"Yeah, me too." He headed back to where they'd been sitting. Charlotte wasn't there. *Where'd she go? She wouldn't have gotten cold feet, would she?* Reece didn't know what to think. He continued past the waiting area and made his way to the airline counter. "Excuse me."

The young woman smiled. "Yes? Can I help you, sir?"

"Can you broadcast a request for Charlotte Delaney to come to the counter, please? Our flight is boarding and I can't find her."

The woman gave him a concerned look. "Oh? Of course." She picked up the telephone receiver and pressed a button on the base. "Would passenger Charlotte Delaney please come to the Alaska Airlines reservations counter? Charlotte Delaney. Thank you."

"Thanks." Reece turned around and scanned the people moving about the airport. No sign of Charlotte.

"I hope you find her. If you have any problems we can change your reservation to a later flight."

"I appreciate it, thanks." Reece moved to the side and waited. After ten minutes he asked the young woman to change their reservation and went back to where he'd been sitting. He dropped the bags onto a chair and sat down. *It doesn't make any sense. Charlotte wouldn't have run off like this.*

Reece sprang forward and snatched Charlotte's flight bag off the seat beside him. He unzipped it and pulled it open. Sitting inside was a note. He picked it up, his heart hammering, and unfolded it. Had she changed her mind? Had she taken off?

He read the words scrawled in black.

'If you want to see your lady again, alive, you'll do exactly what you're told. DO NOT inform the authorities. Board your flight and act as though nothing has happened. If anyone asks, your companion got sick and couldn't make the trip. You'll be given further instruction in Vegas.'

Could this be the work of MacKinnon? Was it his revenge from the grave?

ᚪᚲᚷ

Reece couldn't relax during the flight. All he could think about was Charlotte and what could be happening to her. No one knew where they were going, except for Tommy and Mrs. Jenkins, and he knew neither of them would give the information to anyone. Not even Andre. So who had found out their flight itinerary and how?

The flight was twenty minutes into its forty five minute journey and Reece wished they were already on the ground. He felt confined and useless sitting in the half empty plane unable to do anything. He wanted to get there, head to the hotel and wait for the next communication from whoever had Charlotte. This trip was meant to be a wonderful beginning to their married life and now it had turned into another horrible nightmare.

He had contacted Andre before boarding and hoped he'd be on the next flight out. They had to figure out who these people were, if they were people. Could be more monsters for all he knew. Why Charlotte? Hadn't she been through enough? Was this whole scenario something to do with her or something to do with him? Some kind of payback?

A flight attendant asked if he needed anything and he said no. What he did need was to know Charlotte was still alive.

He pulled the window shade down and closed his eyes. When he opened them again, the pilot announced they were five minutes out of McCarran International and gave a running commentary of the weather conditions. Passengers were requested to fasten their seatbelts and put away all devices before landing.

Reece was relieved and clipped in his belt. He wished he could check his cell phone. Why couldn't someone develop a way for passengers to use their goddamn phones inflight?

The landing was smooth and Reece was glad he had a seat close to the exit. As soon as the plane taxied up the tarmac to the terminal and the door opened he'd be out and on his way to the hotel.

Inside McCarran International, Reece headed to the luggage pickup carousel to collect his and Charlotte's luggage. This should have been the happiest moment of their lives, preparing for their wedding tonight. Instead, he was heading to their hotel alone wondering if he'd ever see her again.

His cell phone vibrated and he whipped it out of his shirt pocket to check the text message. 'At LAX. On next flight out. See you soon.' Reece breathed a sigh of relief. At least with Andre here they could cover more ground. And, if anything or anyone supernatural was involved he'd know. It might give them an advantage.

Reece picked up his rental car, threw the luggage in the trunk and drove out of the parking garage, heading for the older part of Las Vegas, Fremont Street and the Golden Nugget Hotel.

Vegas was a 24/7 hustle. No one slept. Even the roads were congested with a sea of tourist traffic making their way from one venue to the next. It was right on sunset, the time when the city looked her best, and Charlotte would have been in awe of the glitz and glamour of sparkling Sin City. He had seen it all before and it didn't impress him, but he would have loved showing his beautiful bride around.

Reece turned onto South Casino Center Boulevard, continued through the menagerie of pedestrians and cars and pulled into the Golden Nugget's valet parking. He popped the trunk, left the keys in the ignition and grabbed his flight bag. A bellhop informed him his luggage would be in his room by the time he finished at the front desk. Reece handed him five dollars and headed through the brass and glass doors into the foyer.

While he waited in the queue, he noticed a woman dressed in a gypsy costume standing by the steps, watching him. At first he thought he'd imagined it, but after a few minutes he knew he was her target.

After collecting his plastic swipe key for the room, Reece scanned the lobby. The woman was gone. He climbed the steps and headed along the carpeted walkway, past the huge pool and assorted restaurants, to the elevator banks. He pushed the button and waited. While he stood in the center of the lobby, he spotted movement from the corner of his eye and turned his head. The gypsy was at the entrance.

"Is there something you want?" Reece asked, his voice tight. Seeing her again made him feel uneasy. He didn't like it.

The gypsy woman sauntered up to him. "Perhaps there is something *you* want. You are missing something, yes? I have seen your future Reece Daniels. There is *death* in it." She turned on her heel and disappeared into the hotel.

Reece rushed to the entrance and scanned the sea of hotel patrons. She was gone. How did the woman know his name? And whose death did she mean?

CHAPTER TWO

Charlotte woke up in a seedy motel room gagged and with her wrists attached to the old metal bedhead behind her. What had happened? She could smell something. What was it? Chloroform! Someone had drugged her and taken her from the airport. Her heart thudded against her ribs as she gazed around the hazy room and panic washed over her.

Tears stung her eyes. This was meant to be her wedding day. Reece must have been out of his mind with worry. She rubbed her engagement ring finger against her middle finger. The ring was gone! Why? Who brought her here? And where was here? Was she in Las Vegas or still in LA?

Charlotte tried to see over her head in the gloom. She was flat on her back with no pillow under her head. Using her weight to pull herself backwards along the bed, she caught sight of the glint of metal. Handcuffs. She tugged and tugged, but couldn't free herself.

Something else she noticed too. She was in her underwear and her feet were bare. Where were her clothes and shoes? Why had she been undressed? If she could get free she wouldn't hesitate to run in only her underwear. To hell with vanity when your life is at stake.

The room smelt of stale cigarette smoke and beer, so did the bed she was on and a prickling sensation crawled over her skin.

Charlotte lifted her head and glanced at the open venetian blind. An orange light cast intermittent swatches of color across the dirty window pane and she could see a reflection. What was it? Part of the name looked like a number. There were dozens of motels across the country with numbers in their name. She could be anywhere.

The tears she'd held back slid from the corners of her eyes and down her cheeks. How could she get free? She tugged at the cuffs again, knowing the futility of her actions, but this time she felt something slice her skin and the warm sensation of blood trickling down her arm. Charlotte held in the sob threatening to escape. She had to stay strong for her son's sake or she might not get out of this at all.

She pictured Tommy in her mind and was calming down when she heard voices outside the door. A woman and a man. Were they coming in? The woman's laugh was sultry, seductive. The way a woman laughs when she's in the mood for sex. Was she in a hooker motel? The voices passed the door and continued along the walkway. Charlotte let out the breath she'd been holding in one long rush.

An idea came to her. If she bent her thumb as far into the palm of her hand as she could and twisted her wrist in the cuff she might be able to pull free. The blood would act as a lubricant and maybe she could slip her hand out. She worked to free herself but the cuff was too tight. Her head dropped back onto the stale bedspread and more tears spilled.

How long had she been here? It was sundown, so it had to be a few hours. She knew Reece would be looking for her. He'd have the team out searching. But without any clue as to her whereabouts how would they find her?

CHAPTER THREE

By the time Andre arrived at the Golden Nugget it was after 8 PM. He entered the foyer and headed to the elevator banks. Once inside, he called Reece. When he came out of the elevator hub on the fourteenth floor and walked along the hallway, his friend was standing outside the room waiting for him. Andre gave him a man hug and asked if he'd heard anything. Reece told him he hadn't.

Inside the room, Reece showed Andre the note left in Charlotte's bag and told him about the gypsy woman. After reading the instructions, Andre asked if he believed Charlotte was in Las Vegas. Reece said at first he didn't think so, but now he believed she could be. Why would whoever took her have him fly all the way to Vegas unless they'd brought her here?

Andre suggested they go in search of the gypsy woman and question her about what she knew. She had to be involved in Charlotte's abduction, otherwise why would she have approached Reece? Perhaps she was part of an act performing in the hotel or another one nearby. They checked the Vegas entertainment guide in the room and found nothing relating to a gypsy show.

Reece told Andre he needed to get out of the hotel room for a while or he'd go stir crazy, so the pair headed out to Fremont Street. The undercover arcade was packed with tourists, performers and stalls. As the two men wandered through the hordes watching the lightshow, keeping an eye out for anything gypsy related, they spotted a fortune telling wagon on the left not far ahead of them. The sign emblazoned in large white letters on the side of the colorful wooden caravan read *Madame Vadoma Sees All In Her Crystal Ball*. Reece stalked over to the wagon and burst inside. No one was there. The cardboard clock hanging outside the door indicated she would be back in an hour. Was she the woman they were looking for?

Andre held one of the gypsy's scarves and used his senses in an attempt to locate her. An image of a woman in costume appeared in his mind sitting at a table outside the Tasti D Lite ice cream shop half way along Fremont Street. He and Reece pushed through the pedestrian traffic and raced to the store. By the time they got there the woman was gone.

Reece stood with his hands on his hips and did a 360 degree turn, his eyes scanning the entire area and the people moving about. "Where the hell did she go?"

"Don't know. But I sense she isn't going to make it easy for us."

"Yeah? Well we'll keep her wagon under surveillance until she comes back. She'll have to at some point." Reece took a final look around the crowded street. He couldn't believe she'd managed to escape them.

The pair made their way back to the wagon and when they reached it found it was locked. Reece came to the conclusion she had to be working with someone. Were they involved in Charlotte's disappearance? The answer would only reveal itself when they found the woman.

As they headed back to the Golden Nugget, Reece received a text message telling him to be at the Luxor Hotel by 10 PM. And to come alone. Someone would make contact with him there. He wondered how they knew Andre was with him. Were they being watched? He glanced over his shoulder and moved his eyes around the crowd. Could be anyone. How would he know?

Back in their room on the 14th floor of the Carson Tower, Reece and Andre discussed what their next step would be. The room phone rang, interrupting their conversation and Reece gave Andre an uncertain look. He had never felt so unsure of himself. This was personal.

"Answer it. It might be them," Andre told him.

Reece picked up the receiver and took a deep breath before placing the phone to his ear. "Hello?"

"Is this Reece Daniels?"

"Who's asking?" Reece's voice tightened.

"Sheriff Lozano, LVPD. I need to speak with Reece Daniels urgently. It's an official police matter."

"You've reached him. What can I do for you?"

The sheriff cleared his throat. "We've got a couple… unusual cases I'd like your opinion on. Are you available to assist while you're in Vegas?"

"How did you know I was here?" Reece didn't like being so easy to find.

"Not much gets by us. We always know who's visiting our city. We have a good relationship with border protection."

"It still doesn't answer the question, does it?"

"Your girlfriend's babysitter told me. But our guys at the airport do have a good working relationship with border protection." He chuckled.

Reece shook his head. Why had Mrs. Jenkins given a total stranger the information? The sheriff must have been very persuasive. "I'm working a case right now and don't have the time."

The sheriff sighed. "We could really use your input. These deaths are unorthodox to say the least. Look, I understand you're busy and all, but if I could stop by and talk to you it wouldn't take up much of your time."

Reece ran the information around his brain for a moment. Unorthodox deaths? It meant only one thing. Something unnatural was loose in the city. "We'll come to you. Where's your office?"

"Thanks. Appreciate it. Got a pen?"

Reece opened the bedside drawers and took out a notepad and hotel pen. "Yeah, go ahead."

"Four hundred South Martin Luther King Boulevard. Can I expect you in the morning?"

"We'll be there at nine." He hung up and turned to Andre. "The Sheriff's got some deaths they can't explain. He wants us to take a look."

"So we're meeting him in the morning?"

"Yeah. My gut tells me some otherworldly activity is going on here. I don't know how much Sheriff Lozano knows, but I think he's suspicious. Why else would he contact me?"

"Maybe you should talk to him about Charlotte."

"And put her life in more danger than it is already?" He shook his head. "Not an option."

Andre walked over to him. "It might be the only way we can find out if she's here."

Reece gave him a skeptical frown. "How? They would've taken the highway. I doubt they'd put her on a plane."

"They grabbed her at LAX, Reece. Maybe they did."

The PI's cell phone rang and he answered it. "Hello?"

"Bring your vampire friend with you tonight and don't be late," the distorted voice on the other end of the phone said. The line went dead.

CHAPTER FOUR

While Charlotte struggled to free herself, she wondered why no one had come back to check on her or move her or… she didn't want to think about the frightening possibility. What was the abductor's motive? Reece had been concerned about MacKinnon orchestrating some kind of payback from the grave, but Charlotte didn't think it had his style of revenge. He would have implemented a clean sweep and none of them would have ever been found. No it didn't feel like MacKinnon.

Could she have been dumped here? Perhaps no one planned to come back for her. She tried to scream, but because of the gag her voice sounded muffled, small. No one could hear her, or if they did they might get the wrong idea. Kinky sex games. No one would bother to come to her rescue.

If the room had been paid up for several weeks, and no one came back, she would die here. Panic reared its fearful head once again, tears filled her eyes and beads of sweat broke out across her forehead. She tugged and tugged frantically at the cuffs, hoping one would snap open and set her free. They didn't.

How could she escape this nightmare?

Charlotte struggled to turn herself over so she could get onto her knees. It was difficult to do without the use of her hands and by the time she managed it her body trembled from the exertion. She crawled up the bed and examined how the cuffs were attached to the head. She could slide them along the rail to the center floral decal. But what then? She needed something to pick the lock. Her eyes moved to the dark wood, art deco bedside table blending into the gloom, and wondered if anything had been left behind by a previous occupant. A hair pin would make the perfect lock picking tool.

She squeezed her left leg out from underneath her, swung her foot toward the drawers and tried to latch her toes onto the handle. Her foot slipped off. She tried again and her toes gripped the round wooden knob and pulled the drawer open. She used her foot as her hand. A worn Gideon bible sat inside. Charlotte pushed the top drawer shut and aimed for the second drawer. When she stuck her foot inside it was full of candy wrappers, empty cigarette packets and a couple of used syringes. She screwed up her nose and shoved the drawer shut. The bottom one would be harder to maneuver.

Charlotte pushed her left foot onto the floor and tried to stand up but the distance from her cuffed hands to the bedside table was too great and she toppled over onto the Queen-sized bed. She kneeled on her right knee again and aimed for the knob with her foot. After a struggle, the drawer slid open and caught half way. Charlotte dipped her toes inside and felt around. Something soft and rubbery caught between her big toe and her second one and she realized it was a used condom.

She shook her foot several times before the gross sperm balloon flicked from her toes. Thank God it was old. She wasn't sure she wanted to try again, but knew she had no choice. Using her big toe as a feeler she prodded around the edges of the wooden square and felt something wedged into the seam. Her heartbeat quickened. Could it be a hair pin or a paper clip? She didn't care which as long as it unlocked the handcuffs.

The question was, now that she'd found something to help free herself with how was she going to get it out of the drawer?

CHAPTER FIVE

Reece and Andre climbed into the rental and headed for the strip. It wouldn't take more than fifteen minutes, even with traffic, so they'd have enough time to park and make their way into the Luxor. It took longer than expected to locate a parking spot and Reece's gut shrank into a tight ball. He couldn't afford to be late. Charlotte's life depended on it.

As they wandered into the building along the walkway, Reece realized it was some distance to get inside the pyramid-shaped hotel from the rear parking lot. Time they didn't have. The pair stepped up their pace.

Once inside, they took the escalator down to the Grand Atrium and waited in front of the huge stone statues of Ramses II. Reece was edgy and kept checking his watch. 9.58 PM. Two more minutes. Why did they want him to bring Andre? How did they even know Andre was in Vegas?

Time was ticking.

Could the abductors want some kind of trade off? Charlotte for Andre? Reece turned the idea over in his mind. Could he trade his best friend for his girlfriend—fiancée? He hoped he wouldn't have to choose.

One minute after ten.

Reece glanced at Andre. He could tell his friend had put out his immortal feelers to see if he could pick up on who the contact was. Get an anxious vibe, read their mind. With people everywhere, it could have been anyone. The PI checked his watch again, something he never did. In fact, he rarely wore a watch. He hated being governed by a time piece.

Two minutes after ten.

No one approached them. Andre and Reece gazed around the huge, crowded space. Where was the contact?

Above the din of voices, Reece heard his name over the public address system. Andre's sensitive hearing homed in on the entire message. "Come on, they want you over at the reservations counter."

The pair made their way across the crowded atrium and as they approached the long counter a young woman on staff waved them over. "Reece Daniels?"

"Yes. What's this about?" He frowned at her.

"Before I can tell you anything, I need to see some form of ID."

Reece sighed, took his wallet from the back pocket of his jeans and pulled out his PI license. "Will this do?"

The woman took the plastic card, checked to make sure the photo matched the person and passed it back. "Here you are." She handed him a large brown business envelope.

Reece scrutinized the paper parcel then looked at her. "Who left this?"

"Sorry, I wasn't on shift when it was delivered. I can check with my manager if you like."

"Yes, I would. Thanks."

The young woman was gone several minutes. When she returned she said, "It was delivered to the hotel by courier." Her eyebrows rose. "Any help?"

"Not really, but thanks anyway."

He and Andre headed for the car. Reece was anxious to open the envelope but didn't in case they were being watched. He wouldn't give whoever had Charlotte the satisfaction of observing his reaction to its contents.

Out in the parking lot, Reece had the feeling someone's eyes were on them. He had an uncomfortable tingle between his shoulder blades, the kind you experience when you're being followed. He turned around. Too many people moving in and out of the hotel. No one looked suspicious.

When the pair got into the rental Reece ripped open the envelope and turned it upside down. Photos dropped onto his lap. He picked them up. They were pictures of Charlotte unconscious, in her underwear, gagged and handcuffed to a bed in a dank motel room. He handed them to Andre. "I can only hope she's still alive."

Andre looked at the photos. "She is. Just keep believing it."

Reece gave the envelope another shake. A note dropped out. He snatched it up with trembling fingers and opened it.

'Glad you made it on time. For your girlfriend's sake. So far so good. We'll be in touch.'

He balled up the note and threw it at the windshield. "They're playing with us. We have to find the gypsy."

℘℘℘

After the pair dropped off the rental at the valet parking and grabbed a bite to eat, it was almost 11.30 PM. Reece and Andre stepped out of the elevator and headed to the room. The PI was exhausted, but knew he couldn't sleep. He planned to do a bit of research on the Sheriff, just to be sure. When they reached their room the door was ajar. Reece's heckles went up and he pulled his Glock from the back of his belt underneath his shirt. He never went anywhere without it.

He waved Andre back, moved up to the door and pushed it open with his foot. It banged against the wall as he rushed into the room. Andre followed.

Their room had been ransacked. Clothes and personal effects were strewn across the bed and the floor.

What were they looking for?

Half an hour later, hotel security arrived. They went over the events of the evening. What time the pair had left, how long they were gone and what they found when they returned? Did they touch anything? Reece told the guy he was an ex-detective and knew not to corrupt a crime scene.

Andre and Reece were fingerprinted to eliminate them from the investigation, and the room was dusted.

While security wrote up the report, sheriff Lozano entered their room. He'd heard about the break and enter from hotel management and once he knew it was the PI's room drove straight over. He marched up to the pair. "When I heard the break in was here I sent my guy over to assist." He gave Reece a curious frown. "Looks like someone was looking for something. Any idea what?"

"No. There's nothing here anyone would want, just personal effects and clothes." Reece folded his arms. "Maybe someone did it for kicks?"

The sheriff pursed his lips and gazed around the messed up room.

"Don't think so. The Golden Nugget runs a tight ship. Anything missing?" He looked at the PI and raised a questioning eyebrow.

Reece wasn't prepared to tell him Charlotte's suitcase had been taken. Right now he didn't know who he could trust.

"Not sure. We haven't had a chance to check."

Sheriff Lozano closed his notebook and stuffed it into his shirt pocket along with the pen. "Well when you do let us know. It'll need to go in both reports."

"Yeah, ok."

Security was done and so was the crime scene technician, now all Reece had to do was get rid of the sheriff so he and Andre could go through the mess and find out what was missing, apart from Charlotte's suitcase.

It was after 1.00 AM and it didn't seem as though Lozano would leave any time soon.

"Is there anything else, Sheriff? My pal and I are beat, it's pretty late. And we still have the clean up before we can get some sleep." He gestured at the mess.

The sheriff gazed around the room. He knew they weren't telling him the whole story. "I guess it can wait till morning." He was about to walk out the door when he got a call on his radio.

"Hey chief, we've got another one. Can you get forensics over here ASAP? We're in the parking lot behind Circus Circus near the corner of Industrial Drive."

Lozano pressed the button on the speaker mic attached to his shoulder. "Ok. I'll have someone out there as soon as I can." He released the button. "Jesus!"

Reece and Andre frowned at him. "What is it?" Reece asked.

Sheriff Lozano looked the PI in the eye. "It's another one of those unorthodox deaths I was planning to talk to you about tomorrow. Do you think you've got the energy to come take a look?"

CHAPTER SIX

Charlotte lay exhausted after trying for hours to work the wedged object out of the crevice in the drawer. Her arms ached, her toes ached and she had sliced her big toe on the edge of whatever it was she was trying to maneuver out of the corner. Her mind was a jumble of confused thoughts and emotions. What if she never got free? An overwhelming sense of giving up washed over her and tears stung her eyes. She blinked them back and closed her eyes. Her son's face appeared: 'I love you mom.'

"I love you too, sweetie," she said as tears spilled down her cheeks. Her heart ached. Would she ever see Tommy again?

The gloom and silence of the room pressed in on her like a suffocating fog. Would she die in this place?

A sound in the hallway caused her eyes to snap open and her anxious gaze darted to the door. She could see a shadow in the crack of light underneath it. Someone was outside. Someone was about to come in.

Charlotte's heartbeat thumped against her ribs and her breathing became quick and choppy. This was the moment she'd been dreading. Whoever had taken her was here. Would this be her final moments on earth? Was she about to die?

The door opened and bright light from the landing spilled into the dark space. The figure in the doorway was indistinguishable. Could have been male or female. They had something standing on the ground beside them.

Charlotte's eyes widened when she realized it was her suitcase. *How did they get my luggage?*

The person grabbed the handle and wheeled the bulky red case into the room.

Dressed in dark clothing with a hood covering their face, they blended into the gloom and became invisible when the door closed.

Charlotte strained her ears to listen for any movement in the dark space. She was alone with an assailant she couldn't see.

CHAPTER SEVEN

Sheriff Lozano arrived at Circus Circus twenty minutes after the call. He, Reece and Andre stepped out of the vehicle and headed over to the crime scene. The area had been cordoned off with the patrol car sitting at the corner of the parking lot, strobe lights flashing. Forensics was already analyzing the scene and collecting evidence.

Lozano made a beeline for his men. Reece and Andre followed.

Officer Reynolds walked over to the trio.

"Same as the others?" Lozano asked.

"Yeah, boss." Reynolds flipped the visor of his police cap off his forehead, his face pale. "I don't get it. How the hell can a body look like that?" He jabbed his finger toward the covered corpse.

The sheriff shook his head. "I don't know. Any ID?"

"No. But it's male. Just like the others."

Lozano turned to Reece. "Wanna take a look?"

"Sure." He and Andre followed him over.

Officer Domingo had asked forensics to pull back so the sheriff and the PIs could examine the scene. He lifted the cover as they approached.

When the three men reached the body Reece and Andre stared at each other. They hadn't seen anything like it before, although they had researched demons with the capability of killing in this way.

The sheriff stared at the remains. "What could do this to a person?" He lifted his serious gaze to Reece as if he knew the PI had the information he needed.

"What makes you think I have the answer?" He folded his arms.

Lozano stared into Reece's eyes, his serious expression remaining on him. "I've heard things about you." He sighed. "Things I thought were crazy… until this." He motioned toward the body. "You know about this kinda stuff, don't you?"

Andre crouched beside the victim and ran the palm of his hand over the entire length of the body to see if he could pick up anything. He did. Vampire. And something else. Demon?

The sheriff watched him. "What's he doing?"

Reece considered his options, which were minimal. Should he come clean or tell the cop his suspicions were way off? As the two men observed Andre at work, he realized it would be difficult to refute Lozano's insinuation, given the circumstances.

"What do you know, Sheriff?"

Lozano's right eyebrow rose. "What do you mean?"

"Come on, Sheriff Lozano, you've implied my partner and I know more than we're telling. What's your take on what happened here?"

The sheriff blew out a noisy breath. "I think," his gaze moved from Reece to the body, "it's unnatural." He looked at the PI again. "I think there's something dark about these deaths. Something…"

Reece frowned at him. "Supernatural?"

"Yeah." Lozano nodded and crossed himself.

Andre joined the pair. "Can we discuss this somewhere private?"

The sheriff frowned. "Sure. We can go to my office."

On the way back to the car, Andre pulled Reece up. "There are vampires here, but there's something different about them. They don't just drink the blood they suck the soul out of their victim."

The PI remembered reading about demons who drained their host to gain more power. Succubus and Incubus. But they were meant to seduce their victims in their dreams while they slept, not in the real world.

"What do you think it is?"

"It could be a succubus, but I'll need to jump on a computer and do some research. I wish Adrian was here, he'd know the answer."

Reece looked at his friend, his expression pained. They had lost a good man (vampire) in their battle against the Alpha. "So do I, Andre, so do I." He sighed. "What about Sarah? She has an extensive knowledge base on otherworldly creatures and their habits."

"I'll see what I can find out first before bringing anyone else into this. It could be too dangerous."

They reached Lozano's car and the sheriff turned around. "Whatever you two know, I want in. We need to catch whoever or whatever's doing this and get them off our streets before more men are murdered. One of my officers was a victim. I got him lying in the county coroners. He was a good man. His family wants to bury him, but until we have something substantial we can't release the body."

"Ok. Let's get back to your office and we'll fill you in." Reece climbed into the front passenger seat and closed the door.

Lozano remained outside the vehicle staring at Andre. "Why did you run your hand over the body? Are you a psychic or something?"

Andre had no intention of disclosing what he was to the sheriff. "I've had this gift for a long time and it's never failed me. I trust it." He could see the wheels turning in Lozano's brain as the sheriff digested what he'd told him, his eyes never leaving Andre for a second.

Reece pressed the button on the armrest to wind down the window. "Are we going? The sun'll be up in a couple of hours and I'd like to get some sleep before then."

Good save.

⅓⅔

Back at LVMPD headquarters, the three men sat in Lozano's office discussing the deaths. The sheriff showed them crime scene photos of the first three victims and the forensic reports. Which to his mind meant nothing as the information was inconclusive and couldn't shed any light on the perpetrator.

The sheriff sat behind his desk watching the two men paw over the evidence files. What was it about them he couldn't decipher? He wasn't sure about Andre Delacroix; something about the man made him uncomfortable and put his senses on alert. He'd joined the force because he'd always had a sixth sense about people and thought his intuition could do some good.

Andre felt Lozano's eyes on him. Did he suspect what he was? Whether the sheriff knew it about himself or not he was an intuitive.

"So, after looking over what we've got, what do you think?"

Reece glanced up from the report he was reading. "I agree with you. It's definitely not a human perpetrator. Have you heard of succubus?"

Lozano crossed himself and kissed his St. Jude medallion. "I always hoped it was only superstitious mumbo jumbo. You're telling me they're real?"

"There are elements at work here defying explanation. Somehow the boundary between hell and earth has ruptured and the inhabitants have penetrated our world." Reece waited for a reaction.

The sheriff's eyes moved from the pair to his desk. He stared at the case files and allowed the information to settle into the processing center of his brain. Hell had a way in? His gut shrank as the knowledge imparted made sense to him now. He'd seen things, heard things, but didn't want to believe them. Now he had no choice.

CHAPTER EIGHT

Charlotte's nervous eyes searched the shadows in the room. Where was her abductor? How close were they? He or she was playing mind games with her, unravelling her nerves so she would be an easy target. She was an easy target handcuffed to the bed, but she wouldn't give up without a fight. At least her legs were free and she would use them as a weapon. She'd kick out and strike back.

She wished she could talk to whoever was concealed in the dark watching her. If she wasn't gagged, she could try to reason with them. Talk them out of whatever they planned to do to her. Somewhere in the back of her subconscious her detective logic kicked in and Charlotte realized nothing she could say would make a difference. The abductor had an agenda and she was it. Whatever scenario was to play out would happen no matter what she did. She blinked back the sting of tears. She would not fall apart now. Her life depended on it.

The shadow moved toward her and Charlotte's heartbeat accelerated so fast she thought it would burst through her ribs and out of her chest. Her breathing turned shallow, choppy, and her head swam. No! She would not pass out. As the figure moved closer, Charlotte's eyes widened. What were they going to do to her?

A gloved hand reached out of the gloom and ran a taunting finger down her arm. Charlotte gasped and flinched.

"We're done here." The male voice sounded strange. Was it another creature from beyond the boundary of hell? Or did the person have a voice distorting device to disguise their identity? Could it be someone she knew?

The hand grabbed her forearm, squeezing her aching muscles like a vice as it pulled her arm closer.

Charlotte felt the prick of a needle.

Was it lethal? A noiseless way to end her life?

Her ears whooshed, she felt the weight of her body sag into the mattress and her last thought was she hoped she'd wake up again.

CHAPTER NINE

Reece and Andre left LVMPD headquarters at sunrise. There had been no time to sleep because they needed to figure out who had killed the four men lying in the Clark County Coroner's office before another man was attacked.

Sheriff Lozano was very receptive to the information they had offered him. He told them all of his life he'd had a feeling there was something, but didn't want to believe his instincts. He also said he was grateful for their help. Now all they had to do was find the perpetrator.

Reece had concerns of his own to deal with and told Lozano he couldn't devote all of his time to assisting with the case. The sheriff understood it was a professional courtesy.

Andre maintained Reece should talk to the sheriff about Charlotte, but he wouldn't. The PI didn't want to jeopardize getting her back alive and suspected that if the abductors found out—because they seemed to be aware of what was going on—they would kill her. It wasn't a risk he was prepared to take.

The cleanup took an hour out of their morning. And they discovered nothing else had been taken except Charlotte's suitcase. What were they hoping to find inside it?

Without sleep and a bucket of caffeine to keep the adrenalin pumping, Reece set about researching Vegas shows with a supernatural element and the characteristics of the succubus. Andre checked out hotel booking sites. The interior photos of the motels could help them find Charlotte.

While the pair worked at different ends of the room the phone rang. Reece snatched it up. "Hello?"

"Why are you talking to the police?" The voice asked.

"The sheriff asked me to assist with the murders. I'm sure you've read the papers." He jumped up off the bed and paced. "Is Charlotte all right? Can I talk to her?" He knew he sounded desperate but he didn't care. He wanted to know she was still alive.

The line went dead.

"Shit!"

Andre stood up and walked over to him. "They know."

Reece slammed the receiver down. "Yeah. This is why I didn't want to complicate things. Who knows what they'll do now." He dropped down onto the bed and buried his face in his hands. "God, Charlotte."

"We're going to find her." Andre rested a reassuring hand on his friend's shoulder.

Reece looked up at him. "How? We've got nothing."

"Because I found a motel with rooms matching the one Charlotte's in. It's south of the highway."

Reece was on his feet. "Let's go." As he headed to the door his cell phone rang. "Hello."

"It's Enrique Lozano, another body's been found. Can you meet me at the scene?"

"Not right now. I'm on my way to a possible crime scene of my own."

The sheriff sighed. "Ok. I understand. Can we meet up later?"

"We'll come to you after we're done. It's the best I can offer." Reece knew Lozano wasn't happy. His silence confirmed it. But Charlotte was more important right now.

"I'd really prefer to have you at the scene, but if you can't, you can't. I'll see you in my office when you can get there." He rang off.

Andre frowned. "We need to find out who's sucking the life out of these men before more are killed."

Reece took a deep breath and let it out through his nostrils. "This couldn't be worse timing. We need to find Charlotte and deal with whoever took her. I don't have time to chase wanton demons hell bent on sexual gratification as well. Let's just get over to the motel and see what we can find there." Reece hoped the element of surprise could prove advantageous.

ෂ්ටෝ

Sheriff Lozano arrived at the crime scene in record time. As soon as the call came through, he was on his feet and heading out the door. This body made number five in a line of bizarre deaths which left no logical explanation, although he knew part of the reason behind them now. Something unnatural was killing these men for sexual pleasure. All he wanted to know was who the demon was in human form and how to apprehend them. Or eliminate them, whichever was the necessary outcome.

He wished he could clue his officers in on the logistics of the case, but knew he couldn't. He'd be laughed out of the precinct and branded a fear monger. Perhaps in time some of his men might accept the truth, but he knew that time wasn't now.

Lozano got out of his car and headed over to the scene. Officers Lucas and Moreno had been the ones who received the 911 call. The sheriff hoped they'd found something to shed some light on who the victim was. So far it had been difficult for the forensic team to identify the bodies due to the decomposition of the flesh and organs. Well, not decomp so much, more like mummification. Each victim looked like a shriveled raisin. The life force, along with their blood had been sucked clean out of them. Lozano couldn't imagine the agony they must have endured being devoured alive.

The only one to be identified so far was Officer Bobby MacMillan because of the serial number on his hip replacement. He had fallen off a two story building in the line of duty and shattered his pelvis and hip joint. Why he'd been where he was found was anyone's guess. A happily married man didn't frequent the red light district. *And he was a happily married man.* It was obvious to Lozano his officer had been lured there.

The sheriff's men were freaking out about the new find. What was he supposed to tell them?

ෂ්ටෝ

Reece pulled the rental into the parking lot of the rundown motel and he and Andre got out of the car and surveyed the building before making their way to the office. The guy behind the counter wearing a manager's tag didn't bother to glance up when they entered. The bell should have been a dead giveaway, but he was engrossed in some program on the television.

Reece jabbed the counter call bell a few times and the guy moved his unimpressed gaze toward the pair. "You're cops, right?"

"Private investigators." Reece flashed his PI license at the guy.

"No difference. Cops are cops. What do you want?" He turned the volume down on the portable television sitting in front of him and stood up. Reece thought that model of TV had been discontinued years ago. The whole office had an original retro look to it, like something out of the Twilight Zone... or Psycho. Could definitely do with some renovations.

Reece showed him a photo of Charlotte. "Seen this woman?"

"Nope." The guy said without moving his eyes to the picture.

Reece sighed. "It might help if you actually look at the photo." He pushed it at the guy.

"Why, she in some kinda trouble?"

Andre stepped around his friend and stared into the guy's eyes. "You'll tell us what we want to know without any difficulty." He stepped back.

The guy passed the photo back to Reece. "Yeah. I had a phone call saying a woman was arriving. They said she wasn't well and needed to rest up. She wasn't to be disturbed. A cab brought her here last night and the guy took her upstairs then gave me the key and left."

"Which room?" Reece was anxious to get to Charlotte.

"Twenty two." The guy handed him the key.

Reece and Andre were out the door, up the stairs and on the landing in seconds. They counted along the rooms, some without numbers on the door, and when they came to 22 Reece shoved the key in the lock and threw the door open. The room was empty.

CHAPTER TEN

On the way back from the motel, Andre asked Reece to drop him at the Golden Nugget. He wanted to do some more digging into the gypsy's disappearance. She had to be somewhere close by because she wouldn't leave her belongings behind. He also suggested Reece ask Lozano to place an officer on stake out and inform them when the woman returned to her wagon.

The minute Andre entered their hotel room he called Sarah to ask for information about the succubus. He knew he'd missed something at the crime scene and wanted to find out more about the demons and their capabilities. After telling the priest everything leading up to Charlotte's disappearance and the attacks, Sarah was ready to board the next flight out of LA. Andre asked her not to. Not yet.

It was imperative for her to remain close to the historical document files so she could impart authentic information to help trap the demon. He knew Sarah would have to travel to Las Vegas to perform the ritual, because it had to be a member of a religious order, but he wasn't prepared to put her life in danger. Not until it was absolutely necessary. If the succubus discovered what they had planned it would, without doubt, make an attempt on her life. Assuming there was only one demon.

Sarah told him the creatures could only seduce their victims while they dreamt and suck the life force from their body during REM sleep. This was the time when the succubus's powers were renewed. There was nothing to suggest these demons could take on physical human form and fulfil the process in the real world. She told him after everything else they had seen nothing would surprise her. With the threshold between hell and earth violated all bets were off and anything was possible. All too possible.

She asked Andre to keep her up-to-date on Charlotte's disappearance and the police investigation and said she would email him more information as it came to hand. She would pray for Charlotte's safe return. Sarah also told him to be careful and to tell Reece to do the same and suggested they find Bishop's wort and carry it. In ancient Rome, the purple flowers were believed to ward off acts of sorcery and if placed under a person's pillow would keep succubus and incubus at bay.

୫⃝ଓଔ

Reece headed to the LVMPD headquarters and was met in the lobby by sheriff Lozano. He'd been sweating on the PI's arrival. He needed to arm himself with information to protect him and his men while the investigation continued. No male was safe in the city with an active demon on the loose.

Once they were in the privacy of his office, Reece asked him about surveillance on the gypsy wagon in Fremont Street. He told Lozano it was crucial to the case he was working on and would allow him more time to help the department with the murder investigation. It wouldn't, but the sheriff didn't need to know. He had to find Charlotte. She was his main priority. The sheriff said he'd see what he could do but with his officers on patrol searching for the perpetrator he had limited resources.

Lozano leaned back in his office chair and studied the PI. He could sense the case had a personal element to it and decided to ask. "The case you're working, it's personal isn't it?"

Reece frowned at him. Andre had been right. Lozano was intuitive. He didn't want to risk Charlotte's life by telling the cop anything, but realized they needed official assistance.

The sheriff folded his arms and maintained eye contact. "Where's your girlfriend?"

"Fiancée," Reece corrected. "And it's none of your business."

"I could make it my business if something happened to her."

Reece folded his arms. "Do you think I did something to her?"

Lozano sighed. "Of course not, but you were meant to be flying here to get married, weren't you, so where is she?" He folded his arms, his eyes remaining on the PI.

Reece's serious gaze locked onto the sheriff. Lozano must have questioned the hotel manager. "I can't tell you where she is."

The sheriff leaned forward and rested his elbows on the desk. "Why not?"

Reece ran the idea of telling him everything around his brain. Would the abductors find out? They seemed to know everything they had planned so far. Should he risk it? He inhaled a deep breath and let it out. "Because I don't know."

Lozano looked surprised. "So the case you're working on concerns her? Want to tell me about it?"

Reece gave a heavy sigh and straightened in his chair. "Someone took her from LAX before we boarded our flight. I found a note in her belongings telling me to fly here and wait for contact."

"Have they contacted you?"

"Yeah, a couple of times, but they're playing cat and mouse with us. We located the motel where they had Charlotte, but by the time we got there she'd been moved."

"To another room?"

Reece hadn't given the idea any thought. He'd assumed she had been moved somewhere else. He jumped to his feet. "I didn't check." He headed for the door.

"Where're you going?" The sheriff stood up.

"Back to the motel to make the manager open every room."

Lozano shook his head. "Wouldn't do any good. After you left they would've moved her to different location for sure."

Reece slumped into the chair. "How could I have been so stupid?"

The sheriff moved around his desk and rested a hand on the PI's shoulder. "You're too close to the case. Your emotions are invested in the outcome."

"I just want her back."

"Then let me help you. Our undercover guys out in the field can get the information we need."

"There's more to this story than you know."

Lozano sat down. "Ok. Like what?"

CHAPTER ELEVEN

Andre received a call from Reece later in the afternoon telling him the sheriff would see what he could do regarding the stake out on the gypsy wagon. He knew it could take days with the bureaucratic red tape involved, so he headed out to Fremont Street to take another look around. When Andre arrived at the place where the wagon had been sitting he was surprised to find it gone.

What had happened to the gypsy?

He asked several of the street performers nearby, but none of them knew anything. No one spoke to the gypsy woman and they hadn't seen anyone come to move the wagon. It seemed like a dead end but he wasn't about to give up. She had to be somewhere and he *would* find her.

Andre made his way back through the casino to the elevator banks and as one of the doors slid open and he was about to step inside he heard his name called. He turned around to see Sarah coming into the lift lobby, wheeling a bulging suitcase behind her.

"What are you doing here?" He gave her a hug.

"I couldn't sit back in LA not doing anything to help you guys. I need to be here."

"I appreciate you coming, but it's dangerous."

"I think I can handle it." She gave a wry smile.

Sarah was a strong, tough as nails woman with an arsenal to take out any otherworldly creatures. She had dealt with Dracula's minions in the past so she was more than capable of dealing with a demon or two.

"Did you manage to find the ritual to banish the succubus?"

"Yes, I have it on my laptop. We'll need to collect a few things though." The pair stepped into the empty elevator. "Any word on Charlotte?"

"No. And I'm worried. They seem to know our every move. They called and questioned Reece about our police involvement. He told them we were assisting with the murder investigation and they hung up. So we have no idea if Charlotte's ok."

"Mm. They haven't made any demand for a ransom or anything?"

Andre shook his head.

"It doesn't make any sense. What do you think their motive is?"

"I wish I knew. Reece was under the impression MacKinnon had something to do with it."

Sarah's eyebrows rose. "Do you think he could have? Some of the order exacting revenge for his death?"

"No, I don't. It doesn't feel like something he would've orchestrated. He'd have come at us guns blazing. Look what happened at the night club. He was a maniac."

"Yes, he was. We need to look at all the evidence to see if something jumps out at us."

"I have been and nothing has so far."

"Two sets of eyes are better than one." She touched his arm and gave a thin smile.

When the elevator door opened, Andre grabbed the handle of Sarah's heavy case and waited for her to step out.

Once inside the hotel room, he showed her the photos and notes. Sarah's pained expression on seeing the photos of Charlotte tied to the bed made Andre realize how important she was to their group and their lives. He hoped they found her before it was too late. It would kill Reece if anything happened to her.

Sarah swiped a tear from the corner of her eye and inhaled a deep breath through her nostrils. "What else do you have?" Her serious gaze moved from the photos to Andre.

He shrugged. "Nothing. We haven't heard from them since this morning. The last place they had us go to was the Luxor Hotel to pick up the photos. They knew I was here, so they'll know you're here too."

"How?"

"I don't know. But they're one step ahead of us at every turn."

Sarah pawed over the photos and notes again spread out across the queen-sized bed. "None of it makes any sense. Why Charlotte?"

"Exactly. You'd think it would've been one of us. Reece or me or Ed... even you." He gave her a sheepish look and changed the subject. "Where is Ed by the way? I thought he'd be with you."

"He wanted to be here but he couldn't get away. He's heading an investigation."

"Oh? Ok."

"I did bring someone with me though."

Andre frowned. "Who?"

A knock echoed into the room. Andre swung around and stared at the door.

"Aren't you going to open it?" Sarah asked.

He gave her a curious frown, walked across the room and pulled the door open. "Arianne?"

CHAPTER TWELVE

The guy thought all his birthdays had come at once. He couldn't believe his luck. The woman standing before him was a fox. Breathtaking. Gorgeous. Green alluring eyes, milky soft skin and model perfect features. And *she* had approached him in the casino, not the other way around. He knew what she was after and he was going to give it to her. She was certainly equipped with everything a man could want and he knew he'd get lucky tonight. Why else would they be here, right? Wait till he told his friends. They'd be totally pissed.

She had taken him up to the rooftop of the hotel, overlooking the dazzling strip. A place where no one would interrupt them while they hooked up. He'd had a lot to drink, but still felt exhilarated and horny and wanted to get the party started. He was confident he could last the distance.

"What's your name, sweetheart?" he asked, running his eyes over every inch of the red head's sexy curves as she sauntered toward him, licking her cherry-red lipstick. He imagined her voluptuous mouth wrapped around his dick and it hardened inside his jeans. He was ready for her. Everything about this woman oozed sex appeal—long legs, tiny waist, slim shoulders, and firm full breasts—every man's wet dream. He didn't care if they weren't real he couldn't wait to get his mouth on one of those babies.

Her glossy lips spread into a seductive smile. "Do names really matter? We're never going to see each other again, are we?"

"Yeah, you're right." Wow! A woman who knew how it worked: a once off pleasure connection with no complications.

She kneeled down in front of him, unclipped his belt and slid the zipper down on his jeans.

Yes! Fortune had finally smiled on him in Sin City.

CHAPTER THIRTEEN

Reece had called over an hour ago and said he was on his way back to the hotel. So where was he? Andre stood with his cell phone in his hand, staring at the screen and willing it to ring. He'd tried to call his friend but it had gone straight to voicemail. He decided to call sheriff Lozano.

"Sheriff. It's Andre Delacroix. Is Reece with you?"

"No, he left about an hour ago. Why? Hasn't he come back to the hotel?"

"Not yet and I'm worried. It's unlike him not to call if he changed his plans."

"Let me see what I can find out and get back to you." Lozano was on his feet and leaving his office as he spoke.

"Thanks. I appreciate it." Andre rang off and moved his gaze to Sarah and Arianne. "The sheriff's going to get back to me."

"Maybe he stopped for something to eat or to pick up coffee on the way back," Arianne said. She could sense Andre's apprehension and wanted to ease his mind.

Sarah stood up and walked over to him. She rested a reassuring hand on his arm. "He is a grown man, Andre. I'm sure he's fine. He'll probably walk through the door any minute."

Andre's serious gaze met hers. "You know what he's like. He wouldn't have even gone for coffee without letting us know."

She sighed. "Yes, I know. But I'm sure there's a logical explanation."

The musical tone of Andre's cell interrupted their conversation. He touched the screen and pressed the phone to his ear. "Hello?"

"It's me," the sheriff said. "I checked the parking lot and the rental is still here. I also found his cell phone on the ground beside it. Something's happened to him."

"Can you put out a bulletin or something?"

"I'm already on it. I've got a tech checking the car for fingerprints and officers have a description of Reece. It's the best I can do right now."

"It must be the ones who took Charlotte."

"Yeah, I figured. Sit tight. I'll let you know when I hear anything."

"Thank you, sheriff."

"Don't thank me yet. Let's get Reece and his girlfriend back in one piece first." He rang off.

Sarah and Arianne frowned at Andre. "Reece is gone?" Sarah asked.

"Looks like he was taken from the police parking lot. The sheriff found Reece's cell phone near the rental."

"Oh, dear lord. We have to do something."

"Lozano said to sit tight and he'd be in touch when he found out anything."

Sarah's frown deepened. "And you're just going to do what he says? We need to get out there and search for them." She jabbed a finger at the room door.

"Where would we look? The police are better equipped to deal with the situation than we are."

Arianne walked over to the pair. "I agree with Sarah. I think we should get out there and look for them." She turned to Andre. "You and I have an advantage. We can use our senses to pick up Reece's and Charlotte's mortal vibration. We should at least try."

Andre gave her a wry smile. "I know you mean well, Arianne, but in a city overflowing with mortal energy where do you suggest we start?"

She thought for a moment. "What about the police parking lot? There should still be traces of residual energy there. Maybe we can follow it."

"Can you do that?" Sarah asked.

"Yes, to a point," Arianne explained. "If the energy is fresh we should be able to track it."

"Then what are we waiting for? Let's go." Sarah was on her way to the door.

Just as she reached it a knock echoed into the room. She swung it open.

"Andre Delacroix you need my help," the gypsy woman said as she strutted over to him.

❧❧❧

Reece came to in the trunk of a car. His hands zip tied behind him, his mouth covered with duct tape. What the hell happened? He forced his foggy brain to remember. He could still feel the twinge in his muscles. The five second zap from the taser between his shoulder blades had sent his body into spasm and he'd hit the pavement hard. Dammit! He'd dropped his cell phone under the edge of the rental too. No one could track him.

He knew the taser hadn't caused him to black out, so they must have stuck him with a sedative before moving him.

It had to be whoever took Charlotte. At least he'd see her again, if she was still alive.

Reece wondered how long he'd been in the car and how far they had traveled. Were they still in Vegas? He strained his ears to listen. They were on a highway. The sedan was moving at at least 65 miles per hour. He could tell by the rotation of the tires on the hot asphalt.

Would Andre be looking for him? Reece knew he would. But finding him would be another matter.

The car slowed and made a left turn causing Reece's body to roll with the motion. He tried to steady himself with his elbows. Not an easy feat with your hands behind your back in a moving vehicle. Reece braced his left foot against the trunk wall to prevent himself from rolling onto his stomach. He needed to be face up.

He couldn't hear any conversation in the car and assumed only one person was inside. It could give him the advantage he needed when they finally made it to their destination and the trunk opened. Just as the thought crossed his mind the sedan stopped.

Reece held his breath, waiting for the inevitable, and listened to the sounds around him.

Driver's door opening and closing.

Footsteps crunching gravel. *Where the hell are we?*

Key being shoved into the lock.

Trunk latch clicking open.

Blinding glare streaming into the dark space.

SOUL CHASER

Electrical jolt of the taser against his ribs.
His muscles going into spasm. His body jerking.
The prick of a needle in his upper arm.
Blackness.

CHAPTER FOURTEEN

"What do you know about Reece's and Charlotte's disappearances?" Andre asked, his arms folded, his demeanor tense. His serious gaze bored into the gypsy's soul searching for answers he knew she would keep concealed. "And how do you think you can help us?"

"I have knowledge of a lot of things." She wandered around the room, her multicolored full skirt brushing against furnishings as she studied the hotel suite. "I have information about the succubus, but it will not be offered freely."

"You want some kind of payment?" Andre didn't have time for the woman's games. He needed to find Reece and Charlotte before they were killed. "Not interested."

"I did not say I pursued monetary gain. What I need is your help to free me from the supernatural contract I was forced to sign."

"What kind of contract?" Sarah asked.

"One signed in blood. And if I do not fulfill my obligations they will take my soul."

"What kind of obligations?" Arianne was curious.

"To tell the fortunes of young men and guide them to the succubus."

Andre's frown deepened. "So you've been sending men to their deaths by offering them up to demons."

"I had no choice. It was their life or mine."

"How do I know we can trust you? How do I know you weren't sent here as a distraction?"

"You do not. But the information I can give you will certainly save lives, including my own."

"Like what?"

The gypsy's dark gaze rested on him. "Will you help me free myself of this curse?"

"If you can give us something valuable we'll help you." Andre paced for a moment then stopped and stared at the woman. "How many demons are there?"

She gave him a knowing smirk and her right eyebrow rose. "You have an ancient wisdom for one so young."

Andre was taken aback by her intuition. She knew what he was.

"There are three succubus beauties. Katya, Helyna and Oriana. One redhead, one dark and one blonde, each to a man's taste. They are performing at…" Before she could get the words out her face contorted and turned bright red. The gypsy fell to the floor writhing in agony, gasping for air and clutching at her throat.

"Quick! Get her some water," Andre's eyes darted to Arianne.

The young woman dashed to the bar fridge, whipped out a bottle of water, twisted off the cap and threw the bottle across the room to Andre. He lifted the woman's head off the floor and poured a small amount of liquid into her mouth. She coughed and choked, unable to catch her breath.

Andre turned to Sarah. "It must be some kind of spell. What do we do?"

Arianne fell to her knees beside the woman and recited something over and over in Latin until the gypsy's body relaxed and she breathed easy.

"What did you do?" Andre asked.

"It's a protection spell. I wasn't sure it would work without the necessary items but I had to try." She gave him a thin smile and stood up.

Sarah moved beside her. "You know magic?"

The gypsy sat up as though nothing had happened to her. "She has great power. She can vanquish a death spell cast by a demon."

Andre and Sarah's gaze fell on Arianne. "When were you going to tell us?" Andre asked.

"You didn't need to know."

"Does Nathaniel know?" Andre frowned.

"Yes. I'm part of his team."

Andre folded his arms. "Well right now you're part of our team, so you should've told me."

Arianne mirrored his movements. "I wasn't expecting to use my powers... my witch powers, so I didn't think it would be necessary. Is this going to be a problem, because if it is I'll return to LA?"

He ran the idea of her leaving around his mind. He wanted her to stay, he liked her. But he was annoyed she hadn't trusted him with something so important. Andre thought about how he had kept his vampire nature a secret from Reece for so long and understood why Arianne hadn't told him.

"It isn't a problem. I'm sorry."

When the three turned around the gypsy was gone.

Andre raced over to the door. The woman was nowhere. He took off down the hallway to the elevator bank. Not there. Where could she have gone?

Arianne and Sarah met him at the elevators. "We searched both sides of the tower. She's not here," Sarah told him.

"Was this an elaborate hoax?" He gazed over his shoulder. "To get us out of the room." He rushed out of the small lobby and back along the hallway.

Sarah and Arianne followed him. "Is anything missing?" Sarah asked, as the women entered the room.

Andre swung around, hands on hips. "Yes, Reece's suitcase."

CHAPTER FIFTEEN

Reece came to in a boarded up, empty room. The place reminded him of an old motel. There were a lot of those sitting abandoned in the Nevada Desert. It must have been at least 104 degrees, like being inside an oven. He inhaled a deep breath through his nostrils, duct tape still stuck over his mouth, and blinked away the salty sweat dripping into his eyes, his clothes sticking to his body like Saran wrap. Where the hell was he? And where was Charlotte?

He'd been dumped on the filthy floor, his hands still tied behind him but now he had ties around his ankles as well. And his shoes were missing. Lucky for him there were no snakes or scorpions taking shelter here. The desert was a haven for venomous reptiles and arachnids. He tugged at his restraints in an attempt to loosen them, but they were locked tight. The department had incorporated cable tie handcuffs into their armory because perpetrators couldn't get them off and escape. The question was could he?

Reece skidded across the floor on his ass over to a wall and jostled himself onto his feet. It took some doing. He needed to get out of this before someone came back. He jackrabbited over to the window and peered through a crack in the boards. The sun was low over the mountains so it must have been late afternoon. How long had he been unconscious?

He gazed around the hazy room looking for something to cut through the plastic cuffs and spotted a chunk of broken brick lying in the corner. He needed to get to it as fast as possible. Reece laid down on the floor and rolled toward the jagged segment, the skin on his arms and feet being scratched by pieces of debris scattered over the threadbare carpet as he gained momentum.

Once in the corner, he struggled to get his body into a sitting position and wriggled backwards until he felt the brick with his fingers. He ran his hands over the lump of concrete feeling for the sharpest edge. Flipping it with his fingertips to get it into his right palm, he bent his wrist back in an upright angle and hacked at the plastic. At this rate, it would take hours. Time he didn't have.

It must have been later than he thought because the sun slid into the horizon leaving a vague orange hue seeping into the room. He kept sawing at the plastic with the piece of brick; sweat pouring down his face, neck and back as he grappled to free himself. He wondered about Charlotte. What had they done to her? Was she still alive? Losing her was something he didn't want to contemplate.

Reece dropped the brick and prodded the plastic to see if it had given way. He pulled outwards with both hands hoping the cuffs would snap. They didn't. He gave a heavy sigh, worked the chunk back into his palm and continued hacking at the zip tie. "Come on, come on. I have to get out of here."

Time slipped away from him as he worked to get free and the walls surrounding him evaporated into the dark.

Bright light filtered into the room through a crack in the boards and Reece heard the rumble of an engine approaching.

He hacked even harder at the thick plastic. He needed his hands free to defend himself.

୫୦ଔ

Andre, Sarah and Arianne stepped out of the new rental, leaving the headlights on, and gazed around the old motel. Where to begin? There were at least twenty rooms and all of them were boarded up. The headlights only reached so far, and the moon was half full offering very little illumination and making it difficult for Sarah to see. She grabbed a flashlight out of her satchel and flicked it on to make sure it worked. Arianne and Andre had nocturnal vision so they didn't need any light.

"Why don't you two take the ground level and I'll go upstairs?" Andre said, gazing up at the dark balcony.

"All right. Be careful," Sarah told him.

"You too." Andre headed to the concrete stairs at the end of building closest to him, the metal railing jutting out at an odd angle from the staircase, and climbed them.

Sarah and Arianne made their way over to the last door. May as well start where they were and work their way back. The doors were all locked and the windows boarded over. Arianne raised a booted foot and kicked at the door. It flew open. Sarah stepped up to the threshold and ran the beam of her flashlight around the room. "Reece?" she called.

No sign of him. They moved on to the next door.

Andre stood at the top of the stairs and used his immortal senses to see if he could locate his friend. If he was here and still alive he should be able to sense him. They'd pulled into this motel hoping Reece had been brought here. Arianne had lost his energy trail about an hour before and they now had to go on gut instinct and sheer luck to find him.

He had to be out here in the desert somewhere.

𝕤𝕠𝕔𝕩

Reece heard three car doors slam. They had left the headlights on. Why? No element of surprise, unless they thought he was still unconscious. He sawed frantically at the cuffs. He had to get free, had to be able to fight back. He dropped the brick and tugged at his restraints. Snap. One cuff let go. His hands were free. Reece felt down his legs until he found the zip tie around his ankles and pulled and pulled with all of his strength. One loop finally gave way just enough for him to slide his bare foot out. He was on his feet, brick in hand, ready to take on whoever was about to come through the door.

He heard a loud bang somewhere outside and his heart shuddered against his ribs. He backed up to the wall; he didn't need any surprises. Reece's ragged breathing caused his head to spin. He shook the feeling off, sucked in a slow, deep breath and blew it out. He needed to stay alert.

The door burst open and banged against the wall. No one was outside.

It had to be a ruse of some kind and Reece wasn't taking the bait. He remained in the shadows, his back pressed against the warm bricks.

Whoever was out there would either wait out the night or come in after him. Whatever happened he was prepared.

Reece sidled across the wall to the doorway on his left. An old bathroom. The door was missing. *Dammit!* He had nowhere to take cover. He wished he had his Glock but they had taken it. He felt around the doorway and stepped into the small space. No boards on the back window. He climbed into the bathtub and tried to slide the high set window open. It was stuck fast. If he smashed the glass they would know where he was.

Someone had entered the other room. Reece heard footsteps crunching the debris on the floor. He held his breath.

ℰ◯ℭ

Andre, Arianne and Sarah met at the bottom of the first staircase. "Anything?" Andre asked.

Sarah and Arianne shook their heads. "No," Sarah told him. "How many more motels and abandoned buildings are out here? Where do we go next?"

"There's one more motel about ten miles up the highway. We'll check it out and then head back to the hotel."

Arianne frowned at him. "But we have to find Reece before something happens to him."

"I know we do, but we can't drive around in the dark all night. Sarah needs some rest and we do too. We won't be any good to him if we wear ourselves out."

"He's right," Sarah said. "Who knows what we'll face tomorrow? We need to be rested and prepared for anything."

Arianne nodded. "You're right. My only concern is we're running out of time."

Sarah rested a hand on her arm and gave a thin smile. "I know." So was she.

The trio climbed into the car and drove out of the old parking lot heading for the last motel on their route.

ℰ◯ℭ

Whoever was outside the bathroom playing cat and mouse with Reece was trying to unnerve him. And it was working. Why hadn't they made an attempt to attack him? Did they think he was gone? No. If it was a succubus they'd sense him. So who was it? The footsteps moved away, heading toward the busted door. Reece climbed out of the bathtub, edged his way over to the doorway and peered around the frame. Were they leaving? Was he safe?

The figure standing in the doorway was indistinguishable. Could have been male or female by the clothes they had on. Dark hooded jacket and pants. Where were the others? Three car doors had closed when they arrived.

Something dropped onto Reece's back and crawled down the center of his sweat-soaked, clinging shirt. It took all of his resilience not to do the spider dance and alert whoever was there to his presence. The crawling thing kept moving toward his belt. Scorpion? Spider? Lizard? He wasn't sure. He just knew he needed it gone so he could keep his wits about him and focus on the situation at hand.

Keeping his eyes on the figure in the doorway, he reached behind him and prodded the thing on his shirt with a finger. Not a scorpion, thank God. He plucked it from his back and tossed it behind him, breathing a relieved sigh. He hated six and eight legged creatures.

The figure stepped outside into the glare of the headlights, stopped and turned around. Reece ducked behind the wall, his breathing ragged, his heart thumping. Had they heard him?

He eased his body forward and peered around the doorframe again.

Why were they standing there? What were they planning to do?

CHAPTER SIXTEEN

Reece could feel his courage dissolve as he stood in the small dark space, his senses on high alert. With nothing to defend himself he was in deep shit and he knew it. He strained his ears to listen in the silence for any unusual sounds. A lone coyote howled in the distance sending a shiver up his spine. If he died out here he'd be food for the desert wildlife. Could the bang he'd heard earlier have been the others looking for another way in? An element of surprise? Reece gripped the jagged piece of concrete in his hand for fortification, his heart thumping against his ribcage. He inhaled a deep, steadying breath, attempting to alleviate his fears. He couldn't give up now and he wouldn't without exerting every last ounce of strength he had left to protect himself. He had to... for Charlotte.

"Reece?" The female voice echoed into the room. "Are you in there?"

His eyes widened and he peered around the doorframe.

The figure standing in the glare of the headlights at the threshold of the room looked like Charlotte.

Was his mind playing tricks on him? Was he losing it? He darted back behind the wall.

"If you don't come out they're going to kill me." She stepped into the room. "Reece, did you hear me?"

No! It had to be an hallucination. His mind was conjuring up what he wanted to see. He stayed silent.

She moved closer. "Please, Reece, come out to me. They gave their word nothing will happen to you. To us."

Reece's tired and confused mind couldn't make sense of what was happening. Was it Charlotte?

He peered around the wall one-eyed. It looked like her.

"What do they want? Why did they abduct us?"

"If you come out they'll tell you everything." She held out her arms to him, dressed in only a bra and panties. "Come here, Reece. Let me hold you. We've both been through so much."

Reece darted back behind the wall and shook his head to clear his thoughts, his breathing shallow. Was it really her? "If you are Charlotte you'll know the answer to the question I'm about to ask."

"There's no time for questions. If you don't come out right now they'll kill me and I know you don't want that."

Of course he didn't. He would never let anything happen to her ever again. Reece dropped the chunk of brick and stepped into the room.

Charlotte continued moving toward him and when she reached him she wrapped her arms around him. "Thank you." She smiled up at him and raised her mouth to his in a long slow kiss.

Reece pulled her to him and held her tight. "Charlotte," he whispered through the kiss.

"Yes, Reece, it's me."

She lowered them onto the floor and the kiss continued. Reece couldn't believe she was in his arms again. He didn't care how it was possible he just knew he never wanted to let her go.

Charlotte eased herself out of his embrace and kissed his neck, nuzzled his ear, then roamed her mouth down his body to his belt. He groaned. She unclipped the buckle and slid the zipper of his jeans down. Reece closed his eyes and leaned back waiting for her mouth to take him.

An explosion of repetitive gunfire ruptured the silence and their rapture.

Ear piercing shrieks echoed around the dark space shattering the remaining boarded windows. Shards of glass sprayed the room and Reece threw himself into a corner wondering what the hell was going on. He zipped up his jeans and jumped to his feet, his heart hammering, his senses muddled.

Andre and Sarah stormed into the room, high-powered rifles in hand, surveying the area with eyes and weapons.

"Reece, are you ok?" Andre rushed across the room to him.

The PI was dazed. "Huh?"

"Are you all right?" Andre frowned at him. Reece seemed out of it. He shook his friend's shoulder. "Reece?"

"I – I think so, yeah." His eyes scanned the room looking for his fiancée.

"The succubus was about to kill you."

Reece's eyes returned to his friend. "What are you talking about? Where's Charlotte?"

"It wasn't Charlotte," Sarah said as she strutted across the room. "It was a succubus pretending to be her. She would have sucked the life right out of you just like the other victims if we hadn't got here in time."

"But..."

"No, Reece. Sarah's telling you the truth." Andre gripped his friend's arm. "It wasn't her."

"I know what I saw," Reece told him, "what I felt when I held her in my arms."

"She enamored you. It wasn't real."

Arianne entered the room. "All clear. They're gone."

"They're resourceful. It's a pity we didn't kill them." Andre turned to his friend. "Let's get you out of here," he said, taking Reece by the arm.

He shrugged free. "I can walk on my own."

Andre knew the succubus had manipulated Reece's mind into believing he was with Charlotte, and even though he knew the truth no amount of talking would convince him otherwise. Not right now, anyway.

ℰℭ

The spray of hot water relieved the tension in Reece's shoulders and neck as he stood in the shower berating himself for being so stupid, believing the damned demon was Charlotte. In his gut he'd known it couldn't have been her but to his confused state of mind he wanted to believe anything was possible. Maybe the combination of sedatives they'd pumped into him and fatigue had reduced his resistance to the manipulations of otherworldly creatures, because under any other circumstances he wouldn't have been so compliant.

Reece stepped out of the bathtub, wrapped a hotel towel around his waist, walked over to the foggy mirror and swiped the condensation off the glass. He stared at his reflection. *How could you have been so gullible?* He knew how. He wanted Charlotte back in his arms, safe. Not out there somewhere having God knows what done to her. He didn't want to believe she might be dead. He wouldn't survive it.

A knock on the door made him spin around. He was on his guard again. "Yeah?"

"What do you feel like for dinner? We're ordering room service," Andre asked through the door.

"Whatever Sarah and Arianne want, I'm not very hungry, anyway."

Andre opened the door. "You need to keep up your strength, you know. We've got a long battle ahead of us."

"I know." Reece sighed. "Look, about earlier…"

"I get it. You wanted it to be Charlotte. Who wouldn't? I'm sorry it wasn't her."

"Yeah, me too."

"We can talk about it later, if you want." Andre knew what happened at the motel was playing on Reece's mind.

"Maybe."

"Ok." Andre watched his friend for a moment. "We'll order something for you. See you out here when you're done."

"Sure."

Andre closed the door.

Reece put the lid down on the toilet and sat on it. What would he do if something happened to the woman he loved? Having the succubus in his arms resembling Charlotte made him realize how much she meant to him and how he'd be lost without her. A tear slid down his left cheek and he lowered his head into his hands and sobbed.

It was after midnight and Reece couldn't sleep so he and Andre went downstairs to Claude's Bar for a nightcap. Andre wanted to talk to him about the gypsy's visit and how she had revealed the names of the three succubae. They needed to formulate a plan to find the demons before more men were killed. The pair took a quiet corner and sat down.

"The gypsy came up to our room and told us she wanted to help. She said she had a supernatural contract on her life and she was forced to send men to their fate. She also said if we helped her she'd give us the information we needed to destroy the succubus demons."

Reece swallowed a large mouthful of his drink. "Did she give you anything we can actually work with?"

"Yeah. She told us the names of the women. Katya, Helyna and Oriana. They're supposed be performing in some kind of mystical show here in Vegas, but she didn't tell us where."

"Do you know how to contact her?"

Andre shook his head and swallowed a mouthful of Bourbon. "No. In fact, she feigned some kind of supernatural turn and after we helped her she disappeared."

"What?" Reece slid forward on his seat. "So she came to offer help but didn't give us anything."

"I think she was sent as a distraction because as you know while we were looking for her someone took your bag."

Reece stared into his glass of Bourbon then looked at his friend. "Yeah. Remind me to go buy some new stuff, when I have the time." He swallowed the remainder of his drink. "Now they have Charlotte's and my suitcases. What the hell do they want with our things?"

"I have no idea, but we need to sit down with Sarah and Arianne tomorrow and get something in motion otherwise they could leave and we'll never know how to find them. What if they head to LA?"

"Let's hope not. We have enough to deal with there as it is." Reece frowned. "It's obvious now that the demons have Charlotte and not someone else?"

"The gypsy showing up and your suitcase disappearing can't be a coincidence."

"Someone must know where the demons are staying and performing." Reece's cell phone went off and he snatched it off the table. He glanced at Andre. "Lozano. Hello, Sheriff, what…"

Lozano told him a body had been discovered on the rooftop of Caesar's Palace by a maintenance crew and asked if Reece and Andre could meet him at the scene right away.

"Ok. We're leaving now." Reece was on his feet. "They've got another body. Shit, that's six now."

Andre was out of his seat. "We have to find the gypsy and make her tell us where they are. She's the only one who knows anything about them."

"Let's get over to the hotel. Then we'll head to Fremont Street to see if the wagon's back. If not, we'll drive around the other hotels off the strip. Maybe they're performing at one of the lesser-known venues."

CHAPTER SEVENTEEN

Reece and Andre climbed the last few stairs, walked through the doorway and out onto the rooftop. Lozano spotted them and called down, "Hey, up here." Reece eyed the metal ladder beside the door, sighed and gripped the railing. He wasn't impressed about climbing up onto another rooftop after having to take the stairwell. He stepped onto the bottom rung and heaved himself up the ladder, Andre close behind him.

"Glad you could make it," Lozano said, extending his hand to assist the PI over the narrow edge.

Reece ran his eyes over the glistening cityscape. The view was spectacular, but it wasn't the reason they were here. His eyes moved to the sheriff. "Where's the body?" He moved his gaze around the domed rooftop with hands on hips looking for the victim.

"Over here." Lozano walked around the glass dome. "The maintenance guys are pretty shaken up."

"Understandable," Reece said. He and Andre followed the sheriff.

Another shriveled corpse.

"Any ID?" Reece asked.

"Nope. Same as all the other victims."

"Is there any way to gauge how old this guy is?" Reece frowned at the remains. The clothing suggested early twenties.

"By the clothes, I'd say early to mid-twenties." Lozano shifted his gaze to the PI. "Wouldn't you?"

Reece rubbed the stubble on his chin. "Yeah, I was thinking the same thing. Stupid kid, coming up here for some action and getting himself killed instead."

"Yeah." Lozano's eyes moved to Andre.

An image flashed through Andre's mind as he moved closer to the body and ran his hand over it. "I saw the vision of a woman. Long, wavy red hair. Green eyes. Beautiful."

Lozano glanced at Reece sideways. "Does he do that a lot?"

"When it's necessary, yes." Reece gave him a thin smile.

"We know how the guy was lured up here and why. What we need to know is where she went," Lozano deduced.

"Andre and I are going to do a drive around to see if any of the back street venues have a paranormal or mystical show in its lineup. Once we can locate the demons we can deal with them."

"You have a plan?" Lozano's eyebrows rose.

"We have a priest who knows how to, shall we say, imprison them. At least if we can trap them so they can't do any more harm, we can then look for a way to send them back to hell."

Lozano crossed himself. "Amen to that. These bodies are mind-blowing. I can only imagine the pain they endured. Pure hell."

"Yeah, it wouldn't have been pretty."

"If you send them back won't they escape again, with the threshold being breached and all?"

"We're working on it. Sarah, the priest I mentioned, has been researching ancient documents which should point to a way to closing the rift."

Andre joined the pair. "Those creatures have abilities most demons don't because they've been sired by a vampire. We're definitely looking at succubus vampires."

"What?!" Lozano frowned at Andre. "Are you sure?"

"Yes."

"Ay dios mio." He pulled his St. Jude medallion from inside his shirt and kissed it. "How do we get rid of them?"

"These demons are something we haven't come up against before so it's new territory. But we will find a way. Trust me," Reece assured him.

"I hope it's sooner rather than later. I'd like to put a stop to more young men dying."

"So would we." Reece glanced at Andre. "You get anything else?"

He shook his head. "I can't track demon energy. If I could we'd be on our way to where they are."

Reece sighed. "Ok, well, if there's nothing else, Sheriff, we'll take off and do the drive around."

Lozano shook the PI's hand. "I appreciate your help. We would never have figured out what was going on if…"

"Don't thank me yet. We've got a lot of work to do before anyone's safe." Reece motioned for Andre to head back to the ladder and followed him over.

On the lower rooftop, they stopped to discuss their next move. "Once we do the drive around we'll head back to the hotel and see what Sarah's come up with. Hopefully she's found something we can use against those things." He gave a heavy sigh. "God, I hate this job. But somebody's got to do it."

"If we can contain them until we can send them back at least it'll prevent more innocents from dying. I hate succubus. They're insidious. They creep into a person's psyche and manipulate it to the point where the person has no control over their own actions. They believe what they see, like you did."

Reece looked sheepish. He didn't need to be reminded he'd dropped the ball out there in the desert. He was lucky Andre and the others had been looking for him or he'd be one dead PI. "Yeah, I understand how powerful they are after experiencing it firsthand."

Andre gripped his friend's arm. "I'm glad we got there in time. I don't know what I would've done if we'd been too late."

"I'm glad you don't have to find out. Thanks for saving my neck out there. I don't think I said it before."

"You don't have to. We look out for each other." Andre tightened his grip on Reece's arm and smiled. "Right?"

"Yeah." They'd saved each other's skins many times. It was a given in their line of work. Danger and death came with the territory.

The pair left the hotel and cruised the back streets of Vegas looking for any unusual shows being performed off the strip. If only they could find the gypsy. Reece would make her take them to where the demons were holed up.

After driving around for an hour without finding anything useful they decided to call it quits and head back to the Golden Nugget. Reece hoped

Sarah had something they could use to combat the demons with. A way of vanquishing them, if possible. Having Arianne as part of their team gave them some protection against those creatures, if they tried to attack she could use her witchcraft to ward them off. But for how long was anyone's guess.

As they drove past the lower end of Fremont Street, Andre spotted the gypsy. "Stop the car!" Before the car came to a complete stop Andre was out the door and rocketing toward her.

Reece screeched into the curb, pulled the keys from the ignition and bolted after his friend.

When he reached the spot where the wagon had been there was no sign of Andre or the gypsy.

CHAPTER EIGHTEEN

Reece wandered the crowd in Fremont Street and the surrounding area searching for Andre. *Where did he go?* It occurred to him the demons could have used the gypsy as a decoy once again and grabbed his friend. They wanted something, but what? After circling the block for more than twenty minutes, Reece headed back to the rental car.

When he pulled into the valet parking outside the hotel Andre was waiting for him at the entrance. *Thank God!*

"Where have you been? I've been looking for you all over Fremont Street." Reece stalked up to him.

"I tried to catch the gypsy but she eluded me. I didn't want to come back empty-handed so I kept searching. I don't know how she got away."

Reece rested a hand on his friend's shoulder. "Maybe she's one of them. Maybe she's not a gypsy at all. It would certainly explain how."

Andre gave him a disconcerted frown. "You could be right. Why didn't we think of it before? They've been right under our noses playing with us the whole time."

"Yeah. Looks like it." He motioned to the doors. "Let's head up to the room. We need to check for bugs, and I don't mean the six-legged kind."

Once inside the hotel, Reece made a beeline for the elevator banks with Andre close behind. He hoped Sarah and Arianne had found a way to locate the three succubae.

Arianne opened the door before Andre and Reece reached it, her senses alerted to their presence. "Sarah has something to tell you."

The pair followed her into the room and Arianne closed the door.

"I think we've found a locator spell," Sarah told them. "Arianne can perform it to see if we can find the succubae before they kill anyone else."

The look of confusion on Reece's face was obvious. "You're not sure it will work?"

Sarah sighed and frowned. "No, I'm not. We haven't encountered creatures like this before. We can only try it and see what happens." She removed her glasses, sat them beside the laptop and stood up. "Arianne is the best hope we have. Her powers are strong and she should be able to locate them using this spell." She glanced at Arianne and gave a thin smile.

Reece folded his arms. "So how do we go about this? Is there anything you need?"

"Yes, I need a goblet, four blue candles and some tamarisk incense," Arianne told him. "I'll use the bottled water from the refrigerator."

"Where do you think we're going to find those things at this time of night?" It was around three o'clock in the morning.

Sarah folded her arms and gave Reece a stern stare. "Improvise."

Andre tugged his friend's arm. "Come on, there's bound to be somewhere open where we can pick them up. It is Vegas after all."

Reece gave Sarah a disgruntled frown then looked at Andre. "Yeah, I guess you're right." He turned to Sarah and waved her over. When she reached him he whispered in her ear, "Do a sweep of the rooms while we're gone. I think we've been bugged."

Sarah's eyes met his and she gave a sharp nod.

The pair headed for the lifts.

Sarah gazed across the room at Arianne and wondered if the young woman, who was also half vampire, could perform the locator spell. It was difficult enough when trying to find a human let alone a demon. But without her efforts to find the seductresses more men *would* die.

Arianne's eyes met the priest's. "It's all right, Sarah, I will find them."

"I know you'll do your best, Arianne, but it's a difficult spell and demons are harder to track."

"I'm going to meditate until Reece and Andre get back. It will clear my mind and help me get into the zone." She found a spot on the floor between the queen-size beds and sat cross-legged.

"Ok. I'll leave you to it then. Reece asked me to do something for him so I'll start in the other room." Sarah was about to walk through the adjoining doorway when a sharp rap on the door startled her. She spun around. *Who would it be at this hour?* She knew it wasn't Reece or Andre as they had swipe keys to get into the room and they'd only just left. She swallowed the dry lump in her throat and glanced at Arianne, who had stopped meditating and was now standing.

"Who do you…?"

Sarah shook her head and raised a finger to her lips as she moved to the door. Arianne followed.

Another loud rap on the door startled both women and they gasped and jumped backwards.

"Who is it?" Sarah called, hers and Arianne's eyes remaining on each other.

No answer.

Sarah frowned at her companion as she reached for the handle. Her hand hovered above it and she wondered if she should open the door. Her breathing quickened and she swallowed hard, then gave the handle a sharp tug and pulled the door back.

No one was there.

She peered along the hallway in both directions. It was empty.

"Must've been another guest trying to get into the room and realized it wasn't theirs."

Arianne's eyes moved to the carpet outside the door and Sarah's gaze followed.

A brown paper package sat at the threshold.

The women gave each other an anxious look.

Sarah was about to bend down and pick it up when Arianne placed her hand on the priest's arm. "Let me."

"Why?" Sarah gave her a curious glance and stepped aside.

"I sense Charlotte."

Sarah frowned into Arianne's eyes. "You don't think they…?"

"I don't know." She picked up the package carefully and brought it into the room.

Reece and Andre were back within half an hour with everything Arianne needed to work the spell. When they entered the room both men noticed the worried expressions on the women's faces.

"What's wrong?" Reece asked, hurrying across the room.

Andre closed the door and followed him over.

"While you were gone this arrived." Sarah moved aside to reveal the package sitting on the table. "We couldn't bring ourselves to open it." She hesitated for a moment and looked up at Reece. "Arianne can sense Charlotte inside."

Reece swallowed hard and stared at the package.

Andre picked it up and examined it. He could sense her too. He looked at his friend. "Do you want me to open it?"

Reece didn't answer. If Arianne could sense Charlotte in the package did it mean she was dead?

"Reece?"

The PI nodded.

Andre set the package down on the table. "Sarah, do you have a pair of scissors by any chance?"

"I have nail clippers."

"Would you get them please?"

Sarah rushed over to her case and took the nail clippers from her toiletry bag. "Here," she said, passing them to Andre.

He cut the string and pulled it from the package, then opened the crinkled brown paper. Inside sat a medium-sized black cardboard box wrapped with blood red ribbon.

Reece frowned at it. Whoever had Charlotte was toying with them by sending whatever was inside giftwrapped.

The tension in the room was palpable as everyone stared at the box.

Andre reached for the bow.

Reece grabbed his arm. "Wait."

Andre turned to look at him. "We have to open it, Reece."

"I know," he said, giving a heavy sigh, "but what if it's a piece of her?" Tears stung the backs of his eyes. "I don't think I could take it if…"

Andre rested a hand on his friend's arm. "Let's just open it and go from there. Ok?" He could feel the turmoil inside his friend and knew if Reece's fears were real it would tip him over the edge.

Reece nodded. "You can sense her too, can't you? Is her blood inside?"

Andre wasn't sure he should answer but knew he had no choice. Once the box was open they would find out anyway. "Yes, it is."

Reece turned away. "Oh God!"

Sarah walked over to him and wrapped her arms around him. "It might just be her finger, Reece. She can live without a finger." She wanted to alleviate his fears.

He frowned into her eyes. "I know you mean well, Sarah, but even a finger is too much. It would mean they cut it off her while she was awake. I can't deal with her suffering any pain."

"I know." She gave him a distressed look. "But it could very well mean she's still alive. We have to continue to hope. For all our sakes."

Andre opened the box. "Reece."

Reece turned around. "Yeah?"

"It's her engagement ring wrapped in a bloody cloth."

The PI let out the breath he'd been holding. "Thank God!"

"It's still Charlotte's blood."

"I know, but it could mean they cut her. Not cut something off her." His mind wouldn't accept anything else right now.

"There's a note." Andre passed him the blood spattered piece of paper.

CHAPTER NINETEEN

Oriana disliked walking the labyrinth of filthy, pitch black storm tunnels under Vegas, with their graffitied walls, fragmented concrete floor and, in some areas, stagnant pools of water and mud, but she had no choice she had been summoned by their master. All three of them had.

Being a descendant from hell, she could see in the dark, her vision red like an infrared telescopic lens. There were over a thousand homeless living in different sectors of the drains, and as she passed the sleeping vagrants invisibly she searched for her next meal. A lost soul she could devour. They were easy targets and ones that wouldn't be missed.

Although she had enjoyed some of the males being investigated by the police, her sights were set on the private detective working with them. Reece Daniels. She'd almost had him out at the abandoned motel. Almost. She licked her glossy pink lips at the thought of him and hoped he would be her reward at the end of this arduous quest. She despised taking orders and being manipulated by anyone, even Lucifer, but she had no choice about either. If she disobeyed she would be destroyed. Oriana had other ideas. She wanted more than she had now. She had a plan.

The subterranean metropolis stretched for hundreds of miles but where Oriana was heading no one inhabited. It was their master's place of seclusion until the perfect time for him to make himself known. Her sisters Katya and Helyna would already be with him and Oriana wondered why he wanted to see them. Had they not adhered to his demented plan? A plan which could send them back to hell or get them all killed.

She could have assumed her demon form while traipsing through the tunnels, but preferred the human body she inhabited now. She knew it appealed to their master and she wanted to make a memorable impression. Oriana was aware of his tastes and knew he was fond of blondes. She hoped it would save her demon skin from his wrath.

When she reached the obscure section he had chosen as his sanctuary his voice echoed out into the tunnel at her. "Come in, Oriana, we have been waiting for you." His voice was controlled. Too smooth, too even, and she knew they had displeased him. It had to be the incident with the private detective. They were not meant to let him get away so soon.

"I am sorry I'm late, Master," she said, bowing her head in submission. Something she hated doing. Before now, she had been servant to no one except her real master and Lucifer never bothered with trivial acts of subservience.

"Come, join us." He raised his hand and motioned for her to step closer.

Oriana's eyes met her sisters' anxious frowns as she moved across to the intimate group. What had he said to them before her arrival? A threat on their lives, no doubt.

His intense, dark gaze moved around each of the women. "Why did you allow Reece Daniels to escape?"

"His team came in with guns blazing and took him by force, Master. There was nothing we could do," Oriana explained, a nervous tremor in her voice she tried to disguise.

"So your sisters have already informed me." He sat with his hands steepled, pursing his lips in contemplation. "I wanted to detain him for a while longer before he found a way to get free. I wanted his mind to be affected, confused. I wanted him to *suffer*. Now I will have to change my plans." His eyes narrowed, never leaving them for a second.

Katya stepped forward. "We are sorry, Master. We didn't expect his friends to find him out in the desert. We thought the distance from the city would be sufficient, but the vampires are far too sensitive to their humans. They must have followed his mortal vibration."

"Mm. Yes, of course." His gaze remained steadfast. He enjoyed being the cause of their discomfort. "When I have formulated a new scheme I will summon you again. You may go." He waved the trio off.

The women breathed a sigh of relief, bowed, turned on their heels and made a hasty retreat toward the tunnels.

"Next time I will not be so lenient." His words echoed around them as the three hurried out of his presence, before he changed his mind, and made their way back to the entrance.

"We were very lucky," Helyna said. "He could have killed us for such a mistake."

"Who would do his bidding, if he did?" Katya asked, the sting of sarcasm in her voice.

"Let us not forget there are hundreds of demons willing to assist him. We are not the only ones who want to remain among the mortals," Oriana warned.

They made themselves invisible to the human eye as they wandered the inhabited section of the drains. This particular area held quite a few males. Oriana realized a flash flood would wipe out the underground city, and lamented at the waste of good meat, if it happened.

∞⋈∞

"I'm sorry I couldn't make the locator spell work," Arianne said, packing away the candles and incense, disappointed with her lack of supernatural strength. "It appears demons are much harder to track than I thought."

Sarah rested a reassuring hand on her arm. "I did warn you. Don't be too hard on yourself. We'll find another way to locate them."

"How?" Reece folded his arms.

"I don't know. But the research I've been doing points to these particular demons having certain weaknesses. Maybe we can use it to our advantage."

"If we can find them." Reece's left eyebrow rose.

"We will." Sarah sat down in front of her laptop, her determination palpable.

"I wish I could be as confident."

"Here, look at this." Sarah swung her computer around. "They have a strong aversion to conflict of any kind. They will flee rather than face a life-threatening situation." She looked up at him. "Just like at the old motel."

"How does this information help us? We can't fight what we can't find."

"Yes, I know, but it does give us some leverage when we do."

75

"They're insidious creatures," Andre said. "They can suck the life right out of a human and leave a shriveled corpse but they're cowards when it comes to preserving their own existence."

Sarah continued. "If we can release them from their earth bound bodies it will send them straight back to hell. We need to close the rift first so they can't return."

"Have you found anything yet?" Reece's gaze moved to the laptop screen.

"No, but I am working on it. There are hundreds of historical documents to sift through and a lot of them haven't been categorized."

"Ok. Find out what you can as fast as you can. We need to locate the demons and get this done." Reece sighed and glanced at the digital clock. "Andre, we need to keep that appointment. Let's hope it's not another wild goose chase." It was almost five o'clock in the morning, but it didn't make a difference to the demons. Another meeting at yet another hotel, this time The Venetian. What would be waiting for them there?

"We should follow whoever shows up and find out where they go," Andre suggested.

"Let's wait and see if they do show up, then we can decide what action to take. Remember what happened at the Luxor?"

"Yeah, you're right." Andre opened the door to their room. "Ok. Let's get going."

⁎⁏⁐⁑

At such an early hour, the Venetian was relatively quiet. As Reece and Andre passed the fountain and headed to the Grand Canal, Andre sensed they were being watched. His eyes moved inconspicuously around the lobby but only staff were preparing for the day ahead. Still, his senses were on alert. Someone *was* watching them.

"Reece, don't turn around, but we're being watched. I don't know where they are but I can feel their presence."

The PI kept walking without reacting. "Ok. How many?"

"Two. One human, one demon."

"Which means there'll be another package." He sighed. "I wish we could find them. Not knowing if Charlotte's alive or dead is killing me."

Andre glanced at his friend sideways. "I know and I'm sorry you're going through this right now. You should be here on your honeymoon enjoying time together."

Reece's eyes met Andre's. "I only wish."

"We'll find her, Reece."

"I don't doubt it. I just don't know if she'll be alive when we do." He blinked back the tears stinging his eyes. He wanted her in his arms alive and well. "This game of cat and mouse is wearing thin. Do you think you can pinpoint who's watching us so we can follow them?"

"It's hard to say. They're keeping their whereabouts concealed from me so I don't know if I can. But I'll try."

"I hope we can get our hands on them soon. I want to…"

Andre rested a comforting hand on his friend's shoulder and gave him a solemn frown. "I know. And we will."

When the pair reached the Grand Canal a guy dressed as a gondola driver approached them. "Someone asked me to give you this." He passed Reece a business-sized envelope.

Reece took it and frowned. "Can you describe who gave it to you?"

The guy's face contorted into a grimace. "Not really. They were wearing a hood and a bandana over the lower part of their face. And they had some kind of voice distorter."

Andre stepped up to him. "Do you think it was a man or a woman?"

The guy shrugged. "Hard to tell by what they were wearing. But it could've been a dude."

Reece glanced past the guy. "Which way did they go?"

The gondola guy turned and pointed. "That way."

The pair left him standing on the bridge and took off in the direction of the main entrance.

CHAPTER TWENTY

Sarah and Arianne were in the adjoining hotel room searching through books of magic online, looking for a binding spell to contain the three succubae. Once they could hold them they would find a way to send them back to hell and close the rift. Who knew what other creatures had ventured into the world and what kind of havoc they were already wreaking on humanity?

"Any luck?" Sarah asked, removing her glasses and squeezing her thumb and index finger into her tired eyes. They had been at it for hours.

"Not yet." Arianne gave a heavy sigh, stood up and stretched. "Much of the information on the internet is posted by fanatics rather than professionals with any real knowledge. It's difficult to know what will work and what won't."

"I guess it's a case of trial and error, although we don't have a lot of room for error." Sarah switched on the kettle, picked up a sachet of instant coffee, tore it open and poured it into a mug. "Want one?" she asked, turning and gazing across the room at Arianne.

"No thanks. What I could use is some blood."

Sarah gave her a quizzical frown.

"Even though I'm only half vampire, I still need blood from time to time. It boosts my energy levels and clears my mind. And right now I could use some clarity."

"Very interesting. I was unaware."

"You partake of vampire blood, don't you?"

Sarah sighed. "Yes. I do it because I'm searching for…"

"Dracula?"

"How'd you know?"

"Andre told me."

"Oh." Her right eyebrow rose.

"Do you think you'll ever find him?" Arianne walked over and sat on the foot of the bed.

"I pray I will one day. He owes me a huge debt and I want payment."

"Vampire blood has prolonged your life. How much longer do you think you can keep going before it takes its toll on you?"

"I don't know. But while I have breath in my body and the ability to continue I'll keep searching for him, and when I find him we'll face off and deal with the issue." She had the weaponry to destroy him and she would when the opportunity presented itself.

Arianne shivered. "Doesn't he frighten you? The thought of coming face to face with the most infamous vampire of all time scares the hell out of me. He's a danger to everyone, human and vampire alike."

"I'm not afraid. He needs to pay for what he did and I'll make sure he does." The thought caused her heart to shudder against her ribs. Finding the monster and putting an end to him was her sole purpose for living as long as she had. Once she accomplished the task of ridding the world of him she would be free. What then?

Arianne's eyes remained on the priest. "Well, we'd better get back to it." She returned to her seat and her laptop.

"Yes." Sarah watched the young woman for a moment before returning her gaze to her computer. Was she as trustworthy as Andre believed her to be? Half vampire and a witch, something she had kept from them. What else could she be hiding?

ಐ⋅ೞ

Once out of the hotel, Reece and Andre scanned the undercover pickup, drop-off point with desperate eyes. Guests and cars were everywhere. Andre turned his head to the left and spotted the hooded perp heading for the taxi drive through and took off after him. Reece followed, gaining momentum but his running speed wasn't anywhere near as fast as his friend's. When he got to the beginning of the drive, Andre and the contact had disappeared. He heaved a heavy sigh. How could they have gotten away so fast?

Reece pulled his cell from the back pocket of his jeans and speed dialed Andre's number. No answer. He shoved the phone back in place with a disgruntled huff and walked along the path, scanning everyone and everywhere. *Where could they have gone?*

He raced along the left-hand path searching for his friend and the only person who could tell them what they needed to know. Where to find Charlotte's abductors.

When he reached the back corner of the hotel, he found Andre and the hood concealed behind one of the large square columns. Andre had the guy at arm's length pinned against the pillar, his feet flailing off the ground.

"Great work!" Reece slipped behind the column out of sight. Queues of taxis were lined up waiting to drop off guests and they couldn't afford to be seen and reported to security.

"Thanks." Andre said, giving Reece a sideward glance. "He's just a kid. He was paid fifty dollars to deliver the envelope. They told him to give the gondola guy your description and where you'd be waiting."

"Shit!" Reece's intense gaze locked onto the kid. He couldn't have been any more than seventeen.

"What's your name?"

The kid raised his chin in defiance.

Reece gripped his shoulder and squeezed. "Tell me."

"Ow, ok. It's Jeremy." He grimaced and the PI eased off.

"Jeremy what?" Reece wanted to know so the sheriff could keep track of him for his own safety.

"Jacobs."

"Ok, Jeremy Jacobs, can you describe the person who gave you this?" He held up the brown rectangle envelope.

The kid smiled at the memory. "*Oh, yeah.* She was one *hot* babe."

"And?"

"Whaddya wanna know?" The dreamy expression remained on his face.

"A description would be helpful." Reece pocketed the envelope and folded his arms, keeping his intimidating stare on the young guy.

He shrugged. "She was hot."

Reece sighed. "What about hair color, eye color, height, any distinguishing features you can remember?"

The kid thought for a moment. "Um… she was maybe a little taller than me. Blonde. Didn't really pay attention to her eyes but she had great boobs." His smile widened.

Reece sighed and shook his head. Teens and their hormones. "There must've been something else you can remember. Think about it."

The kid frowned. "Oh, yeah, she had a tattoo on the inside of her left forearm."

"What kind of tattoo?" Reece's voice was tight with impatience.

"An upside down cross on top of an old compass. It looked way cool."

"Anything else?"

"Nah. Can't think of anything." The kid gave Andre an irritated glare. "Wanna let me down now?"

Andre released him and stepped back.

"Where'd she meet you?"

"On the strip outside the Bellagio."

Another dead end.

Reece pulled a card out of his wallet and shoved it at the kid. "If you think of anything useful call me." He put two and two together and came up with succubus. "You're lucky to be alive. Don't contact her or go near her again. Understood?"

"But why?" The kid screwed up his face. She had come onto him and his dick had other ideas. He really wanted to hook up with her.

"She's a killer." Reece gave it to him straight. He hoped shock value would do the trick.

The kid chuckled and gave him an incredulous frown. "Yeah. Right."

"He's serious. She and her friends have killed six guys so far and they won't stop there." Andre stared into the kid's eyes and compelled him. "Stay away from her."

"I'll stay away from her." Jeremy's gaze moved from Reece to Andre then back to Reece. "Can I go now?"

"Remember what I said. If you think of anything call me."

The kid nodded, then sidled past the pair and disappeared around the corner of the hotel, heading back to the strip.

"He was telling the truth. He didn't know any more than he told us."

"Yeah, I figured." Reece remembered what the gypsy had said to Andre about the women. One blonde, one brunette and one redhead. There had to be a way to find them.

CHAPTER TWENTY ONE

Reece and Andre headed back to the rental. Once again, Reece didn't open the envelope until they were in the car out of sight. He was determined not to give the demons the satisfaction of witnessing his reaction. He had to play it cool no matter what was inside. The giftwrapped box in their hotel room had been difficult enough. He hoped Charlotte hadn't been butchered when they took the blood from her. He fingered her engagement ring lying inside his shirt pocket. He wanted it close so he could slip it on her finger again when they found her. Deep down, he questioned if she was still alive. Time was running out.

Andre's gaze moved to the envelope. "Are you going to open it?"

Reece sighed. "Yeah, just give me a minute." He needed to steel himself for whatever he was about to see.

"Do you want me to do it?" Andre held out his hand.

"No." He glanced at his friend. "Thanks, I've got it." He tore down the side of the business-sized envelope and spread the opening. A lock of Charlotte's blood encrusted hair lay inside. "Jesus!"

"It still doesn't mean she's dead. They're playing with your emotions."

Reece turned and stared into his friend's eyes. "Maybe she's been dead all along and they're just toying with me. But why? We've never dealt with succubae before so what's their motive?"

Andre took the envelope from Reece's hand. He pressed the end open and inhaled. "I don't know, but we will find out. The hair has Charlotte's essence in it. She was alive when they cut it."

"You're sure?"

"Yes."

Reece let out the breath he'd been holding and swiped at a lone tear sliding down his cheek. "Thank God." He wasn't sure how much more he could take. Charlotte and Tommy were his world now. He couldn't exist without them in it.

"Why don't we head back to the hotel? I'm sure Sarah and Arianne will be wondering what happened."

Reece started the engine and gave his friend a solemn look. "Yeah, we need to get one of those demon vampire bitches to tell us where Charlotte is before we expedite them back to hell."

"Sarah just messaged me. She's found a way to bind the succubae. Now all we have to do is find them."

Once back at the hotel, Reece told Sarah and Arianne about the incident at the Venetian with the kid. Jeremy's hormones were running hot which could be a problem. At least with Andre compelling him he'd be safe. He also told them it was imperative they find the women soon so they could get Charlotte back. She was his first priority.

Reece was curious about binding demons. "So how does the whole thing work?"

"The succubae have to be bound in a barren and uninhabited place, so I thought the center of the Sahara desert would be appropriate. It's so remote not even the nomads travel there. They'll remain trapped until we can repair the rift and send them back to hell."

"And have you found the spell?"

Sarah shook her head. "Not a spell, a prayer."

He gave her a skeptical frown. "And you're sure it'll work?"

"Yes, I have faith it will."

"I think we should do another drive around. They have to be somewhere," Andre said.

"We've covered pretty much everywhere. Where else do you suggest we look?" Reece stood with his hands on his hips.

"There are a couple of other venues we haven't tried."

"Where?"

"The Asylum and Hotel Fear? They're the kinds of places where demons would hang out. And if they are masquerading as performers it would be the perfect location. No one would realize what they were."

"How far out of Vegas are these places?"

"About a ten to fifteen minute drive from here." He typed into the search engine, picked up Arianne's laptop and showed Reece the website. "Maybe we can take a look tonight? Go in as patrons and suss out both venues."

The PI grimaced. "Christ! People really go for this kind of stuff?"

"Everyone loves a good scare and cosplay is huge now." Andre sat the computer on the table.

Reece's serious gaze moved to his friend. "If they only knew what was really out there."

ʀ&#x3;ɣ

Lozano called Reece around midday with an update on Charlotte's case. His undercover guys had asked their contacts if they'd heard any rumors about a woman being held at a motel outside Sin City. No one had. He figured whoever took her covered their tracks so well not even those in-the-know knew anything. He asked if the abductors had made further contact and Reece filled him in on the gift and the envelope. And the kid.

The sheriff was disturbed by the new turn of events and, despite wanting to remain optimistic, his instincts were telling him the PI's girlfriend could be dead. But he would keep his men on it until something came to light or Charlotte's body turned up. He hoped it wasn't the latter.

"Do you want to bring the box and envelope in for forensic testing?" Lozano asked.

"Is there any point? The demons wouldn't have left DNA evidence behind? And what could you compare it to?"

"Look, I know what you're saying and I agree, but who knows? Maybe the bodies they're using have criminal records. If so, their finger prints and DNA would be in the system. We'd have a way to identify them, which could help us locate them sooner rather than later, before anyone else gets killed. The offer's on the table, it's up to you."

Reece sighed into the phone and ran the thought around his brain. "All right. I'll ask Andre to drop them off to you."

"Good. Even the smartest criminals have tripped themselves up by being over confident. Who's to say demons can't do the same?"

"Thanks, Sheriff, I appreciate it."

"No problem. So what's happening with the research for sending the demons back to hell?" He thought about what he'd just said and hoped the precinct phones weren't monitored this week. If anyone heard the conversation they'd think he was crazy. Maybe he should make a point of asking Reece and his team to call him on his personal cell phone in future.

"Sarah can contain the demons in the middle of the Sahara until we can send them back."

"You don't think it would be better to… should I say it, kill them?"

"The whole process is tricky. We can't upset the balance between hell and earth. There's a fine line when it comes to the ratio of humans to demons and…"

"If you kill them the balance will be offset?"

"Exactly. Trust me, I'd love to expedite them into oblivion but unfortunately I can't."

Lozano nodded to himself and gave a heavy sigh. "I understand." His official cell phone vibrated on his desk. "Can you hold for a minute?"

"Sure." Reece heard the muffled conversation but couldn't make out what was said.

The sheriff was back on the line in seconds. "Can you meet me at Meadows Mall as soon as possible? We've got another body."

CHAPTER TWENTY TWO

When Reece and Andre arrived at the mall, the sheriff had the area cordoned off and four police officers were redirecting pedestrian and vehicle traffic away from the crime scene. Three police cruisers with strobe lights flashing blocked the drive and yellow crime scene tape had been secured around the trees outlining the right-hand corner of the complex.

Reece pulled the rental into a parking spot opposite the police cars and he and Andre left the vehicle and walked over to the officers. Reynolds waved them through and told them the sheriff was around the back of Sears department store.

Lozano stepped out from behind the brick wall, talking into his shoulder mic. Reynolds had informed him they were there. "Glad you could make it. This one's the same as the others, except I think he's a lot younger. I figured we were looking at a type, early to mid-twenties, but it looks like they've changed their MO." He sighed and turned on his heel. Reece and Andre followed.

The first thing Reece recognized was the two-toned, fluorescent green running shoes. His gut twisted and a wave of nausea hit him as he moved closer. "Jesus!" His stomach flipped over and bile rose in his throat.

Lozano's eyebrows shot up. "You know him?"

"It's the kid I told you about. Jeremy Jacobs."

"How can you be so sure?"

Reece pointed. "The shoes. And the very distinctive hoodie." It had a drawn design down each sleeve which was definitely not store bought.

The sheriff grimaced. "I'm sorry we couldn't find a location for him. Maybe he was a runaway or one of the many homeless. There are masses of them all over the city now. God. He's just a kid." He shook his head. "What a waste."

"Andre com…" Reece stopped himself.

Lozano's wary gaze rested on the PI. "Andre did what?"

Reece gave him a sheepish look and ignored the question. "We warned the kid not to go near the woman again. I guess his hormones got the better of him." He stood with hands on hips. "Damn stupid kid." *Andre compelled him, why didn't it work?*

"I'll get someone back at the precinct to search juvie records and see if we can come up with an address and family for him. He may not have been an offender and if so we're back to square one."

Reece sighed, his eyes focused on the kid's shriveled remains. He'd been used and eliminated.

Andre motioned with his head for Reece to follow him and they moved away from the scene. "This could be the break we've been looking for."

"How so?"

"We were coming here tonight to check out the horror clubs. This could prove my theory."

Reece frowned. "You think the kid was at one of the venues?"

"What other explanation is there? He probably knew she worked here. The club might have been where he first met her. Are you going to let the sheriff in on what we've got so far?"

"Not yet. We really don't have anything to tell him until we check out those hotspots, and then it all depends on what we find. This is our territory, not his. It's safer for us to do the leg work before bringing Lozano in."

"What about back up?" Andre folded his arms. "We'll need back up."

"I think we got it covered. And besides, what can ordinary weapons do against demons?"

Lozano came up behind them. "Anything you boys want to tell me?"

Reece and Andre swung around. "Not at the moment," Reece said. "We're working on a theory but don't have anything solid to go on yet. When we do we'll fill you in."

The sheriff nodded then locked his serious gaze on both men. "Be sure you do. I want to know what you know, so keep me in the loop. Ok?"

"Will do." Reece pulled a pack of gum out of the front pocket of his jeans, popped a spearmint stick in his mouth and watched the sheriff walk away.

Lozano headed back across the drive, glancing over his shoulder at the pair. He knew they weren't being a hundred percent honest with him but he'd hold off putting a tail on them for a while longer.

Reece's intense gaze followed the sheriff's stout form back to the loading dock. "I hope he didn't hear any of our conversation."

"Lozano's suspicious of us, Reece. He knows we're not telling him what we know. Did you mention the succubae are the ones who have Charlotte?"

"Yeah, but regardless of the two cases being connected now, Charlotte's my responsibility and I don't want law enforcement screwing it up and getting her killed, if she is still alive. We have to deal with this on our own."

"So you're not planning to tell him anything?"

"What he doesn't know won't hurt him. And let's face it, the succubae aren't partial about who they suck the life out of and I wouldn't want to be responsible for the death of a good cop."

"We will need his team's help eventually, you know."

"I know. But right now I want to keep Lozano and his men out of harm's way. We have all the backup we need. Sarah and Arianne are more than capable of watching our backs, and they have the skills and weaponry to do it." He frowned at Andre. "I have a question."

"What is it?"

"Why didn't the compelling work on the kid?"

"I'm not sure. It seemed to, unless the demon made him resistant and he faked it."

Reece's left eyebrow arched. "You think he did?"

"Unfortunately, yes. The kid was horny. He was thinking about having sex with her the whole time we were talking to him."

"Stupid damn kid. I hope it was worth it."

"There's nothing we can do for him now, Reece."

"Yeah, I know. What we have to do is prevent more deaths. And the only way we can do that is to find the blonde succubus so she can lead us to the others."

80CB

Later the same evening, Reece and Andre went back to Meadows Mall and stood in line outside Hotel Fear. As a lot of the patrons dressed in costume, the PIs disguised themselves so they wouldn't be recognized if the women were part of the show and spotted them going through.

It was 6.19. Both venues opened their nightmarish doors at 6.30 PM and the queue of teens and adults waiting to enter was electric. Reece couldn't understand what the attraction was because as a detective he'd witnessed horror on the streets of LA every day. The things people could do to each other defied explanation and was far more frightening than anything these places could offer.

Sarah and Arianne arrived just as the doors opened and people were shuffling forward to enter the venue. "Sorry we're late. Traffic was chaotic." Sarah stepped up beside Reece and Arianne joined Andre behind them.

"Did you bring the stunners?"

Sarah tapped her shoulder bag and gave him a perceptive smirk. "Got everything we need right here."

"Good. I've got a gut feeling the blonde demon is here. Maybe they all are." Reece swallowed his anger. One of them *would* tell him where Charlotte was. If not he'd be more than tempted to upset the balance between hell and earth.

"We're ready for her." Sarah gave a satisfied smile.

Reece's cell phone vibrated in his pocket. He whipped it out and checked the caller ID. "It's Lozano." He pressed the button. "Sheriff, what can I do for you?"

"I'm sending you a picture of a woman believed to be dead. I think it's the blonde succubus you're looking for."

Reece removed the phone from his ear and checked the picture. Now they had something to work with. "Thanks, Sheriff, I appreciate it. Talk to you tomorrow." He rang off and sent the photo to the others. "Now we have a face we can identify."

CHAPTER TWENTY THREE

The gloomy, nerve tingling atmosphere of Hotel Fear sent a shiver up everyone's spine. People's body language was rigid and jerky, their eyes roaming the shadows for whatever was to come. The anxious vibration was palpable as they moved through the darkness in groups of six. 666, the devil's number. Reece and his team could hear the nervous giggles and squeals of fright from patrons further ahead as they wandered the claustrophobic dilapidated hallways, with their peeling, rotting wallpaper, doors opening and banging shut, manic laughter and blood-curdling shrieks. Gruesome characters popped out of hidden recesses along the narrow, pitch black corridors grabbing people in the dark. In some areas the floors moved, causing everyone in the frightened, intimate group to cling to each other to prevent them from falling over.

Reece, Sarah, Andre and Arianne were with a young couple who seemed in awe of the fear-instilling environment, the young woman gasping, jerking with fright then giggling and the young guy pulling her into a snug, protective embrace.

It wouldn't be easy to suss out the succubus in the muted lighting, especially as most of the cast wore costumes and horror make up: pale contacts, blood-splattered, scarred faces, black lipstick and wigs.

The four continued through the hotel of horror with their wits about them, Andre using his immortal senses to try to locate the demon, if it was in the building. Once the succubus realized they were there it would vanish.

"Reece! Over there!" Sarah shouted. She had infrared contacts in her eyes which could spot any demon in the dark.

"Where?" He searched ahead of him through the gloom but his human sight couldn't pick up on the succubus.

"She's making a run for it!"

Reece and the others broke from the group, pushing their way through the patrons, trying to catch up to her before she eluded them once again. She was quick and invisible to the naked human eye.

"Can you still see her?" Reece shoved people out of the way in an attempt to get closer to the woman. He couldn't let her get away. She was his only chance of finding Charlotte.

"Yes, she's scrambling around people trying to get to the emergency exit."

"Can you hit her with the stunner?"

"Not unless you want me to shoot people as well."

"Dammit. Keep moving. She can't get away this time."

People around them thought the dramatic scenario was part of the show. They ducked, weaved, screamed and laughed nervously as the four forced their way through the crowd toward the rear exit.

Sheriff Lozano entered the office of the horror attraction and gave Reece a serious glare. He knew the PI wasn't sharing important information about the case and it didn't sit well with him because he was doing everything he could to cooperate with Daniels and his team.

The four of them were sitting on plastic, stackable chairs lining one wall opposite the busy-looking desk. "The owner tells me you've been disturbing the peace. Why did you come here?"

"We're having a night out. Everyone needed some fun." Reece gave him an equally severe stare.

"You expect me to believe you were here for the fun of it? Want to explain what went wrong?"

Reece sighed and stood up. "We found one of the..."

Lozano raised his hand, motioning for him to stop talking. He turned to the two officers behind him. "Would you both go out and take witness statements? Don't let anyone leave until I've finished in here. Ok?"

The cops gave him a curious frown, stared at the group of four, nodded, then turned on their heels and headed outside to the parking lot. The patrons had been asked to wait until the police finished their investigation.

Once his men were gone, Lozano said, "Ok. Go on."

"It's not a coincidence the kid was murdered at the mall. The blonde works here. Maybe the others too."

The sheriff pursed his lips, his eyes remaining on the PI. "So you weren't here on a night out, you came here to find her. Right?"

Reece glanced over his shoulder at the others then turned to look at Lozano. "Ok. Yeah. We came here to capture her. She knows where Charlotte is."

"Look, I understand you're concerned for your fiancée's well-being, and rightly so, but you can't keep impeding the investigation. I need to know what's going on for *this* very reason." He jabbed a finger at Reece. "Do you want to get yourself arrested tonight?"

"*Are* you arresting us?" Reece frowned and folded his arms.

Sarah, Andre and Arianne stood up, alarm showing on each of their faces. Would they be arrested? They couldn't afford to be locked up now. They had to get out on the street and find the succubus.

"Could be. I'll have to talk to the owners and see if they want to press charges." He turned to walk out the door then turned back. "You better hope they don't."

CHAPTER TWENTY FOUR

Reece stepped up to the glass panel in the door of the booking cell and glowered at Sheriff Lozano. How could he have let this happen knowing what was out there and what they needed to do? They had been in the cell for several hours. Was the sheriff making a point? If so, Reece understood loud and clear. No more keeping secrets. He'd give Lozano everything he had from now on. His team couldn't be out of action for this long. Who knew what had happened since the succubus escaped them?

The grim expression on the sheriff's face turned Reece's stomach to water and an unsettling undercurrent of fear rippled through his gut making him queasy. "What is it, Lozano?"

Enrique Lozano inhaled a deep breath and let it out in a long slow sigh. He couldn't find the words to tell the PI what he'd just witnessed. The officer beside him pushed a key into the dual lock releasing the door and the sheriff raised his hand to the others as they stood up to leave. "I need to speak to Reece alone for a minute. Won't take long."

Andre, Sarah and Arianne frowned at each other, then moved their gazes to the sheriff and their friend. Reece glanced over his shoulder at them as he followed Lozano out of the cell and down the bright corridor.

"What do you think's going on?" Sarah asked, remaining on her feet and staring across the cell.

"No idea. But the sheriff looked... disturbed about something." Andre had picked up fragmented thoughts running through Lozano's head but wasn't about to impart what he'd interpreted to the women. Not now.

Charlotte's name had skimmed past his mind and he had a bad feeling about it. Whatever the sheriff wanted to tell Reece couldn't be good news.

"What do you think it is?" Arianne sat down on the wooden bench and eased herself back against the cream-colored, concrete bricks.

"I guess we'll find out when Reece gets back." Sarah sat next to her.

Andre walked across to the metal and glass door and gazed out. What was the sheriff about to tell his friend?

Lozano ushered Reece into an empty office and closed the door. What he had to say wasn't going to be easy but the PI needed to be told. He motioned for Reece to take a seat but he declined and remained standing.

"What's going on? Why'd you bring me in here?"

The sheriff's gaze remained fixed on the PI. "Because I need to talk to you alone."

"Ok. You've got my attention so what is it?"

Lozano gave a heavy sigh, his eyes never leaving Reece for a second. "Would you please sit down?" He gestured to the chair in front of the desk. His serious expression began to worry Reece and he dragged the chair across the floor and plonked himself down onto it. "Happy now?"

"Yeah." The sheriff moved to the corner of the desk, propped himself there and folded his arms. "Reece…" He cleared his throat. "I have something to tell you and there's no easy way to say it."

Reece mirrored the sheriff's movements and gave him a severe glare. "Say what? Are you going to hold us here longer? You know what we're up against out there. Surely you can pull a few strings…"

Lozano bounced off the corner of the desk onto his feet. "Will you shut the hell up for a minute?" He sighed again. "This is difficult enough without you making it more difficult."

Reece swallowed hard. He could see beads of sweat forming on the sheriff's brow and knew it was serious. He raised defensive hands. "Ok. Tell me."

The sheriff ran a hand over his face and his jaw flexed. "I got a call from the county coroner's office and I went over there." He paced once and turned around. "A Jane Doe was brought in a couple of hours ago…"

Reece jumped to his feet. "You think it's Charlotte, don't you?"

Lozano gestured to the chair again. "Please, sit down."

The PI dropped onto the seat, his face turning a pale shade of gray, tears stinging the backs of his eyes.

The sheriff huffed out a breath. "The description fits. But…"

Reece looked up at him and frowned. "But what?"

"It's difficult to make a positive identification. She's been in the elements a while and, and the wildlife has…"

"Dear God." Reece rested his head in his hands, tears rolling down his face and dripping onto the floor.

"The woman's fingerprints have been removed and…" he cleared his throat again, "her facial features can't be identified by photo. We don't know for sure it's Charlotte."

Reece's head whipped up and he sniffed back the urge to sob. "Have you run her DNA?" He balled his fists and rubbed his eyes.

"Being done as we speak." Lozano rested a firm hand on Reece's shoulder. "Does Charlotte have any distinguishing marks or moles on her body?"

"I don't know." An errant tear slid down the PI's left cheek and the sob remained stuck in his throat.

The sheriff's eyebrows rose. "What do you mean you don't know? You're engaged to the woman. You must've…"

"We haven't been intimate." Reece shook his head. "We were waiting for our wedding night."

Lozano blew out a noisy breath. "Ok." He rubbed the back of his neck where the beginnings of a headache was developing. "We'll just have to wait for the samples then."

Reece was on his feet. "I want to see her!"

The sheriff gripped his arm and stared earnestly into his eyes. "Believe me when I tell you you *don't* want to see her. Not until we know it is her."

"Lozano, I *want* to see her!" Reece loomed over the shorter man.

"And I said *no*." He raised his chin and stared into the PI's eyes. He wasn't about to let the man view a decomposed body ravaged by coyotes that may or may not be his fiancée. "Take a seat."

Reece stood his ground.

So did the sheriff. "I said take a seat."

The PI glowered at him and dropped onto the chair.

Lozano sat back on the edge of the desk. "The coroner thinks she's been out there for a few days, which works with the timeline of when Charlotte was taken, but it doesn't mean it's her. People go missing all the time here, especially women."

Reece swiped another tear from his face and sniffled. "Out where?"

"She was found in the motel where you were being held by a couple of urban explorers. Young guys. Shook them up pretty bad."

"Jesus Christ!" His eyes moved to Lozano. "Then it has to be her." More tears slid down his face, he couldn't hold them back any longer. "Charlotte." Her name left his lips on a sob.

"Don't jump to conclusions so fast. Let's wait and see what forensics gives us. I personally asked Ramirez to deal with it ASAP. Their backlog would've had us waiting three months if I didn't. It'll take a few hours. Then we'll know for sure. She could be just what we suspect her to be, a Jane Doe." Who was he trying to convince the PI or himself?

Lozano left Reece in the office, walked back to the holding cell, gazed through the glass and waved Andre over. He turned to an officer having a conversation nearby. "Hey, Bob, open up will ya?"

"Sure thing, boss." The officer stepped across the corridor and unlocked the cell. The glass and metal door slid in front of the glass wall.

"I need you to come with me." Lozano moved aside to make room for Andre to step out. Arianne and Sarah stood up. "Where are you taking him?"

The sheriff glanced across the cell at the women. "We won't be long. Have a seat."

"What's going on?" Andre's gaze locked onto the sheriff's.

"Let's take a walk."

The pair wandered along the hallway, past the office Reece was in, through a doorway and out to the side of the building.

"I know you and Reece are close so I wanted you to know what happened. He's going to need your support."

Andre folded his arms. "Always. Why?"

"A Jane Doe fitting Charlotte's description came into the coroner's office a couple hours ago..."

Andre's pale complexion turned even paler, if it were possible.

"We haven't been able to make a formal identification because of the condition of the body. It's... pretty bad."

"And you told Reece all of this?"

"He had to know."

Andre frowned. "It would've been better to have waited until you knew for sure. This will throw him completely into a tailspin and we need him focused if we're going to capture the succubae, not have him worrying about whether the body lying in the morgue is Charlotte."

Lozano folded his arms. "Look, I did what I had to do. The man had a right to know and he'd be pissed if it turns out to be her and I didn't tell him."

Andre knew the sheriff was right, but even so Reece's head needed to remain in the supernatural game they'd been thrust into. The demons had to be found and dealt with and he didn't want to be concerned about whether or not Reece could hold it together long enough to accomplish the life-threatening task.

CHAPTER TWENTY FIVE

Lozano escorted Andre back to the office where he'd left Reece and opened the door. Reece wasn't inside. He stepped backwards and gazed up and down the corridor. "Hey, Bob, did you see where Daniels went?"

The officer frowned and shook his head. "Nope. Why?"

Lozano sighed. "Because he's not in here."

"Maybe he had to take a piss," the officer offered with a shrug.

Both men walked down the corridor to the men's room. Empty.

The sheriff's gaze moved to Andre. "Would he go to the coroner's office?" He knew the answer before he'd finished asking the question. He gripped Andre's arm and flinched at the chill of his body. There was no time for his brain to process it, they had to stop Reece before he got into the morgue and viewed the body. "Come on, let's go."

Andre and Lozano raced along the hallway and out into reception. Reece wasn't there. No surprise.

Lozano turned to Andre. "Do you think he'd walk? It's only about ten minutes from here."

"No. He wouldn't be on the street in plain view. He'd hotwire a car."

The pair raced out to the carpark and the sheriff directed Andre to his green Mazda sedan. "We'll take my car." He pressed the remote. "Get in."

Lozano reversed out of the parking spot like his ass was on fire. He couldn't let the PI see the woman's body, not the way it looked.

When they arrived at the coroner's office Reece was stepping out of an early model blue hatchback. Lozano recognized the car. It belonged to one of his men. Given the circumstances he'd have to overlook the theft. The PI wasn't thinking straight.

He and Andre flung open their doors and scrambled from the car. "Reece. Wait," Andre called.

Reece glanced over his shoulder. "Shit!" He gave a heavy sigh and quickened his pace along the concrete path.

Andre raced across the road and caught up to him. "You don't want to do this."

He glowered at him. "Yeah, I do."

Lozano came up behind them. "No, Reece, you don't." He rested a hand on the PI's shoulder. "Wait until we have confirmation." He glanced at his watch. "There's only a couple of hours to go." His brow furrowed. "Please." He felt for the man, he couldn't help it. The situation couldn't get much worse.

Reece's gaze moved to his friend. "Andre could identify her. He's known her almost as long as I have."

"You don't really want to put your friend through that kind of ordeal, do you?" Lozano frowned.

The PI's aloof gaze turned to the sheriff. "We've seen worse. We've watched friends die." He chuckled, thinking *'and return from the dead'* but wouldn't say it out loud.

Reece wasn't making sense and the sheriff figured he was in shock. "I understand what you're saying, but viewing a body like this is different, especially when it's someone so close to you. Don't make him do it."

"It's all right, Sheriff Lozano, I'll go." Andre glanced at the door then back at the pair. "It's better for Reece to know. And I'd rather it was me than him." He looked his friend in the eye then returned his gaze to the sheriff.

"All right, but don't say I didn't warn you." Lozano started along the path then stopped and turned around. "Are you coming?"

"Wait right here, ok? Don't follow us in and don't go *anywhere*. I'll be out as soon as I've taken a look. You want to know, right?" Reece nodded. Andre stared into his friend's aloof gaze then followed the sheriff through the orange façade, glancing over his shoulder before entering the concrete brick building. He had a bad feeling about leaving Reece outside alone, especially in his current state of mind.

Corpses in blue plastic body bags with white and red biohazard labels attached lined the walls. It made death look like an epidemic, which it was, and far too real. Not at all as it appeared on television. Andre followed Lozano and a staff member named Ben along to the last trolley and the guy wheeled it out of the lineup into the middle of the floor. He gave both men an uncertain frown as he reached for the black zipper. "You sure you wanna do this?" he asked, noticing the pallor on Andre's face, unaware he always looked that way.

Lozano gave him a harsh stare, glanced at Andre and nodded. "Go ahead." He cleared his throat and stepped aside.

Andre moved forward and waited for Ben to unzip the bag and fold back the cover.

The face was unrecognizable. Wild animals had eaten away most of it, but the hairstyle and skin tone matched Charlottes. Still, he couldn't be sure it was her. He stepped up to the gurney and his eyes roamed the decimation looking for anything recognizable.

"Is it her?" The sheriff asked.

"Andre sighed. "I – I'm not sure. There's nothing distinctive about her to offer any indication that it is Charlotte."

"That's what I thought. We'll just have to wait for the DNA results." Lozano nodded for the guy to zip up the bag.

"Wait." Andre's eyebrows knitted together as he noticed something familiar and he leaned in to take a closer look. "I think Charlotte had earrings like these." They were hollow, silver heart shaped studs with a red crystal in the center.

Lozano stepped up beside him. "You have to be sure, Andre. Did she or didn't she?"

"I remember seeing her wearing a pair just like those." He closed his eyes and ran the scene through his mind. His eyes snapped open. "It was the day she came to our office to ask for Reece's help with a case she was working on."

"You're sure?" Lozano frowned.

Andre nodded.

"It's not much to go on. The earrings could be commonplace."

Andre shook his head. "They're not. One of our team, Sarah, made a comment about how nice they were and Charlotte said her ex-husband had had them made for her as an anniversary gift when they were together."

"Ok." Lozano sighed. "You've made a positive ID. When the report comes in I'll double check it just to be sure." He was about to place a comforting hand on Andre's back when he remembered what his skin had felt like and dropped his hand to his side.

Andre watched the zipper meet the end of the bag and closed his eyes. How would he tell Reece?

CHAPTER TWENTY SIX

When Lozano and Andre came out of the coroner's office Reece wasn't outside and neither was the blue hatchback. Andre knew he should have trusted his instincts and not let his friend out of his sight. Was he hiding somewhere nearby, waiting until they were gone, so he could go in and ask to see the body? Andre didn't think so.

Lozano stood with his hands on his hips and did a complete 360 degree turn, gazing up and down the street. "Well son of a gun?" His eyes moved to Andre. "Where would he go?"

"I don't know. He's pretty messed up, who knows what's going through his mind."

"Let's get back to the detention center so I can release your friends. You're going to need to find him soon. He could put himself in danger trying to get the information he's after; especially if he thinks the body isn't Charlotte's." The sheriff crossed the street to his car. Andre followed.

"He was pretty shaken up about the kid. Do you think he could be following a lead on him?"

"I wish I knew." Andre turned to Lozano. "You said you thought Jeremy was homeless. Is there somewhere they congregate?"

"There's about a thousand of them living under the strip in the storm water tunnels. Why? Do you think he'd go there?"

"I'm not sure. I'll check our hotel first. Maybe he went back there."

Lozano's right eyebrow rose and he gave Andre an incredulous look. "Wishful thinking, don't you think?"

"I've got nothing else right now."

The two men climbed into the sheriff's car and headed back to the precinct.

After organizing the paperwork, Lozano walked the group out to the front of the building. Sarah and Arianne were in shock. Neither one wanted to believe Charlotte was dead.

A tear slid down Sarah's right cheek and she brushed it away. She never cried, but she couldn't help herself. Charlotte was a lovely person and a valuable part of their team. What were they going to do without her? How would Reece cope? And what about Tommy? Another tear rolled down her face.

"Your rental's over there." Lozano pointed across the parking lot as he handed Andre the keys. "I'm counting on you to find him before he does something stupid and gets himself killed."

Andre nodded and took the keys. "We'll find him."

"I commend your confidence, but if he doesn't want to found..."

"We'll find him." Andre gave the sheriff an irritated frown.

The sheriff raised defensive hands. "Ok. I hope you do. And soon."

The group headed across the parking lot to their car and got in, Sarah in the front passenger seat.

"And you're sure it's Charlotte?" She wanted to hope against hope he'd made a mistake.

Andre turned to her. "You remember the earrings she was wearing when she came into the office to ask Reece to help with the missing teens case?"

Sarah gave him a pained frown. "Yes. Why?"

"Because they're on the body."

Another stray tear slid down her cheek. "Oh."

Andre started the engine. "We have to find Reece before he does something we can't fix. He's not thinking clearly and who knows what he'll get himself into."

"Where do you think he'd go?" Arianne asked from the backseat.

"I'm hoping he went back to the hotel." He reversed out of the parking spot and headed for the Golden Nugget.

෮෬

When the trio reached the hotel room the door was ajar. Andre's instincts told him Reece had been back. He pushed it open and rushed inside. No sign of him. His eyes roamed the furniture and objects in the room searching for a clue as to where his friend had gone. He noticed a piece of paper on the table near the window and rushed over to it.

Don't worry about me. I know what I'm doing. I have a meeting with one of them. She called me while I was waiting for you. I'll make her tell me where the others are and we'll end them. Stay put until I call. Reece.

Andre turned around and passed the note to Sarah. She and Arianne read it. "We have to find him!" Sarah said, her voice tight. "He'll get himself killed if we don't."

"I think I might know where he's headed." Andre opened the laptop and pulled up images of the underground tunnels. "Here."

Sarah gave him a skeptical frown. "What makes you think he'd go there?"

"Because he was upset about Jeremy, and Lozano told me a large number of homeless live down there."

"Do you think the succubae do too?" Sarah shook her head. "They'd be living in style not in some dingy, dirty tunnel."

Andre shrugged and raised his hands. "Then I have no idea where Reece has gone. It was my only theory."

Arianne stepped up and rested a hand on his arm. "We can take a look if you want. You could be right about him going there. Maybe he's looking for someone who knew Jeremy." She gave him a reassuring smile.

Andre gazed into her beautiful dark brown eyes, smiled and placed his hand over hers. "I appreciate your support, Arianne, but Sarah's right. They'd have him go to another hotel just like the other times they've sent us on a wild goose chase."

"The question is which one?" Sarah said.

"We need to figure it out before something happens to him. They murdered Charlotte, what's stopping them from murdering Reece too? God, I wish he wouldn't do this! He's not only putting himself in danger but us as well."

"I think we're already in their sights. Don't you?"

"Why don't we try tracking him again?" Arianne offered.

"Not a half bad idea." Sarah turned to the young woman and smiled.

Andre's serious gaze moved to the women and he frowned at the priest.

"Well it kind of worked before. At least we found him." Sarah shrugged.

"All right. Let's give it a try. But I don't like our chances."

While the trio was out searching for Reece, Andre got a call from the sheriff. Something had happened to the samples. They were inconclusive. Some kind of cross contamination had destroyed the DNA so the forensic pathologist had had to take new samples and rework them. It would take another few hours before they had anything. Lozano told him as soon as he had the report in his hand he'd be in touch.

 

After a few hours of combing the city, the three decided to head back to their hotel. Andre was resistant about giving up the search, but they were all weary and out of ideas.

When Andre opened the door with the card key and rushed into the room he almost collided with Reece stepping out of the bathroom wrapped in a white hotel towel, drying his hair.

"Where have you been? We've been searching the city for you." Andre strutted over to his friend, an irritated frown on his face.

Reece returned the intense gaze. "Why? I told you to wait here until I got back."

Andre folded his arms. "For all we knew you could've been dead. Why did you go after her?"

"Because I wanted to find the others and deal with them before anyone else gets killed. I can't save Charlotte so…"

Andre's serious expression softened. "How'd you know?"

Reece gave a heavy sigh and sat on his bed. "It wasn't difficult to put two and two together and come up with the body in the coroner's office being Charlotte's. She was out at the same abandoned motel, who else could it be?"

"I'm sorry, Reece. I was hoping it wasn't her but the earrings were the ones she had on the day she came to the office to ask you to assist with the Melinda Graham case."

Sarah crossed the room, a pained expression on her face and tears welling in her eyes. "I'm so sorry. Are you all right? Is there anything we can do?"

Reece glanced up at her. "No, I'm not all right, but there's nothing I can do about it. I appreciate the thought, thanks. All I can do is concentrate on finding those demons and putting an end to them. For Charlotte." Tears stung the backs of his eyes and he blinked them away. He had to keep it together, for now at least.

Sarah rested a comforting hand on his shoulder. "I wish…" She was at a loss for words. Losing Charlotte had affected them all.

Reece covered her hand with his. "So do I." He gave her a thin smile.

"So what happened when you met the succubus?" Andre perched himself on the table. Keeping Reece busy was the best thing he could do for his friend.

"She… Oriana, wants a tradeoff. She'll give us the location of the other two as long as we don't send her back to hell."

"What? You didn't agree to it, did you?" Sarah asked, her dark eyebrows coming together.

"Yeah, I did. I want her to think I'm going to help her, but when the time comes she'll be gone just like the others."

"Thank God." Sarah gave a relieved sigh.

"She said they're working for someone but she wouldn't say who. I think I can get it out of her if she believes she can trust me."

"What if she's setting you up? What if you walk into wherever she takes you and it's a trap?" Andre folded his arms.

"Look, if it happens I'll worry about it then. We need to know where they are. We're running out of time and this is the only way we're going to find them."

"She obviously set up another time to meet, so when is it?" Andre wanted to know so he could keep track of his friend.

"Tomorrow at sunset near the fountains outside the Bellagio."

"You want us there as back up?"

"She'll sense you and Arianne, but she won't sense Sarah." His eyes moved to her and he arched his left eyebrow.

"Reece, we need to track you."

"You want to hotwire me?" He gave a thin smile.

"You bet I do. I'm not letting you out of my sight again. Like it or not."

Reece raised defensive hands. "Ok. I get it."

Andre turned to Sarah and Arianne. "Better get some sleep. We've got a busy day tomorrow."

Both women nodded, said their goodnights and stepped through the adjoining doorway into their room.

Andre turned to Reece. "Who do you think is behind all of this?"

Reece shook his head. "Don't know. But if I was a betting man, I'd think your brother was involved."

Andre's eyes widened. "Why?"

"It's his MO. Take away the ones we love so he can weaken us and try to control us. Kill for the hell of it. Don't you think it sounds like him?"

"Jacques is dead, Reece. We watched him burst into flames when he fell from my apartment window. It's obvious someone has a score to settle, but who?"

"That's the million dollar question." Reece stood up, dropped the towel he had around him onto the floor and climbed into his bed.

"Maybe it's one of my brother's adherents. I was sure we got them all, but maybe we didn't."

Reece pushed his left arm behind his head and rested it against the headboard. "Yeah, so did I. One of them might've managed to get out or was already out when we went in."

"What I don't understand is why Charlotte? She had nothing to do with my brother's death."

"Like I said to weaken and manipulate. Make us conform to whoever's will. We've been running around blind doing what they've told us to do, haven't we?"

Andre's eyes moved to his friend. "You really thought Jacques was behind it?"

"It's definitely his style."

"But he's dead." Andre paced.

"You thought he was dead before and he showed up in LA, remember?"

Andre stopped and turned around. "I know, but he burned. We're not like the Phoenix, Reece, vampires can't rise from the ashes."

"As far as you know." They stared at each other until Andre broke eye contact.

"Adrian would've made me aware if it'd happened in the past."

"Ok. Then we need to find out who it is and fast, otherwise one of us will be next."

CHAPTER TWENTY SEVEN

At 6.28 AM Lozano knocked on the hotel room door and waited, his stomach doing nervous flip flops above his regulation issue duty belt. He wasn't sure what he would say, but he had to find out if his suspicions were correct. When the door opened and Andre appeared the sheriff was relieved. He didn't want to have to explain to Reece why he was there at such an early hour of the morning.

"Sheriff," Andre said, his immortal senses connecting with the man's apprehension. "Did you want to speak to Reece?"

"Uh. No." He kept his voice low. "I… can we talk?" He motioned back and forth between them. "In private?" He moved his gaze along the hallway toward the elevator bank.

"Do you want to get some breakfast?"

"Sure. Yeah." He rubbed his sweaty palms together.

"Just give me a couple minutes to dress and I'll be right out."

Lozano nodded. "Ok."

Andre closed the door.

Seven minutes later he was standing at the elevators with the sheriff. He could sense the turmoil raging inside the man and knew whatever Lozano had to say was wreaking havoc with his conscience.

The pair headed for the buffet, found a quiet corner and sat down.

Andre clasped his hands in front of him on the table top and waited for the sheriff to begin.

Lozano cleared his throat, leaned back in his seat and placed his hands in his lap. His eyes took in the man sitting opposite him. Was he really going to ask the question? Yes. He was. He needed to know. "Andre…"

"What's your question, Sheriff?"

Lozano's mind ran through how he could broach the topic without sounding like a lunatic. What if he was wrong? He waited a beat then said, "Th – the other day at the detention center when I touched your arm I noticed something." He watched for a reaction but didn't get one.

"Go on."

He cleared his throat again and ran his hand over his face. "You felt cold."

Andre's right eyebrow arched and he gave the sheriff an incredulous stare.

The sheriff huffed. "I don't mean from sitting in the air-conditioning all those hours. I mean… like someone dead. I've felt dead bodies before and you feel like that."

"What are you asking me?" Andre leaned in to meet his hands. He knew what the man was about to say.

Enrique Lozano straightened in his seat and frowned into Andre's eyes. "Are you a…" he glanced around at the few early patrons and lowered his voice to a whisper, "vampire?"

Andre watched him for a moment wondering if he should reveal himself. Could Lozano be trusted to keep his secret? He realized he didn't have a choice. The sheriff was already suspicious of him, had been since day one. Andre returned his stare. "What if I told you I was?"

A glimmer of satisfaction mingled with fear ran over Lozano's face. "I knew it!" He sat back in his seat and blew out a noisy breath, his gaze focused on the table top, allowing the processing center of his brain to connect the dots. He'd had a gut feeling about Andre from the first moment he laid eyes on him. His gaze returned to the vampire sitting across the table. "How old are you?"

The amazement in the sheriff's eyes was palpable. He sat wide-eyed like a child who had just learned Santa Claus *was* real.

"I'm over four hundred years old."

Lozano ran a hand over his dazed face and blurted, "Four hundred!" It was too incredible to contemplate.

"Yes. What do you plan to do with this information, Sheriff? My life is in your hands."

Lozano snapped out of his reverie and waved a dismissive hand at Andre. "Don't worry, I'm not going to tell anyone. I just needed to know. For myself. I always wondered if creatures…" He grimaced. "Sorry, if people like you existed. Now I know."

"It's imperative no one else finds out about me. You understand, right?" Andre reached across the table.

Lozano snatched his hand away before Andre could connect with him. "Sorry. I'm not ready for the up close and personal just yet."

Andre nodded. "Understood."

"And, yes, I get no one else can find out about you. Your secret's safe with me." His eyes lit up. "I have so many questions."

"Why don't you ask them over breakfast?" Andre stepped away from the table.

"You eat?" Lozano pushed back his chair and stood up, a look of disbelief crossing his face.

"Yes. When I have to."

"Wow, do I have a lot to learn." The sheriff followed Andre over to the breakfast buffet.

ℴℴ

When Reece woke up at 7.45 Andre had just walked through the door. He threw back the covers, swung his legs over the side of the bed and watched his friend cross the room. He could see by the look on Andre's face something was on his mind. "What's up?"

"Lozano figured out what I am." He glanced over at the closed door then returned his gaze to Reece. "He arrived here early this morning and asked if we could talk."

"Shit! So what's he going to do?"

"He said he only wanted to know for himself and my secret was safe with him."

"I think you can believe him." Reece opened his travel bag and rummaged through it for a pair of black boxers and tugged them on.

"I do. I don't think he'd intentionally say anything, but what if he slips up?"

"Who'd believe him?" Reece pushed his head through the neck of his navy blue T-shirt and pulled on his jeans.

"You're right. He isn't about to tell his men demons exist, let alone vampires, so I should be safe."

"He's a good man, Andre. And like you said, he wouldn't intentionally do anything to put you at risk."

"I know. He also asked if we'd made any progress finding the succubae."

Reece headed to the bathroom, leaving the door open. "What did you tell him?"

"I said we'd let him know when we had something to give him. I don't think he bought it though."

"I don't care." Reece came out of the bathroom zipping up his jeans. "The longer we can keep him out of it the better. I don't want any more deaths on my hands."

Andre frowned at him. Charlotte's death wasn't Reece's fault but it was obvious he blamed himself.

"You did all you could to find Charlotte, Reece. You can't take responsibility for what happened. There was nothing you could do."

"I should've gone with her and waited outside the restroom."

"It wouldn't have made any difference. They would've found another way, whether there or here."

Reece eyed his friend sternly without saying a word.

Andre sighed. "Anyhow, the sheriff wasn't happy about me not giving him any information. He told me to tell you he's keeping track."

Reece looked at his reflection in the mirror and ran a hand through his tousled, wavy dark blonde hair. "I hope he hasn't assigned someone to keep tabs on us. It would be a breach of professional ethics as far as I'm concerned. And mutual respect."

Andre shrugged. "He could have. I guess he's concerned about not knowing what's going on."

"Yeah, well, if he has I'll be down at the precinct so fast his head'll spin. I'm trying to keep him safe."

"But he thinks you're withholding vital information."

Reece sat on the bed and pulled on his boots. "I am for his protection. He knows we deal with otherworldly creatures on a daily basis, so he should have some trust and a little faith."

Sarah rushed into the room. "Reece, is your phone off? The sheriff's been trying to call you." She shoved hers at him. "Here."

Reece frowned at her and glanced over his shoulder at the bedside table. His phone was where he'd left it. He pressed Sarah's Samsung Galaxy to his ear. "What can I do for you, Sheriff?"

Lozano told him they had another body only this one was different. He asked Reece to meet him on the top floor of Harrah's parking garage as soon as he could get there.

Reece handed the cell phone back to Sarah and frowned at Andre. "Let's go."

"I wonder what he meant by different." Andre said as he and Reece headed for the lifts. His immortal hearing had picked up the telephone conversation.

"I don't know, but I don't like the sound of it." Something crawled through the tangle of nerves in his gut and he knew whoever was behind the deaths and Charlotte's abduction had just upped the stakes of the game.

CHAPTER TWENTY EIGHT

Oriana's glossy red lips spread into a wide smile as she sat in front of the lighted Hollywood vanity mirror brushing her long blonde hair. She would remain on earth. Reece Daniels had given his word. She could live the life she was meant to live. Have all the mortal men she desired. She didn't even feel a pang of guilt for her sisters. They were senseless and did everything their new master told them to do. Why? They could have killed him and escaped his control long before now. They were demons, after all. Hell's spawn. The smile disappeared from her face as she realized so could she. What stopped the trio from ridding themselves of such a monster? Her searing demon blood chilled in her veins and the human body she inhabited shivered, goosebumps spreading like a rash up her arms. Oriana knew the reason.

Something about him frightened her. Frightened them all.

Something dark and sinister, more evil than Lucifer, made her demon heart shudder in her chest. They hadn't tried to end his life because they knew he would destroy them if they failed.

Katya wandered into the room and noticed Oriana's pallid appearance. "What is wrong, sister?"

"Nothing. I'm fine." Her smile erased the mask of fear and guilt from her face as she glanced past her sister. "Where is Helyna?"

"Running an errand."

Oriana's eyes narrowed. "What kind of errand?"

"Nothing you need be concerned about." The corner of her mouth twitched into a smirk as she turned on her heel and sauntered out of the room.

Oriana lay her hairbrush down, pushed back her chair and followed her sister. What was she up to?

By the time she reached her door and glanced along the hallway she spotted Katya leaning against the outer brick wall talking to a young man. Who was he? And why was her sister flirting with him? She wasn't thinking about taking his life here, was she?

Oriana walked briskly along the passage to the open front door. "Katya, who is this?" She gave him a thin smile and returned her gaze to her sister.

Katya looped her arm through his. "This is Curtis. He offered to buy me a drink after the show." She ran her other hand along the bare skin of his arm, feeling his mortal heat for her and batted her eyelashes at him. "Isn't he delicious? And sweet?"

Oriana did her best to control her shock. "Yes, isn't he? Can I talk to you inside for a moment?"

Katya untangled her arm from the young man's and gave him a seductive smile. "Don't go away. I'll be right back."

The guy shook his head and gave her a lovesick puppy grin. "I won't."

Katya followed Oriana along the hallway to her room. "What?"

"Sister, dearest, you cannot kill him in broad daylight. Someone is bound to see you."

"Oh, Oriana, don't be ridiculous. I'm not planning on killing him here. And no one will see me."

"You can't risk it, you'll endanger us all."

Katya hugged her sister. "You worry too much. I know what I'm doing."

"Did *he* tell you to do this?" Oriana stepped backwards out of her sister's embrace.

Katya didn't answer. She crossed the room to the doorway and gazed along the hall at the young man waiting on the front steps. She would enjoy every last drop of him. She turned her head, smiled at Oriana and sauntered along the hallway to her next meal.

80C3

Helyna wandered the deep, shadowed subterranean tunnels making her way to her master. She had to warn him, had to make him aware. If she didn't there would be serious consequences when he discovered the truth by some other means. She hated the underground drains. Even in the daylight they were dark and foreboding. It reminded her of hell. Bleak and dangerous. With the gateway open between earth and hades, who knew what supernatural creature could be lurking in the shadows waiting to strike.

Her breathing quickened as she sucked in an anxious breath and picked up her pace, her eyes darting around the gloom. As she continued rushing along the tunnel a shadow emerged out of the darkness.

"Why are you here?"

She lowered her head, her eyes remaining on the dirt covered concrete. "I – I came to tell you something."

He moved closer, reached out and raised her face up to meet his scrutinizing gaze. "What?"

Helyna's heartbeat shuddered in her breast and she thought it would fly right out of her chest. "It – it's Oriana."

"What about her?"

Her breath caught in her throat. Should she betray her sister? Would he punish her? "She – she's up to something."

"What do you think she is up to?" His eyes narrowed in the dark but he could see her face perfectly.

"I don't know but she goes out and won't say where she has been…"

"Perhaps she is feeding and doesn't want you and your sister to know about it."

She shook her head. "I don't believe she is. I think it's something else."

"Like what exactly?" He reached out, gripped her forearm and tugged her closer to him.

"I'm not sure, but I think she is trying to find a way to stay among the mortals."

His fingers loosened around her arm and he stepped back. "I want you to keep an eye on her and inform me when you know exactly what she is doing."

Helyna's head bobbed up and down. "I will, Master. I will."

"You may go."

She turned on her heel and hurried back the way she had come. She would have to think of a convincing story to tell Oriana when she returned to their residence, otherwise her sister would become suspicious. Helyna had to find out what her sister was up. She knew her life was now in danger. She had revealed what she knew, and if she didn't satisfy their master's demand for information she would most certainly die.

CHAPTER TWENTY NINE

The LVPD had the entire top level of the hotel's parking garage cordoned off and when Reece and Andre arrived they couldn't drive up because patrons' cars had blocked both the exit and entry ramps trying to get to the lower levels to find other places to park. It was like a feeding frenzy. He pulled the rental into a corner and turned off the engine. It would have to do as there were no available spots anywhere and he wanted to get up to the fourth floor as fast as possible.

He jabbed the elevator button a dozen times. "Come on, come on."

"I wonder if this body has had the life sucked out of it," Andre said.

"Lozano didn't want to elaborate over the phone so we won't know till we get up there. If the damn elevator ever gets here."

The lift doors slid open and a couple of cops they hadn't met before stepped out.

"You can't go up there," one cop said, raising his hand and blocking their path. "Official personal only."

Reece flashed his PI license. "Lozano's expecting us."

"*Sheriff* Lozano to you, and is that right?" The cop's right eyebrow rose and he gave each of them a cool stare then gestured toward the elevator. "Then I guess it's ok for you to go on up."

The second officer held the door, his eyes following them as they moved toward the lift.

"Thanks." Reece eyeballed them as he and Andre stepped into the elevator, wondering what the attitude was all about.

"No problem," the second cop said. Both officers stood with hands on their duty belts watching the doors close on the pair.

"Did you think they had a problem with us?" Andre asked.

Reece's eyes remained on the closed doors and he pressed the top floor button. "Yeah, I did."

"You don't suppose the sheriff said anything about our conversation, do you?"

"Who'd believe him?" He sighed and folded his arms. "No, something else was going on with those two."

"Perhaps it's a turf war. Vegas verses LA. Maybe they don't like us stepping onto their territory."

"Maybe, although we haven't met any opposition so far."

"There's bound to be someone. There always is."

The elevator stopped with a jolt and the lift doors hissed open.

Lozano was waiting for them, hands on hips.

"Sheriff," Reece greeted as he and Andre stepped out.

"What took you so long?"

"Have you seen the other levels? It's chaos down there. We're parked on the ground floor because we couldn't drive up." Reece's voice was tight. He didn't need the third degree. Maybe he should remind Lozano they were there as a courtesy. He decided to let it go.

The sheriff let out a frustrated breath. "Ok. Follow me. The body's over here. You're not going to believe it when you see it."

Reece and Andre frowned at each other.

Lozano strutted ahead of them and as they reached the crime scene he motioned for Reynolds to lift the cover off the body.

"Jesus Christ!" Reece's stomach roiled. He'd seen a lot of dead bodies in his time but nothing like this.

"It's the gypsy we've been looking for," Andre said.

The body wasn't shriveled like a raisin. It had been drained of blood and the head ripped clean off the neck, the face distorted in a horrified grimace, mouth and eyes wide with terror.

"The woman's head was over there." Lozano pointed to the far left back corner of the building. "And the body was here. It's been completely drained of blood. The couple that found it is over there talking to Officer Domingo. This isn't the initial crime scene. The body was dumped here."

Reece had turned a pale shade of gray. "Shit."

The sheriff eyed Andre. "Do you have any idea who could've done this?"

Andre frowned and lowered his voice. "You think I know every vampire living in the US?" He raised his left hand. "And before you get any ideas. No, I had nothing to do with it."

"Ok. But you'd say it was a vampire attack, right?" Lozano's eyes moved to the body then back to Andre.

"May I?" Andre gestured at the gypsy. "I might be able to pick up something."

Lozano stepped aside and motioned for Reynolds to take a walk. "Go right ahead." He moved up beside Reece and folded his arms.

The PI gave him a stern frown. "You didn't really think Andre had anything to do with this, did you?"

The sheriff sighed. "He's the only vampire I know. Of course the thought crossed my mind."

"Andre doesn't kill to survive, Sheriff. He's one of the good guys and don't forget it."

"Ok, ok. I understand." He watched Andre run his hand over the body and examine the neck wound. "I'm sorry. I should've known better."

"Yeah, you should."

"Look, this is all new to me. Getting my head around the fact he even exists and there are more of them out there... it blew my mind, you know?"

"But now you're aware..."

"Yeah, yeah, I won't say anything to anybody." He crossed himself and raised his eyes upward.

"Good."

Andre joined them. "Definitely a vampire. It's difficult to tell which kind with the head severed from the body. There could have been bite marks but we'll never know for sure."

The sheriff frowned at him. "So there are different kinds?"

"Yes. A neophyte could have done this. They're savage until they get their bloodlust under control. But it looks more like the work of a master. If the body was intact and there were no bite marks we'd know without a doubt."

Lozano expression turned blank. "What do you mean no bite marks? Don't they all leave them?"

Andre shook his head. "No. A master has the ability to heal the wounds. It helps avoid detection."

"It's fascinating. I want to talk to you more about it at a later time but right now I need to focus on this murder. Did you get anything at all from the body?" Lozano was praying for a miracle.

"Unfortunately, no. It's been exposed to the elements for too long."

"How are we going to stop these creatures if we can't find them?" Lozano ran his hand over his face.

"Leave it to us, we're working on it." Reece turned and headed to the elevator. Andre followed.

"Where're you going?" Lozano called.

Reece glanced over his shoulder. "To do my job."

Once the pair was inside the lift and on their way to the ground floor Reece turned to Andre. "Ok, what did you find out?"

CHAPTER THIRTY

The dark tunnel seemed endless as Reece raced along it, peering over his shoulder wondering if the creatures were still in hot pursuit. He had to find a place to hide until the sun came up. The stark white beam of his flashlight app bobbed against the graffitied walls as he ran, but within seconds the glow faded, flickered and died, leaving him in total pitch black. Reece lurched to a stop and smacked his phone against his hand hoping it would jolt a few more seconds of life into the battery. It didn't. "Shit!"

His heart rose in his throat and he sucked in a strangled breath, unable to inhale a full ribcage of air. The claustrophobic atmosphere was thick around him and he felt like he was suffocating. *How did they find me so fast?* He thought he'd have more time.

Manic laughter resonated out of the deep shadows in the underground drains and Reece's eyes darted around the gloom. They were almost on top of him.

He broke into a panicked run, stumbling over broken concrete, cans, bottles and other rubbish strewn along the fetid, damp passage. He tripped on something soft and landed on top of it, the small amount of oxygen he'd managed to inhale whooshing out of him with the heavy thud. Feeling around, unable to see, and his brain making the connection, Reece felt buttons, material, a hand, a face... a sticky wet crater where the nose had been. Another face... holes where the eyes should have been. Bodies!

Bile gushed up his throat and he staggered to his feet, his heart beating so fast it felt like butterfly wings against his ribs. He spat the bitter liquid onto the ground and rushed into the shadows. He had to find a way out or somewhere to hide before they reached him or he'd be another rotting corpse amongst the body count.

"Reece." A voice echoed out of the blackness ahead of him.

Charlotte? His eyes roamed the dark and he wished he had Andre's nocturnal vision.

"This way."

He followed the sound of the voice. Was it Charlotte? *It couldn't be. She's dead.*

The laughter grew in intensity, encircling him. He spun around unable to see, his heartrate accelerating; his breathing ragged. Where were they?

Something touched his shoulder, his arm, the back of his leg.

More laughter.

Reece continued his frenzied spin. "What do you want from me?" he yelled, his strained voice ricocheting off the concrete walls.

Silence.

He stopped, panting in fear.

He could hear the kerthump, kerthump of his heart as though the sound was outside of his body. Loud, fast, uneven. Why hadn't he brought his Glock with him?

The voice again. "Hurry! This way."

Reece followed it.

A dull light appeared not far ahead of him and he stopped in his tracks. His body stiffened and he opened and closed his fists to keep the blood pumping. Something was wrong. Someone was leading him into a trap.

He spun on his heel and headed back in the direction he had come from. The entrance was miles away, but if he could just keep going… he knew he would make it out alive.

Another dull light flashed on in front of him and he froze.

A darkly clad male figure appeared from a crevice in the wall.

Every instinct in Reece's body screamed for him to run. Flight. Flight. Flight! Not fight or flight this time. There was no choice. He had to run. Had to get away. Had to stay alive.

He tried to suck air into his lungs but they wouldn't expand. He opened his mouth and heaved his chest, his heart pounding so hard he thought it would burst through his ribs.

The figure moved toward him.

Reece's blood whooshed in his ears making him dizzy. He staggered backwards and straightened to prevent himself from falling over. He wouldn't show fear.

"I've been waiting a long time for this moment, Reece Daniels."

He recognized the voice. Every nerve ending in his stomach constricted and his gut turned to lead.

No! No, it can't be. Reece's mind went into overdrive. *How is this possible?* His eyes widened as the figure stepped closer. "You're not real."

Laughter. This time from the figure.

"I can assure you I am *very* real."

Reece took another step back.

Someone grabbed him with strong hands.

He struggled, watching the figure get closer. "Let me go." His high-pitch cry echoed off the surrounding walls.

The figure lunged at him, fangs bared.

Jacques!

Reece wrestled the covers, threw them back and launched himself out of bed, making a dash for the door, unable to breathe, his heart hammering.

Andre turned on the lamp and rushed across the room to him. "It's ok, Reece, it was just a bad dream."

The PI's raspy breaths sounded as though he'd run a marathon.

"Look at me. You're ok." Andre gripped Reece's arm, led him back to his bed and sat him down. "You had a nightmare. You're fine now."

Reece gazed up at him, dazed. "It felt so real. I thought…"

"You called out Jacques' name."

Reece sucked in a deep breath and ran his fingers through his tousled hair. "Yeah. He was in the dream. God, I thought I was going to die."

Andre went into the bathroom to get Reece a glass of water, came back and handed it to him. "Drink this it'll help." He realized his friend's state of mind was far more fragile than he had thought. He'd have to keep a close eye on him.

"Thanks." Reece took a large swallow. "I heard Charlotte's voice in the dream, too. Could she still be alive? Could the body at the Coroner's office be someone else?"

"I wish it was. But we both know it has to be her. It adds up. Your dream was all of the things you've been stressing over. That's all."

Reece ran his hand over his face. "I guess you're right." He sat the glass on the bedside table, climbed back into bed and pulled the covers over him.

"Try to get some sleep." Andre sat on his bed watching his friend. He wouldn't sleep. He'd remain awake for the rest of the night just to be sure Reece stayed put.

Reece turned over to face the window, his back to his friend. How could he sleep when his mind couldn't shut off after such a vivid dream? *Andre said a master vampire had definitely killed the gypsy. Could Jacques still be alive? He'd managed to return from death once before. Why not again? Could Andre be wrong about him burning to ash? Was the dream warning me?*

CHAPTER THIRTY ONE

Next morning, when Andre came out of the bathroom Reece wasn't there. His eyes roamed the large space looking for a note. None. He stood with his hands on his hips and frowned into the empty hotel room. He couldn't believe his friend had managed to get out without him hearing. *Where would he have gone?*

Sarah and Arianne came through the adjoining door and wondered why Andre was standing in the center of the room staring into space.

"Everything all right?" Sarah's forehead creased into a curious frown.

"Reece isn't here."

"I noticed. Where is he?"

Andre spun around. "Good question. I went to take a shower and when I came out he was gone."

"Could he have gone downstairs for coffee?" Sarah walked over to him. Arianne remained in the doorway.

"Maybe. But it's not like him to go without letting me know." He folded his arms. "He had a nightmare last night and it shook him up pretty bad."

"Did he tell you about it?"

"He didn't have to. I woke up to him calling out Jacques' name." His serious gaze met hers.

"But Jacques is dead."

"I know. But for some reason Reece has it in his head Jacques is behind this whole situation. He said it feels like my brother's handiwork."

"What?" Sarah's brow wrinkled even more. "He can't honestly believe Jacques has anything to do with this."

"Well he does. He said Jacques had returned from the dead once before, and he's right, he did. But not this time."

Arianne crossed the room. "Is there any chance he could be right?"

Sarah and Andre turned to her and both said, "No."

"He was ash on the pavement, Arianne," Andre told her with conviction. He didn't want to believe it could be even remotely possible.

The door opened and Reece walked in with a tray of coffee and everyone turned to look at him. He frowned. "What?"

"We were worried about you," Sarah told him.

Reece closed the door, walked across the room and set the tray down on the table. "Look, you have to stop worrying about me. I'm fine." He picked up the cardboard cups two at a time and passed them around. "I won't do anything to endanger any of our lives. My head is ok."

His friend shot him a skeptical gaze.

"Andre, I'm fine."

"You weren't fine last night after the nightmare."

Reece sighed. "Yeah. Ok. I know. But I am now."

"Are you sure?" Sarah gave him a concerned look.

"Yes." He picked up his coffee and took a cautious sip. "We need to get Lozano to look into rental properties leased a few weeks prior to the murders. Perhaps it'll give us a lead on where the succubae are holed up."

"Great idea," Sarah said, sipping her coffee. She pointed to the tray. "What's in the bag?"

"Oh, yeah. I bought scones if anyone wants one. The Starbucks downstairs has them."

Sarah walked over to the table and picked up the brown paper bag with the green mermaid logo and peered inside. "Mm, blueberry. My favorite." She took one and passed the bag around.

"I called the sheriff. He'll be here in half an hour. After what happened the other night I thought we'd better make good on our promise to provide him with whatever information we have. We don't want to wind up in another holding cell for some minor infringement." He checked his watch. "After the meeting I have somewhere to be."

"Where?" His three companions chorused together.

"Can't a man have any privacy?" He took a bite of his scone.

"Not when it means risking your life." Andre gave him an intense stare.

"I said I'm fine and I am. Will you trust me?"

His friend didn't answer.

Reece's left eyebrow rose. "Andre?"

"I've always trusted you. But..."

He sighed. "But what?"

"I don't want you disappearing and someone grabbing you again."

"It won't happen."

"You can't be so sure. We're all in danger until we can find out who's behind this."

Sarah glanced from Andre to Reece then back to Andre. "And we have to trust each other otherwise everything will fall apart."

"I just want to keep us all safe, Sarah," Andre said, his voice tight.

She reached across and touched his arm. "If Reece has somewhere to go we have to let him go. He has a right to some personal space when he needs it. We all do."

"Let's get breakfast over with Lozano will be here soon," Reece told them. "And Andre, I'll be ok. I just need some time on my own." He wouldn't tell them the blonde had contacted him again and he planned to meet her alone.

By the time they finished breakfast a knock echoed into the room. Lozano was punctual. He had some news for them too. Some very important news.

Andre opened the door. "Hello, Sheriff, come in."

Lozano stepped into the hotel room and walked over to the other three. "Hi. Thanks for meeting with me."

"Not a problem, Sheriff." Reece gestured to the two chairs at the table. "Take a seat."

"Thanks." Lozano wandered over and sat by the window. "There have been some important developments."

Reece folded his arms and frowned at the sheriff. "What kind of developments?"

Lozano stood up, a smile spreading to his eyes. "The forensic report came back and the body isn't Charlotte."

Arianne, Sarah and Andre's faces lit up and they hugged each other. This was wonderful news.

Reece's knees unlocked beneath him and he stumbled backwards and sat on the foot of the bed to prevent himself from toppling over. Tears stung the backs of his eyes and he inhaled a deep breath and blew it out. His gaze moved to Lozano. "They're sure?"

"Yeah, one hundred percent." He walked over and gripped the PI's arm. "She's still out there, somewhere, Reece."

"What about the earrings? They're hers."

Lozano placed his right index finger to his lips and pondered for a moment then said, "My guess is they wanted to throw you off your game. Have your head in another space. Grief." His eyes moved to the PI. "Didn't you say they took her suitcase?"

"They took both hers and mine."

"Maybe they were planning to disguise another body to make it look like you," Lozano reasoned.

"They mangled an innocent woman's face and sheared off her finger prints for Christ's sake. You think they were going to do that to someone else?"

The sheriff rested his hand on Reece's shoulder. "It seems like it. They want to make you all suffer. Why?"

Reece's irritated gaze met Lozano's. "Does there have to be a reason?"

He nodded. "Yeah, I think there does. Who'd you piss off?"

"In our line of work it could be anyone," Andre told him. "We've come up against too many otherworldly creatures to count."

Lozano shook his head. "This is personal. I've been a cop too long not to know that." He turned to look at Reece again. "Wanna tell me who you think it is? You must have a theory."

The PI gazed up at him. "I thought it was Andre's brother, Jacques. But he's dead. It's his modus operandi."

The sheriff's left eyebrow rose. "Take someone you love and make you believe they were dead, you mean?"

"Well, yeah, kind of. He liked to weaken and manipulate people. Use it to his advantage."

"Reece." Andre wasn't happy about discussing his brother regardless of what he'd done.

Reece gave a heavy sigh and his eyes moved to his friend. "Sorry, Andre, but I can't help thinking it's him. It's too close to how he operated."

"Like I already said, I think it's one of his adherents or a vampire we missed in the raid."

Lozano looked from Andre to Reece then back to Andre. "What raid? When did this happen?"

Reece stood up. "It was about three years ago. Andre thought he'd killed Jacques back in 16th century France, but turns out his brother tricked him. He arrived in LA wanting to rekindle his brotherly bond and all hell broke loose. I lost my partner because of him. We thought we got all of his entourage, including him, but one must've got away or was outside the church when it all went down."

The sheriff wiped his hand over his face. "Man! But didn't you think it was MacKinnon?"

"Yeah. At first. But not now."

Lozano frowned at Andre. "And you know your brother's dead? For sure?"

Andre crossed the room. "Yes. He fell out of my apartment window into the sun and burned. As I said to Reece, no vampire could survive it."

The sheriff sighed. "Ok. Then it has to be someone who knew him, knew how he operated. Maybe there were others you didn't know about. Maybe he had two places to keep low."

"We're beginning to think so." Sarah walked over to the trio.

At least the one good thing to come out of all this was Charlotte was out there. Somewhere.

Reece couldn't get his head around the fact that his beautiful fiancée was still alive. After grieving for the dead woman in the coroner's office, thinking it was Charlotte, he never believed a miracle like this could happen, but it had. She was alive!

The one question roaming his mind? Where was she?

CHAPTER THIRTY TWO

In the Valley Hospital ICU, Dr. Eric Benson pulled the patient file from the holder at the foot of the bed and ran his eyes over the pathology report. He frowned as his index finger moved down the list to the blood work. Had this patient tried to commit suicide with an overdose of Midazolam? High doses of the chemical had been detected in the sample. He sighed and glanced along the bed at his unconscious patient. Only time would tell and he'd need some answers when she woke up.

The hospital hadn't informed the police yet. Eric wanted an opportunity to question her, to make sure she hadn't tried to kill herself before handing her case over to the authorities. Things… ugly things went down in Vegas on a regular basis. Things the tourist industry kept quiet. And this could be one of those dreadful situations. He'd seen many over the years of working in the ER.

A nurse entered the room to check patient vitals and Dr. Benson stepped aside to give her room to do her task. "Any new developments with this one? he asked.

She shook her head while adjusting the drip attached to the woman's arm then placed a digital thermometer in the woman's ear. "No, Doctor, nothing yet. We're hoping to see some sign of life soon."

He closed the file and slid it back into place. "Well let me know the minute anything does. I need to speak to this patient before we proceed further." He had a feeling there was more to this case, and once his patient was awake she would be able to confirm his suspicions.

The nurse smiled. "I will, Doctor Benson."

He eyed the woman with plastic tubes hooked up to a heart monitor, drip stand and ventilation mask before turning and heading out of the room. He hoped she would wake up soon.

CHAPTER THIRTY THREE

Reece stepped into Serendipity 3 at around 10.30 AM and scanned the restaurant for the blonde. He thought it was an unusual place to meet, but well-populated. Was it for her benefit or his? The old fashioned ice cream parlor décor brought back memories of Disneyland with his parents when he was a kid. The black and white checkered floor and white metal chairs with faux red leather padded seats gave the place a feel-good vibe, and the sweet, fruity aroma of home-made apple pie prodding his nostrils made his stomach growl. He made a mental note to come here for a meal some time. He spotted her sitting near the display shelves and weaved his way through the scattered tables to join her.

When he reached her she smiled up at him. "Thank you for coming." She gestured for him to take the seat beside her.

Reece pulled out the opposite chair and sat down. "Do you have something for me?"

Oriana flashed him a dazzling cherry gloss grin. She was beautifully mesmerizing and he had to keep his wits about him. "I have bestowed a gift to you, Reece Daniels."

He frowned into her honey colored eyes. "What kind of gift." He had already been the recipient of their gifts and didn't like the sound of it.

She sipped her soda. "One you'll be delighted with. A token of good faith."

"What do you mean?"

"You will find out soon enough." Her alluring smile widened.

Reece glowered at her and flattened his palms on the tabletop ready to push back his chair and leave. She was toying with him again.

She raised her hand. "Don't go yet. I have information."

He sighed and folded his arms. "Well."

Oriana spoke in a low tone. "One of my sisters is planning to dispatch a young man in daylight hours. She already has one in mind."

Reece's left eyebrow arched. "Who?"

"I only know his first name. Curtis. I have no knowledge of where he lives or…"

"Then what good is the information you're offering if you can't provide facts to help me find him?"

Oriana leaned forward, revealing her firm rounded breasts to him in the low-cut dress she had on. "I will find out and call you as soon as I can. Promise." She gave him another dazzling cherry red smile.

"What about this master of yours? Who is he and where is he staying?"

Her seductive smile vanished and her face paled. Her eyes roamed the other patrons making sure she wouldn't be heard. "If – if I tell you he'll end me."

Reece leaned forward. "We had a deal. You give me the information I need and I help you remain on earth. Remember?"

She nodded. "Yes, I am aware. But I need more time."

He pushed back his chair and stood up. "There isn't any time left. If you don't come up with something we can use the deal's off." Reece turned to leave.

"Wait. Please." She sidled out of her seat and sauntered up to him. "As I said when you first arrived, I've given you a gift in good faith." She reached up and twisted a wavy lock of his dark blonde hair around her fingers. "I will provide the information you need. I will not let you down, Reece Daniels."

He grasped her hand and moved it away from him. "Don't try to charm me, Oriana, it won't work." He turned on his heel and stalked out of the restaurant.

Oriana's perfectly sculpted right eyebrow arched and her plump glossy red lips spread into a smirk. She already had out at the abandoned motel.

೮౩

Heading back to the Golden Nugget, Reece wondered about the tunnels under the city and the homeless who lived there. He had wanted to investigate the meandering dark depths, but after the dream he'd decided not to. Jeremy's face popped into his head. Could the kid have been living in the storm water drains? Did someone down there know him?

Against his better judgment he turned the rental around and headed for one of the entrances into the subterranean city.

The opening into this section of the two hundred mile floodway lay opposite the McCarran Field Executive Terminal on South Las Vegas Boulevard. He parked in a vertical parking space in the center of the dual carriageway, grabbed his cell phone off the passenger seat and stepped out of the sedan. The 'Welcome to Fabulous Las Vegas Nevada' sign stood proudly on the center island with several tourists taking happy snaps.

Gazing along the road at the traffic whisking past, he waited for a break in the flow, crossed the street and headed past the bus stop to the end of the chain-link fence. Making his way down to the double entrance ahead of him he stopped short. What was he doing? Checking out the tunnels for Jeremy's sake. He'd have family somewhere who would want to know what happened to him. Someone, somewhere, must know him. And he wanted to satisfy his own curiosity. This would be a place Jacques would hide, if he were still alive.

Reece swiped the face of his phone and pressed the flashlight app. Although the sky was a beautiful azure blue and bright streams of mid-morning sunlight fell upon the unpainted, gray concrete exterior, from what he could see the endless underground labyrinth was pitch black. No sign of light or life where he was about to enter. He swallowed the thickening lump in his throat and his body shuddered as the thought of the nightmare he'd had the previous evening resurfaced in his mind. *Am I really going to do this?* He inhaled a deep breath, ignored his churning gut and stepped into the dark. This time he did have his Glock, loaded with sanctified silver cartridges.

ജാ

Sarah sat down, opened her laptop, keyed in the password and clicked on the tracking device program. Unbeknown to Reece, Andre had attached a GPS tracker to their rental as a safety precaution, so he'd know where his friend was at all times. Sarah frowned at the screen. "Andre, you need to take a look at this."

Andre crossed the room, leaned in to view the screen and frowned. "Where is he?"

"It looks like he's gone into the tunnels," she said, gazing up at him.

"What is he thinking going in there alone? After the dream he had I thought he'd changed his mind about checking them out." He crossed the room and snatched up the phone. "Hi, yes, can you connect me to the Las Vegas Police Department? Thanks."

"What are you doing?" Sarah stood up and walked over to him.

"The only thing I can do. Get the cops out there to find him before something happens. We don't have any transport." The call was answered. "Can I speak to sheriff Lozano please?" Andre waited to be connected.

The sheriff picked up.

"Hi, Sheriff, can you send a patrol car over to the tunnels on South Las Vegas Boulevard? Reece has gone in there alone and I'm worried about his safety. Please call me when they've found him. Thank you." He dropped the handset into its cradle.

"Reece isn't going to like this," Sarah said.

Andre's brooding gaze met hers. "I don't care. He can't keep going off doing things on his own. It's too dangerous. We have to stay together and watch each other's backs. What if someone else is tracking him?"

CHAPTER THIRTY FOUR

When Reece turned around to gauge the distance, the entrance looked like a pinhole of light. The further he ventured in the darker it became. After traipsing through the gloom for what seemed like an hour he spotted a shaft of daylight ahead of him and rushed into it—blue sky above a rectangle grate. He breathed a sigh of relief, realizing his heart was pounding. He could feel the heavy, rapid beat in his throat. Was he stupid to be in here alone? Probably, but he had to find out if the dream he'd had meant something. So far no people. If they weren't down here where were they?

Reece checked his phone's battery. 53%. How long would it last if he kept the flashlight app on? Maybe an hour if he was lucky. His gut churned and the acrid taste of bile rose in his throat. This scenario was more like his dream than he cared to admit. He remained under the grated blue sky for a few minutes longer before turning and facing the dark. He inhaled a deep breath and continued his trek into the black unknown.

Reynolds drove up over the curb, across the sidewalk, down the concrete slope and skidded to a stop at the double entryway into the tunnels. Sheriff Lozano told them it was imperative they find Reece Daniels as fast as they could. His life could be in danger. The PI had a good head start and could be anywhere by now. The officers climbed out of the squad car and stepped inside the concrete opening. Reynolds pressed the button on his shoulder mic. "Hey, Chief, no sign of Daniels so far. We're going in."

Static.

"Chief?" Reynolds gave Domingo a sideward glance. "Wonder why the radio's acting up?" His eyes roamed the murky gray depths and he heaved a heavy sigh. "Probably too much concrete blocking the signal."

Domingo tried his. "Hey, boss, you copy?" He played with the controls on his radio. "Dispatch, do you read?"

More static.

He shrugged. "Guess you're right." He pulled his cell phone from a side pocket in his khaki uniform pants and checked its coverage. "Half a bar. It'll be out of service once we get deeper inside."

Reynolds didn't like going into the underground without communication. Anything could happen down there. What if they needed backup?

𝄢𝄢

Andre was at the valet parking outside the Golden Nugget. He'd asked the hotel to arrange another rental car for him and was waiting to pick up the keys from the clerk behind the counter. A tourist couple was ahead of him and weren't happy about having to wait for their car. It should have been out front already. Sarah and Arianne would meet him across the street. They were organizing weapons. Sarah had a stash in her suitcase, undetectable during security checks because they were inside a narrow lead-lined box under the lining of the lid. And besides, she knew they wouldn't check her luggage because she was a priest.

It had been two hours and he couldn't wait any longer for Lozano to make contact. He had a bad feeling about Reece, so he and the women were going in after him. At least they were equipped to deal with anything otherworldly. The cops weren't.

He stepped up to the desk, gave his name and collected the keys to a silver JEEP Cherokee Trailhawk. It would come in handy if they had to transport Reece to a hospital, but he hoped it wouldn't be necessary. Andre climbed up into the four wheel drive, started the engine and drove out onto South Casino Center Boulevard. Sarah and Arianne were waiting on the opposite corner.

☙℘℘

Reece came to a junction in the drains. He aimed the bright beam of his phone's flashlight into one dark length littered with rubbish and graffiti, then into the other. Which way? Still no sign of life yet. A shiver crawled over him, making all the hair on his body stand on end. He attempted to shrug it off. No turning back now. He stepped into the left tunnel.

As he continued down the center of the concrete corridor, avoiding the black widow spider webs adhered to the edges of the walls he kicked something.

"Hey!" a voice echoed out of the gloom. "Watch it, will ya." A pale, thin-framed guy dressed in black jumped into the stark glare of Reece's flashlight, raising a hand to his face to shield his eyes from the brightness.

"Sorry, pal. I didn't see you." Reece stepped backwards and directed the beam of light away from the guy's face.

"No worries. It's pretty dark in here." He gave Reece a curious frown. "Whaddya doin' down here anyway?"

"I'm trying to find someone who knew a kid by the name of Jeremy Jacobs. Did you know him?"

The guy's forehead wrinkled and he thought for a moment. "Nah never heard of him." He grimaced. "You couldn't spare a few bucks, could ya? I really need to eat."

Reece knew the guy would probably spend it on alcohol instead of food. But he wasn't in a position to argue. He dug into the pocket of his jeans and pulled out a ten dollar bill he'd stashed there earlier. Just in case. He wasn't about to show his wallet. He passed it to the guy.

"Gee, thanks, buddy. Really appreciate the generosity." He thrust out his grimy hand.

Reece shook it. "No problem. I'd better keep moving. Are there any other people in this section?"

"Not for a mile or so, depending on which way you go. Most of 'em live down the other end of the strip."

"Ok, thanks." Reece sidled around the guy and glanced over his shoulder as he headed into the oppressive blackness. Now he understood why they were called mole people. The guy's vision had adjusted to being in the dark. Reece picked up his pace. He didn't need any surprises.

Reynolds and Domingo stopped and held their flashlights at shoulder height, aiming the bright beam of light into the gloom to get a better idea of how far the pitch black flood channel traveled. Both officers trudged the stinking drain, stepping over bottles, cans, rotted clothing and other debris lying in the muck. The thunderstorm a few nights before would have deposited the pools of now fetid water into the storm tunnels.

The pair continued forward hoping to find the private investigator soon and get the hell out of the subterranean labyrinth. Reynolds wasn't fond of the dark, neither was Domingo.

A shadow darted between the overlapping circles of light.

The cops stopped in their tracks.

Reynolds held his flashlight above his head for a longer aim and panned the tunnel. "Who's there?" His wavering voice echoed along the walls.

No answer.

He gave Domingo a sideward glance. "You saw that, right?"

The officer nodded. "Hell, yeah. What do you think it was? A homeless person?"

Reynolds frowned. "Don't know. Fuck! I wish we had communication down here." His heart hammered against his ribs. No one would know where they were.

"Do you wanna go back?" Domingo hoped he'd say yes.

Reynolds sighed. "Yeah, but we can't. We've been told to find Daniels, so we'd better just keep moving." He didn't like it, but he had his orders. He stepped forward. Domingo didn't follow. Reynolds turned around. "Come on, Miguel, let's go."

"But…"

"I hate pulling rank, but as your senior officer, that's an order." Reynolds gestured for his partner to move ahead of him.

Domingo's eyes widened and the color drained from his face. His mouth gaped and he pointed behind Reynolds. As the officer went for his gun something reached out of the shadows, grabbed him and dragged him into the dark. Domingo pulled his weapon and fired into the black void, the explosive sound ricocheting off the thick walls, until the clip was empty. The last thing he heard was a blood-curdling scream.

Reece spun around and thrust the light of his phone into the darkness. He recognized gun shots when he heard them, but it wasn't close. He pulled his Glock from the back of his belt and edged forward. He stumbled over chunks of concrete and other debris heading back in the direction he had come from. Someone else was in the tunnels. Who? Did they need help?

He broke into a run. When he passed the place where he'd spoken to the vagrant the guy wasn't there. Neither were his belongings. Had he been the one firing the gun? Reece raced along the length of concrete, the flashlight beam bobbing up and down along the floor and surrounding walls. He kept moving. After a while he was back at the fork. He continued forward trying to get to the entrance and daylight as fast as he could.

A shadow stepped into his path out of nowhere.

Reece recoiled and aimed his weapon.

"It's me," Andre said. "Let's get out of here."

When they reached the opening, Sarah and Arianne were waiting next to a police car.

"Where are the cops?" Reece asked.

"We don't know. When we arrived the car was here unmanned." Sarah gazed around the exterior. "They were looking for you, Reece. Sheriff Lozano sent them."

Reece gave Andre a disapproving stare. He knew his friend was behind the cops looking for him. "I heard gunfire inside. They must be in trouble."

"Then we have to help them," Sarah said.

"Let's grab some of your weapons and go back in." Reece's eyebrows rose when he saw the JEEP. "Are they in the back?"

Sarah nodded. "Where else?" The group moved around the four wheel drive.

CHAPTER THIRTY FIVE

Sheriff Lozano was worried. He'd been trying to contact his officers since they arrived at the tunnels. He had also tried to contact Andre without any luck. Rather than wait around, he grabbed his cell phone, holstered his weapon and headed to the parking lot. He'd be at the location in about ten minutes, give or take, as long as the traffic played nice.

Not today. Traffic was the usual stop, start shuffle, so Lozano turned on his siren and forced his way through the cars, across the huge intersection past MGM Hotel, New York, New York, Tropicana and the Excalibur, and sped along South Las Vegas Boulevard. He almost overshot the mark and screeched up over the curb a few feet past the fence and across the sidewalk. He spun the wheels on the grass, roared down the concrete slope and stopped behind Reynolds' and Domingo's black and white cruiser.

Reece and his team were gearing up to go into the tunnels.

Lozano got out of his car and strutted over to the group. "Where are my men?"

"We don't know. When we arrived they weren't here," Andre told him.

"Did you find Reece?"

The PI came around the vehicle. "We kinda found each other. Look, Lozano, I heard gun shots inside. I think your guys are in trouble."

The sheriff's eyes widened. "You mean supernatural trouble?"

Reece nodded. "Yeah, it would be my guess, considering no one lives in this section."

Lozano pulled his weapon and checked the clip. "All right, let's go in."

"I don't think it's a good idea, Sheriff. We know what we're doing, you don't," Reece warned.

The shorter man gazed up at him, anger flashing across his eyes. "I sent my men in there after you so don't tell me I can't be involved in their rescue."

Reece sighed and glowered at him. "Got a flak jacket in your car?"

Lozano nodded.

"Then go get it. You'll need it."

The sheriff marched over to his car and was ready to go in seconds.

"Ok. Stay close and watch each other's backs. Here." He passed Lozano an infrared headset. "You'll need this too."

The group entered the tunnel, weapons raised.

They wandered the concrete shaft, their senses on high alert. Reece and Andre were at the forefront, followed by Lozano, Sarah and Arianne.

The sheriff stepped up beside Reece. "Should we call out for Reynolds and Domingo? Maybe they'll respond."

Reece frowned at him. "And let whoever or whatever's down here know where we are?"

His eyes widened. "Ok. Yeah. You're right."

"Just remain behind us and hopefully we'll all get out of this alive."

Lozano swallowed the thick lump of nerves lodged in his throat and stepped back with the women. He had no idea what he'd gotten himself into.

The team picked up their pace. The sooner they could locate the cops and get out the better.

After more than an hour of trudging the drains there was no sign of Lozano's men.

Reece stopped and panned the walls and ground with his infrared headset. He noticed something lying about ten feet ahead. "Wait here." He made his way toward the object and picked it up. Carrying it back to the others he knew something terrible had happened to the officers. He held up the gun.

Lozano almost choked on his tongue. "It's police issue. Must be Reynolds' or Domingo's." He gazed around the concrete tomb. "Where the hell are they?"

"My guess is something otherworldly got them."

"You mean they're dead?" The color drained from the sheriff's face.

"We can't be sure, not yet," Sarah said, stepping up beside him.

"Yeah, we can." Reece wasn't about to baby Lozano. "If one of your officers drew his weapon and fired until the clip was empty then I'd say something deadly went down in here. We need to be prepared for anything."

They continued moving through the gloom. When they reached the fork they took the right as Reece had been in the left when he heard the gun shots.

After travelling through it for what seemed like hours Andre stopped. "Wait. Do you hear that?"

Everyone stayed motionless, listening.

"What is it?" Lozano asked.

"I don't know but I don't like the sound of it." Reece moved up beside Andre. "Is it ahead of us?"

"Yes. I don't think the others should come with us."

Reece frowned. "You think the cops are up there?"

"Unfortunately, yes." He turned to the others. "Stay here. Reece and I will be right back."

"Where're you going? If you know something now's the time to tell me." Lozano's pale face was strained with anxiety.

"We're going to scout up ahead. If nothing's there we'll turn around."

The pair left the group and headed further into the drain, disappearing into the dark.

"Why'd you send the cops looking for me? If they're dead it's on your head, you know."

Andre glared at him. "Are you serious? If you were honest with me I wouldn't have had to."

"I'm a grown man, Andre. I don't have to tell you everything. I can take care of myself. I don't need you babysitting me."

Andre stopped. "Baby...? If you didn't act like an ass and do things that could potentially get you killed I wouldn't have to *babysit* you." He strutted ahead. "The cops were doing their job. It's no one's fault if they died in the line of duty."

Reece caught up to him. "You think so, huh?"

"Yes, I do. And besides, if anyone's to blame it's you for being down here in the first place."

"Well it's good to know..." Reece tripped over something lying on the ground and landed in a gooey red mess. Andre whipped him up off the concrete and onto his feet with one hand. Both men backed up.

"Jesus!" Reece's stomach felt like a washing machine sloshing back and forth and his breakfast erupted from his mouth onto the ground at his feet, the red sludge he'd fallen into was smeared all over his hands, arms and the knees of his jeans.

"Well now we know what happened to them." Andre walked around the double pools of ooze. "And it wasn't a succubus." He searched the ground for something to clean Reece off with and found an old newspaper. "Here, you can't go back to the others covered in bloody slime."

A sound echoed out of the dark. Both men spun around and recoiled.

Lozano peered through the infrared viewer. "What's taking them so long?" The headset lit up the tunnel like a bright red neon.

"Don't worry, they'll be back soon," Arianne assured him.

The sheriff turned around. "Do you think they've found something?"

"Possibly," Sarah said.

"You don't think they're in any trouble, do you?"

The thought had crossed her mind. "I'm sure they'll be here any minute."

Arianne pulled Sarah to one side. "Maybe we should go look for them. They've been a while."

"I was thinking the same thing."

The women walked over to the sheriff. "I think we'll head in and see if we can find them," Sarah said.

"So you're worried about them too?"

"Not worried. But it can't hurt."

The trio trudged along the center of the tunnel.

Reece and Andre burst out of the dark, hurtling toward them. "Run!"

The three turned on their heels and took off along the drain, Andre and Reece close behind. They raced out of the second shaft and down the main tunnel to the entrance. The sun had almost set and the sky was dusky pink. How long had they been down there?

When they reached the opening, Reece and Andre peered over their shoulders to see if the creature would venture into the remaining light. It didn't. Thank God.

"What was chasing us?" Lozano asked.

"A flesh-eating demon," Andre told him. "One that can liquefy a human body with its venom." The rift was transporting more and more threatening demons to earth.

The sheriff crossed himself. "Holy mother of God." His eyes met Reece's. "It got my men, didn't it?"

Reece gave a heavy sigh. "I'm sorry, Lozano."

Lozano's eyes moved to the ground then darted up to the PI. "How am I supposed to explain this to their families... and my men?"

"You can't. We're going to have to abandon the car out in the desert and make it look like they were abducted or got lost while investigating out there."

"What? You can't be serious."

Reece stood with his hands on his hips. "Do you have a better solution? If you send forensics in, not only will they be in danger of the same fate, but how are they going to explain what's down there?"

The sheriff paced then turned around. "So we're staging a crime scene?"

The PI gave him an intense stare. "It's the only way. We don't have a choice."

"And what about the remains? Can we do something about them?"

"There are no remains, Lozano. Your men were liquefied."

The sheriff couldn't get his head around it. Two of his best officers were dead because of him.

CHAPTER THIRTY SIX

Lying in bed that night, Reece thought about what Oriana had said to him at the restaurant. She had bestowed a gift upon him, one he'd be delighted with. Nothing had arrived at their door so what did she mean? *What kind of gift? And where is it?* He thought about Charlotte. *Could she still be alive after so long? If so, where is she?* He hated having so many unanswered questions rolling around inside his head. A knock on the door echoed into the quiet room dragging him from his thoughts. Everyone else was asleep.

Reece glanced at the clock radio on the bedside table between his and Andre's beds. 12.02 AM. He frowned, threw back the covers, stepped out of bed and pulled on the pair of boxers lying on top of his jeans on the floor. Grabbing his Glock from under his pillow, he made his way across the room without a sound and squinted into the peephole. Black.

He pressed his ear against the back of the door. No one was talking. Was only one person outside? Could it be the gift Oriana had promised? He crossed the room, picked up his jeans and shirt and yanked them on. Better to be prepared. "Andre, wake up," he whispered. He knew it would be difficult because when immortals slept they were pretty much dead. He shoved his friend. "Andre." He grabbed his shoulders and shook him. "Andre, wake up!"

Andre opened his drowsy eyes and sucked in a deep breath as though he'd been holding it under water. "What's wrong?"

"Someone's outside. They knocked a few seconds ago."

He sat up and attempted to shake off the lethargy. "What time is it?"

"After midnight."

Andre threw back the covers and was on his feet. He slept in boxers and T-shirt while sharing adjoining rooms with Arianne and Sarah. "Did you check through the peephole?"

"Of course I did. Couldn't see anything. Whoever's out there is blocking it."

Andre nodded and crossed the room. He leaned close and inhaled.

Reece walked over to him. "Anything?" he mouthed.

"Vampire," his friend mouthed back.

The PI's eyes widened and he raised his weapon, aiming it at whoever was out in the hall.

Andre moved him aside and slid back the latch.

Reece grabbed his hand. "Don't! What are you doing?"

"It's all right." He swung the door open.

Nathaniel's large frame took up most of the doorway.

"Come in," Andre offered.

The large black vampire entered their room. "Thank you."

"What are you doing here?" Reece asked, a curious frown on his face.

"I am here to assist you." He set his suitcase down beside the adjoining door. It opened and Arianne and Sarah came into the room. "We asked him to come," Arianne said. "We need his help."

Reece frowned at her then moved his gaze to Nathaniel. "We've been fine so far. You really didn't need to come all this way."

"I am happy to do so." He gazed around the room, then looked at Reece and Andre. "We can discuss the situation in the morning. Why don't you all get some rest, I will be fine."

The women said goodnight and headed back to their room. Reece followed.

"Why did you call Nathaniel?" He glared at them.

"Because we can't do this alone, Reece. We've had no luck in locating the succubae, and now we know Charlotte is out there somewhere we need him." Sarah walked over and sat down on her bed. Arianne remained standing.

"Look, I understand you think we're not making progress, but we are. The meetings I've had with Oriana are producing the results we want. She's almost ready to give her sisters up. You brought Nathaniel here prematurely."

"I don't think so." Arianne stepped up to him. "We haven't made any progress at all. You and Andre have been running around following the demons' every command in the hope to get Charlotte back and we still have no idea where she is." She folded her arms. "We do need his help, whether you care to admit it or not."

Reece's stern gaze remained on the young woman for a moment, then he gave a huffy sigh, turned on his heel and marched out of their room. No point in arguing with strong-willed women. And he didn't want to admit they were right.

Nathaniel had made himself comfortable in a chair at the table. Andre in the other. It looked like no one would get much sleep tonight.

"Do you want to retire or would you prefer to bring me up to speed?" Nathaniel asked, resting his large hands in his lap.

"What did Sarah tell you?" Reece crossed the room slid the Glock under his pillow, walked around his bed and sat on the edge.

"She told me the gypsy warned you someone would die. You were kidnapped and taken into the desert. You have been assisting the sheriff with the succubus killings and he knows about the creatures." His eyes moved to Andre. "And Andre." He returned his gaze to the PI. "A woman's body was found which you first believed to be Charlotte. And you have met with one of the succubae who wants to remain on earth and is willing to make a deal. Am I correct, so far?" His dark eyes met Reece's. "Oh, and you thought Jacques could be behind it."

Reece's eyes narrowed and he gave Nathaniel a sour look. "Well that about brings you up to speed, doesn't it?" He folded his arms. "We've had no luck locating Charlotte, if she's still alive. And we've had no luck finding out who the succubae are working for. Oriana is too afraid to tell me. She said she will soon, but I don't believe her. I think she would rather return to hell than risk her life."

"And you are sure both incidents are related?"

The PI frowned at the vampire. "Of course. The succubae were the ones sending me the notes and macabre gifts. And they're definitely killing young men here. Why?"

"No reason. I only want to be sure of the facts."

"What do you think about my theory?" Reece watched Nathaniel's expression for a reaction. He didn't get one.

"You mean about Jacques being alive and behind all of this?"

"Could I be right?"

"I have been looking into your theory since I received Sarah's phone call and I believe anything is possible.

CHAPTER THIRTY SEVEN

The next morning, around eight o'clock, Reece and the others sat in his and Andre's room going over what they knew so far. Sarah told Nathaniel about the prayer she'd found which would bind the succubae in the middle of the desert until they could repair the breach and expedite all three back to hell. Andre filled him in on the gypsy's body and his conclusions about a master vampire being the perpetrator and Reece offered to introduce him to Sheriff Lozano later in the day. He'd already set up a meeting.

Nathaniel informed the group he had been researching vampires coming back from ash and had contacted immortals in Europe who had witnessed the phenomenon firsthand. He wasn't convinced Jacques had risen from the dead for a second time, but he also wasn't ready to rule out the possibility.

Reece's body tightened at the thought. They had rid their world of Jacques a couple of years ago, or so they thought. Was it possible he'd returned to wreak havoc on them once again? If so, Charlotte was only a pawn in his demented game and once she was no longer of any use to him she would be dead. They had to find her!

"The knowledge bestowed upon me regarding vampires returning from ash is from a reliable source. If he has returned, it is quite possible Jacques had other adherents I was not aware of collect his remains and take them to a sorcerer for reanimation. According to the information given all they would need is a vial of his blood, some of his ashes and an awakening spell."

Nathaniel's words made Reece's insides turn to ice. The PI trusted him and knew he wouldn't impart what he had learned if he didn't believe it was relevant. "I had a feeling it could be him. This whole scenario reminded me of the way he operated." He turned his gaze to his friend. "Andre didn't believe me. He thought I was slipping over the edge."

"And I still don't think it's my brother. Why haven't I sensed him? If Jacques were here I would have by now."

"Perhaps not. He would block you. He did it once before." Nathaniel's gaze rested on him.

Sarah stood up and paced the room, a worried frown on her face. "So should we be looking for him specifically?" Jacques was Andre's identical twin. A homicidal maniac master vampire who had no qualms about who he killed to get what he wanted, and if he had found a way to come back they were all in danger. His games always ended in death. They had lost good people battling him the last time.

"It may not be him, Sarah, but as long as we are aware it could be we will be better equipped to deal with the situation." Nathaniel stood up and looked at Reece. "Where were you taken when the succubae abducted you?"

"Out into the desert to an abandoned motel off the highway."

"Can you take me there?"

"Why?"

"I want to examine the location to see if there are any residual vibrations we can follow." He looked at his protégé. "Did you not think of using your immortal senses, Arianne?"

"Not at the time, no, we were more concerned with finding Reece before they killed him. I don't think there would be anything out there now," Arianne said. "It was days ago."

Nathaniel gave her a stern stare. "Nevertheless, I am interested in having a look around." His eyes moved to the PI. "Will you drive me out there now?"

"Now?" Reece's eyebrows rose in surprise. "Yeah, I guess. But I don't know what you expect to find."

"When I find it I will tell you."

"What do you want us to do while you're gone?" Sarah asked, moving to the open laptop sitting on the table and taking her seat.

Reece ran his eyes around his team. "Andre, check with Lozano and see if anything unusual came back on the gypsy. Sarah, I'd like you to continue researching a way to close the rift. It's our number one priority. Arianne, check through the realtor lists and see if anything stands out about the clients. Maybe we'll get lucky and find the succubae by their rental agreement. The three of them would've had to sign it."

He turned to Nathaniel. "Ok, let's go. It's going to take a good couple hours or so to get out there."

When Reece swung the door open Lozano was in the hall about to knock. "Hey, Sheriff, what are you doing here? Weren't we meeting up later in the day?"

"Yes, we were but I just got a call from a…" he opened his notebook, "Dr. Eric Benson from the Valley Hospital intensive care unit and wanted to tell you in person. They have Charlotte."

‟⇣

Reece's heart boomed in his chest as he raced through the hospital entrance to reception. Charlotte was alive and he was about to see her again. He rushed over to the woman behind the counter to ask where the ICU was and once he had the directions made his way there in record time. He wanted to see his lovely lady, hold her in his arms, place the engagement ring in his pocket back on her finger. Marry her before anything else happened.

When he entered the intensive care unit a doctor walked up to him extending his hand. "Hello Detective Daniels, I'm Eric Benson. I've been treating your fiancée since she was admitted three days ago. She was unconscious until early this morning and we initially thought she was in a coma until the toxicology report came back. She'd been heavily sedated, hadn't had any food and was very dehydrated. Please don't react when you see her because she hasn't seen herself yet. She's confined to bed rest."

Reece frowned into the doctor's eyes. "So she's in pretty bad shape?"

The doctor nodded. "She's lucky to be alive."

The PI's jaw clenched and tears stung the backs of his eyes. He blinked and squeezed his thumb and index finger into them to stop the flow and inhaled a deep breath through his nostrils. "Ok. I'll do my best not to react but I can't promise I won't. It's been days since she was abducted and none of us knew if she was alive or dead."

Eric Benson gave a sympathetic smile. "I understand. Just do the best you can, for her sake."

Reece shrugged off the intense anxiety he felt and gave a sharp nod. He had to be strong for Charlotte.

∞⌘

When Lozano pulled the patrol cruiser up outside the dilapidated motel and turned off the ignition he glanced sideways at the large, black immortal sitting in the passenger seat beside him. Another vampire. A monster of a vampire. He had to be at least six feet eight inches tall and was broader than a gridiron quarterback. He swallowed the nervous lump in his throat, swung the car door open and climbed out.

Nathaniel stepped out of the vehicle, along with Andre who had been sitting behind him, and ran his gaze over the rundown, vacant premises. He already had an image in his mind of what had taken place here and could also sense the death of the woman his friends had believed was Charlotte. She had screamed herself hoarse while they assaulted her. Stripping her fingerprints from her hands while she was conscious and biting off the features of her face so she wouldn't be recognized. She had bled out during the attack. The vision disturbed him. He frowned and moved toward the room the woman had been held prisoner in.

The sheriff and Andre followed.

Nathaniel tore down the yellow crime scene tape and stepped inside. He moved around the room, stopping in certain places and closing his eyes. The vibration of fear hung densely in the atmosphere like thick fog. "Coyotes did not mutilate her, the demons did."

Lozano swallowed hard. "I thought…"

"Yes, it would be easy to assume wild animals had attacked her out here in the desert."

"How terrible." The sheriff ran his eyes over the blood-splattered room.

Andre walked over to the bloody table. *Thank God it hadn't been Charlotte.*

Nathaniel turned to him. "Yes, it is good news Charlotte is still alive and unharmed, but unfortunate for the woman who took her place. I understand why Reece thinks Jacques is involved. It is the kind of deranged game he would play."

Andre's eyes darted to him. "Do you think it is?"

"I cannot be sure. There is nothing here to suggest it is."

Lozano stood with his arms folded. "If it's not Andre's brother then who?"

"A question which requires an answer I cannot give."

"Any idea who the woman is lying in the coroner's office?" Andre asked the sheriff.

"Not yet. Her DNA didn't match any on file so she wasn't a working girl."

"Why hasn't she been reported missing then?"

"Maybe she was one of the homeless. Hopefully we'll have some answers soon."

The three headed to the room where Reece had been held captive.

CHAPTER THIRTY EIGHT

Reece hesitated before stepping into the room. When he arrived he'd been ready to rush into the ICU, scoop Charlotte into his arms and never let her go, but after hearing what the doctor had to say he wasn't even sure if he could hold it together long enough to step through the open door. He swallowed hard, the tangle of nerves lodged in his gut causing a rolling wave of nausea, and glanced at Dr. Benson standing beside him. This was going to be harder than he thought.

Oriana's words echoed inside his head. Had this been the gift she promised? Had *she* freed Charlotte? He let the thought go. Nothing else mattered now except getting his beautiful bride-to-be back on her feet. They had her son to raise.

He inhaled a deep breath into his constricted lungs and walked into the glass cubicle. Hot tears stung his eyes when he saw how pale and fragile Charlotte looked lying in the bed with plastic tubes everywhere, the heart monitor beeping its rhythmic beat. He blinked and watched her before approaching the hospital bed. She had been through so much and he hadn't been there to protect her. Reece sat down on the visitor's chair and reached for Charlotte's hand. Every fiber of his body ached to touch her. Her hand felt cool and clammy. A tear slid down his left cheek and he swiped it away. Her recovery depended on his strength.

Charlotte's sunken, dark-rimmed eyes opened slowly and widened when she saw him. "Reece!" Her weak voice sounded like a small child's behind the oxygen mask.

He put on a brave face and smiled. "Hello sweetheart. You don't know how good it is to have you back." His heart thumped as he gave her hand a gentle squeeze.

Tears slid from the corners of her eyes and Reece was on his feet scooping her gently into his arms, holding her close. It shocked him when he wrapped his arms around her. Charlotte was normally of slight build, but he could feel the bones beneath her skin. She was much frailer than she first appeared.

"I... never thought... I'd see you again," she told him, more tears sliding down her face. "I thought I was going to die."

"You're safe now, sweetheart. All you have to do is concentrate on getting well." He held her close willing all the strength he had to penetrate her weak frame and help her recover quickly. He eased himself out of her embrace. He'd wanted to place her engagement ring back on her finger but would have to wait until she gained more weight. Those threatening tears continued to sting the backs of his eyes and he blinked them away.

Charlotte reached up and touched his unshaven face. "I love you," her voice was a whisper. "I never thought I'd get to say those words to you again."

He took her hand in his and kissed the palm. "I love you too."

"How long have I been gone?"

"Several days. It felt much longer though. We've been looking everywhere for you."

She gave a thin smile, knowing they would have. "Do you know who did it?"

"We do now, although it took a while to figure out. They were very shrewd. Sent notes and messengers to do their work for them."

Charlotte stared into Reece's eyes. "Was it the usual suspects?" She meant otherworldly creatures but couldn't say it in front of the doctor.

Reece nodded.

Dr. Benson crossed the room. "She needs to rest now. You can come back later."

Charlotte protested weakly. "I want him to stay. Please don't make him go."

The doctor rested a comforting hand on her shoulder. "You need plenty of rest if you're going to make a full recovery. He won't be far away."

Another tear slid down her face and she nodded.

"Good girl." He turned to Reece. "Can I talk to you before you go?"

"Sure."

"I'll give you a minute." The doctor stepped out of the room.

Reece leaned in to Charlotte, lifted the oxygen mask off her face and planted a gentle kiss on her lips. "Sleep, sweetheart. I'll be back soon. Do you need anything?"

Charlotte shook her head. "Only you."

He smiled and gazed into her eyes with a profound look of love. "You have me. For life."

⟋⟍

By the time Reece arrived back at the hotel and pulled into the driveway, Andre and Nathaniel were stepping out of Sheriff Lozano's car. The PI handed the rental's keys to a valet and walked over to the pair. "Any luck out there?" He was curious to know what Nathaniel had picked up on.

"Let us go up to the room," Nathaniel told him. "We can discuss it there."

"How's Charlotte doing?" Andre asked.

"She's in bad shape. Those bitches didn't feed her or give her any water and they kept her heavily sedated. Her arms look like a junkie's. She's always had a slight build but now she's skin and bone."

"I'm so sorry, Reece. She didn't deserve any of it."

"Yeah, you're right, she didn't. The doctor looking after her seems to know what he's doing so hopefully she'll be out in a few days."

"Can we see her?"

"Maybe in a day or two. I was kicked out of there after only a few minutes. The doc said she needs plenty of rest to make a full recovery. She doesn't look like herself either. I almost lost my shit when I saw her. Imagine what Sarah and Arianne would do."

"You're right. Women get too emotional."

"Yeah, they do. And it's the last thing Charlotte needs right now."

The three men made their way to the elevator banks.

Just as the doors slid open, Oriana rushed into the lobby. "I need to speak with you."

Reece frowned. "You should've called first."

"This cannot wait."

The PI glanced at Andre and Nathaniel. "I'll see you up there. Won't be long."

Nathaniel eyed the young woman. A succubus was a deadly companion. "Perhaps she should come with us?"

"No, it's all right. You go on up. I'll be there soon."

Andre and Nathaniel were reluctant to step into the elevator.

"It's ok." Reece turned to look at the pair. "I'll be fine."

"If you're not back in fifteen minutes we'll come looking for you," Andre warned.

Reece nodded and his friend pressed the button to their floor. Both vampires eyed the woman as the doors closed.

"Your friends care about you a great deal."

"We care about each other. Now what do you want?"

"I believe you received my gift of good faith," she said, giving him a seductive smile. "I hope it met your expectations. And I hope it will mean my safety."

"You let Charlotte go? Why?"

"I wanted you to know I meant what I said. I will assist you if you help me stay here." She sauntered toward the lift lobby exit. "Coming?"

"Where?" He followed.

"I want coffee. There's a Starbucks just over there." She gestured down the walkway.

Reece stepped up beside her and they made their way to the café.

"You get the coffee and I'll wait over there." She pointed to an empty table near the window.

"How do you take it?"

"Black." She gave him a wink. She knew he would get her witticism. Black as the bowels of hades.

Once the order was ready, Reece took the cardboard takeaway cups over to the table and sat down opposite Oriana. "Here." He pushed the drink across the table.

"Thank you."

"Tell me about the woman."

Her perfectly sculpted right eyebrow arched. "The woman who took Charlotte's place?"

He frowned into her eyes. "Don't play games with me. You know who I mean. Who was she?"

Oriana removed the plastic lid from the cup, breathed in the aromatic, nutty aroma rising in the steam then sipped the coffee cautiously. "No one."

Reece glowered at her. "She was *someone*. Someone's mother, daughter, sister, friend."

"She was a homeless woman living in the tunnels. Nothing more. I knew she wouldn't be missed and she fitted your girlfriend's body shape and hair color."

"Fiancée." Reece sighed. He was tired of correcting people.

Oriana's glossy red lips spread into an amused smile. "Fiancée then. No need to be so touchy."

"So what happened?" Reece took a cautious sip of his latte.

She sat her cup on the table. "We took Charlotte's earrings and underclothes and placed them on the woman. Then we removed her fingerprints and her facial features to make her unrecognizable. So now it's up to you to keep your *fiancée* hidden."

"She's in the intensive care unit." Reece folded his arms. "You took her to the hospital, didn't you?"

"I could have left her in the tunnels but she would have died so I dropped her outside the emergency room. Our master believes the body found was Charlotte's so she should be safe for a while."

Reece didn't like the sound of that. How long did 'a while' mean? He gave her an intense stare. "Is that the reason our luggage was taken? Did you plan to substitute me as well?"

She raised her chin and looked at him from under her long lashes. "It wasn't my doing. We were ordered by our master."

"Who is this master of yours? You said you'd tell me."

Oriana gave him an assured glossy smile and sipped her coffee, despite her internal turmoil. Inside, the human form quaked with fear. She dreaded revealing it and wasn't sure she could, even though she had given her word. Demons rarely kept their promises, but she had to if she wanted to remain in the mortal realm. And she longed to stay. If her master discovered she was the one who gave his name to the private eye he would destroy her in the most excruciating way possible. Hell had nothing on him.

CHAPTER THIRTY NINE

"I followed my sister and she met with the private investigator. She is up to something, Master. I told you," Helyna said. "She has been meeting with him regularly and I am sure it is to bargain for her life." She knew her sister wanted to remain on earth and would do anything to make it happen. They each craved it, but she and her sister, Katya, were not so reckless as to blatantly go against their master and have him end them.

"Yes, I am aware. My informant has also been following her." He steepled his fingers under his chin. "Something will have to be done. Something... drastic." He gave her a fanged smile.

Helyna shivered. Had she done the wrong thing by telling him? Would he kill her sister for her disloyalty?

"Oriana is a liability. One I cannot afford. If she has been providing information to the PI he will be one step ahead of me. I cannot allow that to happen." His dark gaze moved to the woman standing before him. "I want you to dispatch her."

Helyna's mouth gaped. "But, Master, I..."

"You will do as I say or you can take her place." His eyes narrowed.

"Please, Master, don't make me do it. She is my sister."

He gave her a satisfied smirk. "Perhaps you should have considered that before coming here to betray her."

Helyna lowered her head and closed her eyes. How could she kill her own sister?

He clicked his fingers to gain her attention. "And make sure it is done quickly." He held out his hand to her with a vial of something dark purple. "This will do the task."

The demon's eyes widened. "What is it?"

"Belladonna, also known as deadly nightshade. It will kill anything, mortal or immortal."

The succubus reached out a trembling hand and took the small glass bottle then bowed, turned on her heel and rushed out of the cavern into the tunnel, tears sliding down her cheeks. *What have I done? How can I do what he has commanded?*

CHAPTER FORTY

Reece slapped the palm of his hand onto the bedside table and groped around for his jangling cell phone, his foggy brain wondering what time it was. He snatched up his iPhone and pressed the button. "Do you have any idea what time it is?" His blurred vision moved to the red digital numerals on the clock radio and a fuzzy 2.23 AM stared back at him.

"Yeah, I do," Lozano said, "but we've got another body. I'm at the scene now."

Reece sat bolt upright in bed. "What? Where?"

Andre turned on the lamp and threw back the covers.

"It's behind the Mandalay Bay, first right turn off Russell Road under the up ramp. We've got the section cordoned off. Do you want to come down?"

"Was it a succubus?"

"No. It's… well it looks like another vampire killing."

Reece was on his feet. "We'll be right there." He hung up and wrestled on his underwear and jeans. "You heard?"

Andre was dressed and ready to go. "Yes."

Sarah and Arianne came into the room wrapped in hotel robes. "What's going on?" Sarah asked, her voice thick from sleep.

"There's been another vampire killing." Reece shrugged into his faded denim shirt and clawed at the buttons, starting from the bottom and working his way up.

"Where?"

"Behind Mandalay Bay Hotel."

"Do you want us to come along?"

"No, go back to bed and get some sleep. We'll take a look."

"Who could be doing this?" Arianne asked. "Why now?"

"I don't know, but we're going to find out." He headed for the door. Andre followed him.

As Reece opened it, Nathaniel appeared in the hallway. "I am coming with you."

The PI gazed up at the tall, broad vampire realizing his immortal hearing had tapped into the conversation with Lozano. "Ok. Let's go."

∞

Reece made a right turn off Russell Road into Frank Sinatra Drive and pulled up in the red NO PARKING ZONE beside the concrete ramp not far along from the crime scene. He and the others climbed out of the four wheel drive and walked back to Lozano. The sheriff was on his radio telling his men to do a thorough sweep of the area. He turned around when he heard footsteps behind him. "Glad you could make it." He gazed up at Nathaniel then his eyes moved back to the PI. The sheriff leaned in to Reece and spoke into his ear. "Do you think the big guy can help?"

"Yeah, I do. He's an excellent tracker and he can pick up things the rest of us can't, like what you're saying right now." He glanced over his shoulder at Nathaniel and raised his chin in a gesture of camaraderie.

"Oh, ok" Lozano gave Nathaniel a quick sheepish look then returned his gaze to Reece. "I've cleared the area. Wanna take a look?"

The three men followed him behind the tacked up black polythene tarpaulin and yellow crime scene tape.

Nathaniel moved closer to the remains. This time the head had not been ripped from the body, which meant the gypsy had been a revenge killing. The one relevant aspect he noticed was there were no bite marks, although the body was completely drained of blood.

"This is the secondary crime scene. God knows where this young woman was attacked." The sheriff was disturbed by the new turn of events and new killer. He had thought the gypsy woman was a one off, a loose end being tied up. Lozano paced once then stopped and turned around? "Do we have two homicidal otherworldly maniacs to worry about now?"

Nathaniel moved his gaze to the sheriff. "It would appear so." He straightened and walked back to the men. "This was a superior master vampire." His eyes moved to Andre. "It is not Jacques. There is a certain energy here, but it is not his."

"Do you know whose it is?" Reece asked, standing beside him with his arms folded.

Nathaniel's eyes moved back to the exsanguinated young woman. "You would not believe me if I told you."

Reece frowned. "You should know me better by now, Nathaniel. Maybe once I wouldn't have been so receptive but today I'll believe whatever you tell me. Our lives and the lives of everyone else depend on it."

The large black vampire moved his scrutinizing gaze around the three men, taking in the expressions on their faces. "I believe the vampire we are looking for is…" He hesitated.

"Who?" Reece urged.

"Dracula."

Reece was on his cell phone within seconds calling Sarah. He knew she was in search of the infamous forefather of blood drinkers. "I need you to come down here. There's something I want you to do."

"What's wrong?" She could hear the tension in the PI's voice.

"Nathaniel just told us the vampire killing these latest victims is Dracula."

"What?!" Sarah threw back the bed covers and was on her feet. "I'll be right there. Do you want me to bring Arianne?"

"I think we'll need all the manpower we can get."

"We're on our way."

"Sarah?"

"Yes?"

"Bring your weapons. We're going into the tunnels.

ஐ

Sarah had waited an extended lifetime to meet the vampire who had killed her family. She had once been a wife and mother but Dracula had taken it all away from her. And she had had to decapitate her beloved husband and children to prevent them from returning as hungry, blood drinking savages.

Why was her nemesis in Las Vegas? And why had he orchestrated the abduction of Charlotte? If he wanted her why hadn't he come after her? Sarah knew why. He enjoyed playing games with humans. Toying with their emotions and weakening their resolve. She eased the rental down the concrete slope, pulled in behind the four wheel drive and she and Arianne climbed out.

The four men were waiting for them outside the entrance into the storm water drains. This time they planned to find the monster they were seeking and eliminate him. Sarah's unique weaponry would accomplish the task. She had had her arsenal created for the purpose of ridding the world of a vampire people believed was a character in a gothic horror story.

Lozano wouldn't take no for an answer. He'd wanted to join them in their quest to find the most dangerous, psychotic predator known to man. He believed the demon that had killed his men had been unleashed by the vampire and if his intuition was correct, and he was certain it was, he wanted payback.

Sarah called Reece over to the car and opened the trunk. Inside sat her oversized suitcase. She unzipped it and pushed the lid back. Her weapons were deadly to any otherworldly creature—demon or vampire. The PI particularly liked the high-powered, double-chamber crossbow with pure solid silver arrows. He had used it before and it was his weapon of choice for this particular mission. He knew he wouldn't miss.

Reece, Sarah and Lozano slid on their infrared headsets. The sheriff had provided each of them with a Kevlar jacket and also a cache of silver bullets he had confiscated from a kid who believed he was a werewolf hunter a year ago. Maybe he was after all. Lozano's gut had told him they would come in handy one day and was glad he'd kept them out of the evidence locker.

Sarah blessed the bullets. The thought of the night in the underground caverns of St. Gabriel's church when they were fighting Jacques' coven of vampires popped into her head. She had dropped the zip lock bag of silver bullets in the dark, which Dave Colson had pilfered from the precinct, and had cursed out loud to Reece's disbelief. An amused smile crossed her face.

"What's so funny?" Reece asked.

"I was thinking about St. Gabriel's and the time I dropped the bag of bullets."

Reece gave her a smile. "Yeah, I remember. I had no idea priests swore."

"We don't usually but I was under extreme pressure at the time."

"Yes, you were. We all were." He glanced around at his team, Nathaniel, Andre, Arianne, Lozano and Sarah and wondered what awaited them inside the pitch black tunnels? Would they all make it out alive? He checked his watch. "Oriana should be here any minute."

"Why is she coming with us?" Nathaniel gave the PI an intense stare.

"To show us where Dracula is hiding out."

Andre stepped up to him. "You really believe she'll betray him? You said she was afraid for her life, what makes you think she isn't setting us up?"

"If we don't use her to get to him we could end up lost in the labyrinth of tunnels down here and be picked off instead of using the element of surprise to get to him first." Reece glanced at his watch again. She was late. His phone went off and he pulled it from the back pocket of his jeans.

A message from Oriana.

'Sorry, Reece, but I can't come with you. It would be committing immortal suicide. I've attached a map for you to follow. It will take you to where he's hiding. I hope you make it out ok.'

Reece gave a heavy sigh. "Dammit!"

"She's not coming, is she?" Andre's eyes met his frown.

"No. She sent a map." He ran his hand over the stubble on his face. "Jesus."

"Do you think it's a trap, like Andre said?" Sarah asked, walking over to the pair.

Reece shook his head. "Her not accompanying us into the tunnels could mean it is. If any of you don't want to go in I'll understand."

Lozano stepped up to him and gripped his arm. "We're here so let's do this. Someone has to stop him and his demons from killing any more innocent people."

The PI gazed around his team. They each knew the risk. "Thank you."

"Let us go." Nathaniel's black clad form dissolved into the dark tunnel.

The others followed.

After traipsing through the stinking, dank concrete passages for almost three hours and finding nothing Reece was ready to call it quits. Oriana had sent them on another wild goose chase. Was the vampire even in this section of the storm water drains? He could have been anywhere—a five star hotel even. Who would know? Reece was angry with himself for putting his trust in a demon. He should have known better.

As the group continued into the depths of the labyrinth, Reece thought about Charlotte and what she had gone through. Had she been a prisoner down here? His body tightened at the thought of her being in such a foul place. She had been so badly emaciated from lack of food and water she could have died in these tunnels and never been found. At least he had his fiancée back safe and sound, and even though he didn't want to admit it he owed Oriana. She had set Charlotte free.

Andre and Nathaniel stopped ahead of the group and used their immortal hearing. Nothing.

"I think Oriana lied to us," Andre said. "There's nothing down here."

"Yeah, I'm inclined to agree with you." Reece gazed along the length of the tunnel through the infrared viewer. "There doesn't seem to be any openings or gaps in these walls. I think she steered us in the wrong direction on purpose."

"Maybe we should keep going for a bit longer," Sarah suggested. "Perhaps we haven't reached the section on the map yet."

Reece turned around. "What makes you say that?"

Sarah pushed her cell phone forward and pointed to the diagram Reece had messaged to each of them. "Look here. I think this intersection is further ahead. We haven't come across anything like it so far."

Everyone checked their maps.

"I think Sarah's right," Arianne said. "If you calculate how long we've been walking and the distance on the map we haven't come to it."

Something vibrated along the tunnel causing a frigid wave to move through the airless atmosphere around them. Sarah, Reece and the sheriff shivered.

"What was that?" Lozano said, his breath pluming in white clouds, his eyes wide. He swung around and focused his infrared gaze on the darkness ahead of them. He could see nothing unusual.

"Let's keep moving." Reece joined Nathaniel and Andre. The others followed.

When the group reached the intersection in the tunnel Reece checked the map again. "We need to go left."

They continued along the drain keeping their wits about them, their anxiety wrapping itself around them like their black surroundings. If the map was correct they were close now.

A metallic clang echoed out of the dark ahead of them and everyone stopped in their tracks.

Nathaniel whipped his large frame into the gloom and disappeared from sight.

"Where's he going?" Lozano asked, stepping up alongside Reece.

"To check out what's up ahead before we venture any further."

"What do you think made that sound?"

"Could be a homeless person living down here. Although the guy I spoke to said no one lives in these sections. They congregate at the other end of the strip."

"So could it mean there's something down here guarding the area for Dracula?"

"Yeah, it could."

"Maybe the flesh dissolving demon?"

"Possibly."

Lozano swallowed the wad of nerves lodged in his throat and took up his position with Sarah and Arianne, his weapon raised in shaky hands, his finger poised on the trigger. He realized he was out of his depth but he wasn't about to back out now. The more firepower the group had the better.

Nathaniel emerged out of the shadows. "I dispatched the demon. We can continue."

"There could be more, right?" Reece glanced along the tunnel.

"We will only find out once we move on."

Reece gave a heavy sigh and stepped up beside Nathaniel. "I hate surprises."

The group continued through the murky gloom. The deeper into the tunnels they traveled the denser the air became and the more their senses were on high alert. They could hear each other's labored breathing.

Nathaniel raised his hand and motioned for everyone to stop. He stepped away from the group and used his immortal hearing and vision to scope out the area ahead. Something awaited them in the dark, something only he could see.

CHAPTER FORTY ONE

At 6.30 AM Charlotte snatched up her cell phone from off the cabinet beside her hospital bed and keyed in Mrs. Jenkins' number. It had been almost two weeks since she had been abducted and she wanted to hear her son's voice. Something she thought she would never do again. The line rang for quite a while before anyone picked up. She knew they'd be awake because it was a school day and Tommy would be getting ready.

"Jenkins residence."

"Hello, Mrs. J, it's Charlotte. Can I speak to Tommy please?"

"Charlotte! How did the wedding go? Tommy was wondering why you didn't send photos."

Tears stung the backs of Charlotte's eyes and she couldn't speak.

"Is everything all right?" Mrs. Jenkins soft voice was filled with concern.

Charlotte cleared her throat and attempted to sound cheerful. "Yes, everything's fine. We've just been so busy. I didn't mean to forget."

"It's all right, dear, don't fret. Here's Tommy. Have a wonderful rest of your honeymoon."

"Thank you, Mrs. J, we will."

"Mom!"

"Hi honey, sorry I didn't send the photos I promised. We've…"

"It's ok, Mom, you're on your honeymoon. I get it. How are you? How's Reece? Did you visit the Grand Canyon yet?" Her son's voice was brimming with excitement.

"We're both fine. No, we haven't yet, but we will. How are you? What have you been up to?"

"Just school and stuff. I'm ok. Mrs. J is taking good care of me so don't worry." Tommy went quiet for a moment, then he said, "Mom?"

"Yes, honey?"

"There's something I want to ask you about." Her son's voice took on a serious tone.

"What is it, sweetie?" Charlotte frowned and tears threatened to spill. Her emotions were all over the place right now but she had to hold it together for Tommy.

"Do you think... never mind."

"No, honey, go on. Do I think what?"

He gave a huffy sigh then continued. "Do you think Reece would mind if I called him dad? I've been thinking about it and I'd really like to."

Tears spilled down Charlotte's face and she covered her mouth with her hand to stop the small sob threatening to escape.

"Mom, are you still there?"

Charlotte swallowed the aching lump in her throat and steadied her voice. "Yes, honey, I'm here. I think he would love you calling him dad. He cares about you so much."

"Yeah, I know. And I really care about him too. He's been like a dad to me."

"Yes, he has."

"Do you think I should ask him?"

"If you want to, honey. But I'm sure he won't mind either way."

Tommy let out a soft sigh. "Ok. When you get home I'll ask him."

Dr. Benson walked into the room.

"Honey, I'm sorry but I have to go. I'll call you again in a couple of days, ok? I love you."

"I love you too, Mom. Say hi to Reece for me and have a fun vacation."

More tears spilled down Charlotte's face. "I will. Thank you, sweetie." She pressed the end button and slid her cell phone onto the cabinet.

"Your son?"

Charlotte nodded as she brushed the tears from her cheeks and sniffled.

"How is he?" He walked around the bed and passed her the tissue box.

"He... he's good. Happy. Mrs. J takes good care of him." She plucked a tissue from it and wiped her eyes.

"And how are you doing? Physically you're improving by the day, but what about emotionally?"

Charlotte sighed. "I don't know. I almost died. Talking to my son seemed so surreal. I never thought I'd get to do that again."

"You have to try to move forward, Charlotte. I know you've been through a terrifying ordeal but you're safe now. Nothing can happen to you here. In a couple of weeks you'll be heading home to your son. Take comfort in that."

She gave him a forced smile and nodded. "You're right."

He moved to the visitor chair and sat down. "Would you like to speak to a trauma specialist?"

Charlotte flashed him a daggerous glare. "No, I wouldn't."

"It might help you sort out your feelings."

"I don't *need* a counselor." She folded her arms.

"Are you sure? There's no shame in talking to someone about what you experienced."

She glowered at him. "I know there's no shame in talking about it, but I don't want to."

Eric Benson sighed. "Ok, the offer's there if you decide to change your mind." He stood up.

Charlotte realized he was only trying to help. "Thank you, I know you're looking out for me, but I'll be ok. I've been through a lot worse and survived."

"Yes, I imagine you have. Being a detective is a risky occupation."

"You don't know the half of it," Charlotte said under her breath.

He studied her for a moment. "I think it's time to get you out of bed and moving. I'll send a nurse in shortly and she can help you to the bathroom so you can take a shower and freshen up properly."

Charlotte smiled. "Thank you. It would be wonderful to feel human again."

"Just don't overdo it. You're not out of the woods yet."

171

CHAPTER FORTY TWO

Nathaniel darted backwards, raised his weapon and fired continuously into the dark. Reece threw the crossbow to Arianne and pulled his Glock loaded with silver from his belt, the clip held seventeen rounds and he knew it would do more damage than two silver arrows. He and Andre flanked Nathaniel and opened fire, the flare of their weapons lighting up the tunnel around them and making their attackers visible. An army of snarling homeless men and women vampires stalked toward the group in the murky pools of pungent water while others crawled along the ceiling like oversized spiders, their eyes glowing in the dark.

Sarah raised her automatic HK53 loaded with silver high-velocity 5.56mm rifle ammunition and fired non-stop. It held forty rounds and would take out as many as she could hit. Screaming vampires dropped to ground one by one and exploded into bloody spray while others scrambled over the top of the fallen and kept coming.

Arianne aimed the crossbow and fired off two silver shafts then reloaded and fired again. The arrows rocketed through the gloom and hit two teenaged vampires directly in their hearts. Both young men's bodies turned black and disintegrated into ash where they stood. Still, an unending stream of vampires stalked toward them.

"Move back!" Reece yelled, the urgency in his voice ricocheting off the concrete walls. Everyone continued to fire as they ran backwards along the tunnel to the section that led to their vehicles.

"There are too many of them," Lozano shouted, firing into the stampede of ravenous vampires, his gut tight as a drum, beads of sweat on his brow.

"Keep firing and keep moving," Reece told them. He had planted plastic explosives at the entrance into this section of the drains as a precaution. Once they were all out safely he'd set it off. They would have to find another way into Dracula's lair.

The swarm of crazed, bloodthirsty vampires continued to descend upon them. Reece stopped and fired off more silver into the throng. Several creatures went down but more surged forward.

"Reece, come on!" Sarah called out. "We have to go."

Before he could turn and make a run for it, three vampires dropped from the ceiling, knocking him to the ground and hungrily tore flesh from his body, lapping at his blood. Reece fired randomly at the trio but they kept biting and sucking.

Nathaniel, Andre and Arianne whipped along the tunnel and tore the ravenous creatures off of him, twisting their necks and tossing the bodies across the drain into the others to slow them down. Nathaniel scooped Reece up with one hand as though he were as light as a feather and threw him over his shoulder. The group raced along the tunnel to the exit into the next section. Sarah set the plastic explosives and they made a dash out of the way to protect themselves from the explosion just as it rocked the drains around them. Chunks of concrete rained down on the opening they had escaped from, blocking the remaining vampires inside. They were safe.

Nathaniel eased Reece down onto the dirty ground. The PI's breathing was shallow and blood poured from several bite marks saturating his faded blue denim shirt and turning it murky brown.

Andre leaned in to his friend. "Reece can you hear me?"

Reece's eyes opened slowly and he nodded.

"I need to give you some of my blood. It's the only way to heal you."

Reece raised his shaking hand. "No!" His voice was a labored whisper.

"It will not turn you," Nathaniel assured.

"Get... me... outside to... the cars," Reece breathed, his chest heaving.

"You won't make it if I don't heal you." Andre frowned at him. His friend had lost too much blood.

Reece's dazed eyes stared into Andre's. Realizing his fate he nodded.

Andre bit into his wrist and pressed it to Reece's mouth.

"We need to keep moving," Sarah said. "There might be another way in we don't know about."

173

Nathaniel lifted Reece up off the rubbish strewn concrete and led the group out of the tunnel. He opened the four wheel drive's front passenger door and eased Reece onto the seat. "How are you feeling now?"

"Like I've been run over by a bulldozer, but I'll live." He gave a wry smile. "I was under the impression if I drank vampire blood after being bitten I'd turn."

"Only if you drink from the vampire who bit you and he in turn drinks from you to the point of death." Nathaniel told him in a matter-of-fact fashion before turning on his heel and moving to the back of the vehicle to assist the ladies in packing away the weapons.

Reece's left eyebrow rose. "Good to know."

Andre shrugged out of his button through shirt, pulled his T-shirt off over his head and handed it to Reece. "Here, put this on. You can't walk through the hotel lobby looking like you've massacred someone." He slid back into his gray shirt and buttoned it.

"Thanks, Andre. For saving my life again."

"You don't have to thank me, Reece. I've always got your back the same as you've got mine." The right corner of his mouth lifted. "Are you feeling ok?"

"Better than ok, actually." He glanced at his arms. The bite marks were disappearing.

Arianne appeared at the door. "Ready to go?" She glanced at Andre and smiled. Andre's eyes met hers and her cheeks flushed. She turned and walked around to the other side of the car.

Reece's eyes moved to his friend and he lowered his voice. "Something I need to know about?"

"There's nothing going on."

"But you'd like there to be, right?"

"Maybe."

"So why haven't you done anything about it?"

"I think we've had too much on our plate to even contemplate it right now, don't you?"

Reece sighed. "Yeah, I get your point. I wish we'd managed to locate Dracula. He's one step ahead of us at every turn."

"We'll find him," Andre assured. "Sarah won't rest until we do. She has a score to settle."

CHAPTER FORTY THREE

Later the same afternoon, Reece drove to the hospital to visit Charlotte. When he walked into the ICU Dr. Benson approached him with a smile on his face. "Hello, Detective Daniels." He reached out his hand. Reece shook it. "I'm happy to say Charlotte's been moved to a private room. We had her out of bed earlier today so she could take a shower and get a little exercise and as she's doing so well I thought it was time to make her more comfortable."

"That's great news. Where is she?"

"Let me walk with you." The doctor gestured for Reece to move ahead of him and they left the intensive care unit. "She still needs to rest and regain her strength, but I thought it would help her recovery if she wasn't reminded of the reason she was here."

"Thanks, I really appreciate it. She's been through a lot."

"Yes, she has. She doesn't want to talk about what happened, and I respect her wishes, although I believe it would help her emotionally. Maybe you could encourage her to open up. She needs to get it out of her system for her own mental wellbeing."

"Charlotte's a strong woman, Dr. Benson. She's been through worse and came out of it ok."

"So she said." He stopped. "Look, I understand about not letting outsiders in but I really believe she needs to talk to a trauma specialist. This could all come back to haunt her later if she doesn't."

Reece's serious gaze rested on Dr. Benson for a moment. Perhaps he was right. Charlotte hadn't allowed herself time to work out the situation with her ex being the Alpha and her shooting him in the head yet. Maybe both traumatic scenarios so close together could be her tipping point. "I'll see what I can do."

"Thank you. It's for her own good."

They continued on to Charlotte's room.

Eric Benson stopped at the door. "Here we are. Visiting hours are different for private rooms. You can visit and stay as long as you like within the set timeframe. I'll leave you to it." He smiled, turned and walked along the corridor.

Reece stood outside the door. His heartbeat ticked up a notch or two. He plucked Charlotte's engagement ring from the pocket of his shirt and held it up to eye level. After everything they'd been through, all he wanted to do was make her his bride. Mrs. Charlotte Daniels had a nice ring to it. He dropped the ring back into his pocket and opened the door. "Hello, sweetheart, how're you feeling?"

"Better now you're here." She smiled. "I have a message from Tommy. He said to say hi."

"When you call him again tell him I said hi too. It's good you talked to him." He was amazed at how human she looked. A couple of days ago he barely recognized her but now she looked more like her old self again. She was still attached to the drip and heart monitor though, but that would change as she got stronger. He closed the door, walked over to her, leaned in and planted a soft kiss on her lips. "You're looking so much better today." He sat down on the chair beside the bed.

"I had a shower and freshened up. One of the nurses helped me with the makeup and I'm starting to feel like me again." She gave a quiet sigh and frowned at him. "How are you? You look a little pale. Everything ok?"

Reece leaned back in the chair and folded his arms. "Everything's just fine. Don't worry about me. It's probably the lack of a good night's sleep."

"You'd tell me if anything happened, wouldn't you?" Her eyes remained on him. She knew there was something he wasn't telling her.

"Of course I would."

"You're sure?"

"You know me well enough to know I…"

"Wouldn't want to worry me while I'm recuperating." She gave him a wry smile.

Reece leaned forward and took her hand in his. "Nothing happened. I'm fine."

She sighed. "Ok, I'll take your word for it."

"Good." He waited a beat. "Want to talk about what happened with you?"

Tears welled in her eyes. "I don't think I'm ready. I may never be ready."

"It'll help, you know." He patted her hand then brought it to his lips and kissed the palm. "At least I understand what you went through."

"Yes, I know you do, but..." Her eyes moved to the bed cover. "Thinking I was going to die in that horrible motel and never see Tommy or you again almost killed me before... before they had a chance to." She blinked back the tears threatening to spill. "When they injected me and I was slipping into unconsciousness I thought I wouldn't wake up again. I thought it was a quiet way for them to end my life." An errant tear rolled down her left cheek and she brushed it away.

Reece stood up, moved to the bed and sat down next to her. "But it didn't, sweetheart. You're still here and you're safe. And I won't let anything happen to you ever again."

"You can't make that kind of promise, Reece. Look what happened already." She raised a finger to his lips. "And before you say anything it wasn't your fault."

He kissed her hand again. "Do you have any idea where you were? Did anything jump out at you? A logo? A hotel name?"

She shook her head. "I woke up in a luxury hotel suite. The shades were drawn and I was handcuffed to the bedhead so I couldn't move around. It was certainly an improvement on the dump of a motel I was in."

"Anything specific about the suite you remember?"

Charlotte thought for a moment. "It had to be a penthouse. The double doors to the room they had me in were open and the rest of the place was huge."

"Doesn't really give us much to go on, there are dozens of penthouse suites in hotels around Vegas."

She grimaced. "I know. I'm sorry."

"Don't be. I didn't expect you to remember anything with the amount of drugs you had in your system." He kissed her forehead. "Do you remember being taken to the hospital?"

"Vaguely. I think a blonde woman was driving the car."

"Any idea which direction. Were you coming from the southern or northern end of the strip?"

Charlotte shook her head. "I honestly don't know."

Reece brushed gentle fingers down her left cheek. "It's ok, sweetheart. Maybe it'll come back to you when you're stronger."

"I hope so. I'd like to come face to face with the person who abducted me. I've wracked my brain trying to figure out who it could be and why. I thought MacKinnon might've orchestrated some kind of revenge before he died, but…"

He remained pokerfaced. "I don't think it was MacKinnon. We're working on it."

Charlotte frowned into Reece's eyes. "You know, don't you?"

"Why would you think that?"

"The look on your face just now." She sat up in the bed. "Who kidnapped me, Reece? I have a right to know."

A knock echoed into the room and the door opened. A bunch of colorful balloons adorned with Get Well Soon across them squeezed through the opening followed by Andre, Sarah and Arianne.

Charlotte's eyes widened. "It's so good to see you all!"

"How are you feeling?" Sarah asked, crossing the room and giving Charlotte a big hug.

"Much better." She eased out of the priest's embrace. "How are you?"

"We've been so worried about…"

Reece shook his head and Sarah stopped mid-sentence.

Andre walked over, kissed Charlotte's cheek and tied the large bunch of purple, pink, white and blue balloons to the bedhead. "It's great to see you. You're looking really good."

Arianne stood at the foot of the bed. "I'm so glad you're ok, Charlotte."

"Thank you, Arianne. I appreciate it."

Reece motioned with his eyes for them to leave. He wanted some alone time with his fiancée, wanted to place her engagement ring back on her finger and tell her how much he loved her. The others could come back in a couple of days to see her. She wasn't being discharged for another week or so.

"We won't stay, we just wanted to see how you were," Sarah said, her eyes moving to Arianne and Andre.

"Please stay. I'm fine. Really." Tears stung the backs of Charlotte's eyes. It had been so long since she'd seen them.

"Sarah's right. You need your rest. We'll come back in a day or two." Andre moved to the door. Sarah and Arianne followed. "Get well quickly. We've missed you," Sarah said.

"Thank you for coming. You don't know what it means to me to see you all."

"I think they do. We've all felt exactly the same." Reece squeezed her hand gently.

"See you in a couple of days." Charlotte smiled and waved goodbye. Once their friends were gone she turned to Reece with a serious frown on her face. "Now tell me who took me."

CHAPTER FORTY FOUR

Helyna stirred the Belladonna into the purple passion cocktail and gave a heavy sigh. Could she really go through with it? Would she kill her sister? She knew if she didn't he would destroy them all. He had the power to do so and had threatened them on many occasions. He did not tolerate betrayal. She never expected him to order her sister's death. She thought he would punish Oriana by making an example of her. Some example. They already feared what he could do to them so why end her life?

She picked up the cocktails and carried them along the hall. When she reached the open doorway she mustered her best smile and waltzed into the room. "Here, sister, let us drink a toast." She sat a glass in front of Oriana and raised hers. "To better times ahead."

Oriana gazed at the purple concoction then gave her sister a curious stare. "Why are we toasting?"

"Because Katya and I are devising a plan to liberate us from our current master. If it works we'll be free to roam the earth and devour as many young men as we wish without hindrance from him or anyone else."

Oriana lifted the cocktail to eye level and gazed at the deep purple color. "What is it?"

"Purple passion. Fitting, don't you think?" Helyna brought her drink to her lips and feigned a sip. "Mm, it's delicious. Try it."

"Why didn't you tell me about your plan?" She knew something was wrong. She could sense discomfort in her sister.

"We wanted to be sure we could orchestrate it before we told you. In case he became suspicious and questioned you. At least when you told him you knew nothing it would have been the truth. He couldn't have read your mind and discovered our secret."

Her sister's answer sounded plausible but something was definitely off.

Helyna sauntered over to her and handed Oriana her cocktail. "Here, have mine." She eased the other glass out of her sister's hand, smiled and took a sip. She had given Oriana the non-toxic drink as a ruse, knowing she would be suspicious.

Oriana smiled and took the glass. "To better times ahead for us all, dear sister." She sipped the concoction.

"Isn't it good?" Helyna took another sip of her cocktail.

"Yes, very good." Oriana sipped more of the sweet purple potion. "Thank you for making it."

Helyna gave a thin smile and watched Oriana finish the drink. Her insides squirmed as she realized she had just murdered her sister.

₧ℌ

As Reece stepped out of the automatic doors to the hospital his messages went off on his cell. He snatched the phone from the back pocket of his jeans and glanced at the display. It was an unknown number. He sighed and pressed the comment box. The message was from Oriana. 'I've been poisoned. My sister Helyna. The drink was deep purple. If you don't come and find me I will be dead. I am alone in the house now. Please help me!' She provided the address. Reece was in his car and on his way within seconds.

He could easily let her die, it would be one less demon to worry about, but he owed her Charlotte's life. He was on his cell. "Andre. Does Arianne know of a poison that's purple? Oriana needs our help."

Andre asked her.

"She said it could be Belladonna. It's the most potent form of poison and will kill anyone, human or otherworldly. Warm vinegar or a mixture of mustard and water will help, but Arianne can't guarantee it will save her. It will neutralize the effects to some degree and prolong her life for a while longer."

"I can't let her die, Andre. She saved Charlotte's life."

Andre turned to Arianne. "Is there anything else that can save her life?"

"I'll have to check my spell book," Arianne said.

"Arianne is going to check. I'll call you back when we have something. Do you need me to meet you?"

The PI ran a red light and heard the whirr of the police siren before he spotted the red and blue lights in his rearview mirror. "No. Just find an antidote."

Reece screeched the four wheel drive to a halt in the driveway of the two story, yellow brick house, flung the door open and climbed out. He rushed around the vehicle, raced along the path and up the three steps to the open front door. "Oriana?" he called into the building, stopping at the threshold. No answer.

He ran his wary gaze along the hallway, noticing another open door at the end. *Could it be a trap?* He swallowed hard and stepped into whatever fate had in store for him. As he eased himself along the hallway Reece pulled his Glock from the back of his tan leather belt and checked the clip. He still had five of the seventeen rounds of silver bullets in it. He held his weapon in both hands low in front of him, his finger on the trigger ready to aim and fire, and continued down the hall to the room, his eyes taking in his surroundings and his ears listening for any movement in other areas of the house.

"Oriana?" he called again. *Where is she?*

Reece pressed his back against the wall when he reached the doorway and peered around the jamb. No one. He frowned. She couldn't have gotten far with the poison spreading rapidly through her system. A demon's pulse was five times faster than a human's.

He scanned the room as he stepped into it. A cocktail glass sat on the dresser. He walked over, picked it up and sniffed. Odorless. He frowned as his eyes surveyed the entire space. He noticed a closed door and assumed it was a closet. He moved across the room, gripped the handle and swung it back. A bathroom.

Oriana laid hunched in the claw-footed tub her legs dangling over the rim.

Reece raced over and leaned in to check her breathing. She wasn't. He pressed his fingers into the carotid artery in her neck. Nothing. "Shit!"

CHAPTER FORTY FIVE

Arianne slipped out of the hotel room she shared with Sarah and made her way down the hall to the elevator banks. It was 4.37 AM. The others were still asleep and it was the perfect opportunity for her to get away without being asked where she was going. She took the elevator to the lobby and wandered through the hotel to Fremont Street. The sun had not yet appeared over the mountains so she knew she would be safe from prying eyes. She shoved her hands into the pockets of the black hoodie she had on and stalked along the near empty street to north 4th Street.

A black sedan idled at the curb in front of the Neonopolis and as she crossed the road and stepped onto the sidewalk the passenger door flew open. "Get in."

Arianne climbed into the car, closed the door and the vehicle pulled onto the road, heading north.

"Did you get it?" the driver asked.

"Yes." She reached into her left pocket and pulled out the black leather box she had taken from Sarah's suitcase and hesitated before passing it to him. She knew it was a bad decision but there was nothing she could do about it now.

He opened the box and glanced at its contents, a devious smile spreading across his face. "Good work. The master will be pleased."

"Tell your master I'm not doing this anymore. If he wants anything else in future he'll have to get himself."

"He will not be pleased with your decision." The driver reached in front of her, opened the glove compartment, sat the device inside then snapped it shut.

"I don't care if I please him or not."

"It's Delacroix, isn't it? You've let your feelings for him interfere with the task assigned to you."

"This has nothing to do with Andre. I'm tired of doing my father's bidding. I do have a life of my own, you know." She folded her arms and glowered at him.

The driver stared deep into Arianne's dark eyes for a brief moment then returned his gaze to the road. "You know there will be repercussions for your actions. There always is."

Arianne frowned at him. She hadn't considered her father's reaction at all. She just wanted out. Her mouth went dry. "What kind of repercussions?"

"He would never do anything to harm you, so he'll target one of your friends."

"You tell him to leave them alone."

"If you're intent on betraying his trust he will retaliate."

Arianne sighed. "Then take me to him. I'll talk to him myself, make him see reason."

"You know I cannot."

"Why not?"

A smirk lifted the right corner of his mouth. "Because, dear Arianne, then you would know his whereabouts. And he doesn't want you to."

"Why?"

He chuckled, reached across, picked up a lock of her brunette hair in his gloved hand and ran it through his fingers. "It would be easy for you to tell the others, wouldn't it?"

"Are you insane? He's my father and I know what he's capable of. I might want my freedom but I would never go that far."

The driver's left eyebrow arched. "Are you sure? The freedom you are seeking always comes at a price."

⦵⦵

Arianne opened the door and quietly entered the room. She shrugged out of her hoodie and slid off her boots then climbed into bed fully clothed with a soft sigh. No one had realized she'd been out of the hotel. The lamp between the two queen-sized beds flashed on and Sarah, Reece and Andre were sitting on Sarah's bed waiting for her return.

"Mind telling us where you've been?" Reece walked over to her.

"I – I went for a walk to clear my head. I couldn't sleep."

Andre and Sarah got up and joined him.

"So where's the ultraviolet device from my suitcase?" Sarah asked. She knew something had always been off with Arianne but had chosen to ignore her instincts. How foolish.

Arianne threw back the covers and flew out of bed. "Are you accusing me of taking it?"

"It was there when I checked before bed." Sarah folded her arms. "I always do an inventory of my weapons before going to sleep."

"Then why didn't you ask me when you found it was missing?"

"I couldn't be sure it was you, and I hoped it wasn't for Andre's sake." She gave him a sideward glance. "I know he cares about you. I wanted to see how the situation played out and you walked right into it."

Andre frowned into Arianne's eyes. "Tell me you didn't take it."

Arianne's gaze moved to the man she secretly loved. Tears stung the backs of her eyes and she let out a heavy sigh and dropped onto the bed. "You won't understand."

"Try us." Reece folded his arms and gave a heavy sigh.

Arianne gasped and jerked awake. She sprang up in bed and gazed around the shadowed room, a cold sweat beading her brow. It had all been a dream. She let out the breath she'd been holding and dropped back onto the pillows. She would never betray Reece and Andre. Never. The images in the dream ran through her mind and she remembered telling the driver she wouldn't do her father's bidding anymore. A shiver ran the length of her body. Was she Dracula's daughter? *No, I can't be, can I?*

She threw back the covers and got out of bed. Only one vampire could give her the answers she needed. She slipped out of the room, walked down the hall to Nathaniel's door and knocked.

Nathaniel opened it and gave her a curious frown. "What is it, Arianne? Why are you here at this late hour?"

Arianne barged past the huge, black vampire. "I had a dream and I need to know the truth." She stopped in the center of the room, turned around and folded her arms.

"Would you care to elaborate?"

"Is Dracula my father?" She blinked back the stinging tears to prevent them from spilling down her face.

Nathaniel closed the door and crossed the room. He gestured for her to take a seat. She sat at the small round table in the corner by the window and he joined her. "Yes, he is. Your mother wanted to keep it from you for your own protection. She knew one day he would seek you out and use you to his advantage." He studied her face for a moment. "There is no familial love in his heart for anyone, Arianne." He reached across and rested a hand on her arm.

The tears spilled and she looked at him through welling eyes. "You knew my mother?"

"I did, yes." He squeezed her arm gently. "She loved you very much. When your father was cursed and became a bloodthirsty monster she knew she could not keep you safe. She sent you away to protect you. He turned two of his sons, your half-brothers, and it would not have been long before he condemned you to the same fate of becoming a true vampire."

"What happened to my mother?"

Nathaniel's solemn gaze moved from hers and he glanced at the mottled gold carpet. "Sadly, she took her own life. She could not stop loving the man who had become the monster and she could not live with him either."

"Oh, my God," Arianne's voice was a whisper.

"I am sorry to be the bearer of such bad tidings."

A lone tear slid down Arianne's right cheek and she brushed it away. It was very sad, but even so she didn't remember her parents and she couldn't allow it to affect her now. "How old am I? And what is my real name?"

"You are approximately five hundred and fifty years old. You were born Countess Marja Zaleska Tepes Dracul, but was known to family and friends as Zaleska."

"Am I truly a half breed?"

"Yes. Your mother was mortal. Her name was Cneajna Bathory, Princess of Moldavia."

Arianne's eyes widened. "But doesn't that mean...?"

Nathaniel knew what she was thinking. "Your mother married your father a hundred years before Erzsébet Bathory, or Elizabeth as she is known today, was born. Do not concern yourself with bloodlines. You are distant relatives. Her blood does not run through your veins." He gave a reassuring smile.

"At least that's something, I guess." Arianne frowned at Nathaniel. "Why didn't I remember any of it?"

"Your memories... some of them, were blocked by a warlock to protect you from your father."

"My *father*." She huffed a laugh. "Vlad the Impaler, son of the dragon. My descendants were all bloodthirsty savages." She sighed and stood up.

"Your family does not define who you are, Arianne. You would do well to remember that."

"I'm still part vampire, part Dracul, aren't I, so it does." She gave him a wry smile. "Thank you for being honest with me, Nathaniel. Now, how to figure out a way to tell Andre, Reece and Sarah." She blew out a noisy breath. "I'm sure that'll go down well."

CHAPTER FORTY SIX

At the beginning of the following week, Reece was at the hospital bright and early to pick up Charlotte. It had been so long since they'd been together in the outside world that he couldn't wait to have her to himself for a while. He'd arranged another room on the same floor at the hotel and he and Charlotte would share it after their wedding. In the meantime, his lovely bride-to-be would stay with Sarah and Arianne. Just to be safe.

He carried her bag and walked alongside the wheelchair out to the car. Dr. Benson stopped beside the passenger door, opened it and helped his patient into the front seat. "It's good to see you leaving so soon, Charlotte. You've made a dramatic recovery. Take care of yourself."

Charlotte smiled up at him. "Thank you for taking such good care of me, Eric. I appreciate everything you've done to get me on my feet so quickly."

"He smiled and waved the comment away. "All in a day's work."

"No, it's not. You believe in what you do. Saving lives means everything to you."

Reece reached out his hand and the doctor shook it. "Thanks Dr. Benson. Charlotte couldn't have been in better hands."

"You're welcome, Detective Daniels."

"Please, call me Reece."

Dr. Benson smiled. "You're welcome, Reece. Take good care of your future wife and one of my favorite patients."

"Come to the wedding." Reece glanced at Charlotte.

"Yes, please do come, Eric. It would be wonderful to have you there."

The doctor gazed from one to the other. "I'd love to come. Just call and let me know when and where."

"Surely you can guess where? It is Las Vegas." Charlotte gave him a huge smile.

"The Little White Wedding Chapel?"

"None other," Charlotte said with a chuckle.

"All right. Let me know when and I'll be there."

Reece moved around the car and opened the driver's door. "We will. Thanks again." He climbed in beside Charlotte and started the engine. "Ready to get back into the real world?"

Charlotte sighed. "I think so."

Reece reached across and gave her hand a squeeze. "I love you, Charlotte. I won't let anything happen to you again. I give you my word."

She gave him a heartfelt smile. "I know and I love you, too." Her stomach grumbled and they both laughed. "Oh, my, that's embarrassing. Let's go. I'm so looking forward to some real food."

The PI chuckled. "Yeah, hospital food is definitely an acquired taste. It's so good to have you back, sweetheart." He reached into the top pocket of his checked shirt, slid out her engagement ring, took her hand and slipped it on her finger.

"Oh, Reece." She gazed into his eyes, leaned over and kissed him. "I'm so grateful to be here with you right now."

He smiled at her then pulled the car away from the curb and headed toward the Golden Nugget. In a couple of days they would finally tie the knot and he couldn't wait for Charlotte to be his wife. His heart was overjoyed.

Charlotte glanced out of the passenger window and unbeknown to Reece a single tear slid down her left cheek and she discreetly brushed it away. She hoped she was ready to be out in the real world again with its monsters and danger. Her abduction had changed her and she wasn't sure how just yet.

Reece pushed the keycard into the slot on the door of his and Andre's hotel room and turned the handle. When he swung the door back everyone yelled 'Surprise!' They had decorated the room with a colorful WELCOME HOME banner, streamers and balloons, and a huge cake sat in the center of the round table along with a bottle of champagne and six glass flutes.

Charlotte felt her cheeks flush as she stepped into the room and Reece closed the door behind them. "I never expected anything like this. Thank you so much!"

Sarah came over to her and gave her a tight hug. "It's so good to have you back, Charlotte," she said, blinking back the tears stinging her eyes. They had all thought the Jane Doe was her and coming to terms with the loss had been incredibly difficult. Charlotte had virtually come back from the dead.

"It's good to be back." She also blinked back tears.

Andre hugged her so tight she thought he'd break her in two. He was a vampire, after all, with superhuman strength. "We missed you, Charlotte." His thoughts returned to the coroner's office and identifying what he'd believed to be her remains. "I'm so glad you're safe."

"Thank you, Andre. I missed you all too. And I'm truly grateful to be here." She eased herself out of his embrace and attempted to lighten the somber mood. "That cake looks delicious. Let's have some."

A knock echoed into the room and everyone turned around.

Reece pulled his Glock from his belt and moved to the peephole. He breathed a relieved sigh and opened the door. "Lozano. What brings you here?"

"I wanted to bring these to Charlotte." He held out a large bouquet of colorful flowers. "That's all right, isn't it?"

The PI moved aside and the sheriff stepped into the room. "Sorry to be a gatecrasher. I just wanted to meet you, Charlotte, and say how happy I am you're ok."

Charlotte picked up a plate with cake on it, and a fork, walked over and handed it to Lozano. "Thank you for coming, Sheriff. And thank you for the lovely flowers."

Lozano passed the bouquet to her and took the plate. "You're more than welcome. Thanks for the cake."

Charlotte went into the bathroom to sit the flowers in some water in the sink until she could arrange for a vase. She stared at her reflection in the soft light and tears slipped down her cheeks. Everyone, including people who didn't know her, had been worried for her safety. What would have happened if she'd died? How would Reece have explained it to Tommy?

She brushed the tears away and sniffled. *It doesn't matter now you're safe and Tommy will never know what happened.* As she turned off the light and joined the others a thought ran through her mind. *Will any of us ever be truly safe?*

After the welcome back party had ended and Charlotte laid down for a nap, Reece and the others sat down with Arianne. It had taken her a week to work up the courage to tell them what Nathaniel had imparted to her and the revelation of her being Dracula's daughter had sent everyone into a spin. The PI wasn't sure whether to send her back to LA or keep her close by. She had to be the reason they'd been targeted. Her father had to know Arianne was part of their team. At first he'd thought it was Sarah the vampire was after, but now he knew the truth it all made perfect sense.

"I think we should send you back to LA for your own protection," Reece said, staring into her face.

"But why? I'm more help to you here. What would you have me do there?" She popped out of her seat, folded her arms and paced. "You don't trust me, do you?"

"If your father is trying to manipulate you into joining him it will only be a matter of time before you give in. He'll make sure of it." Reece stood up and walked over to the young woman. "Do you want him to keep picking us off one at a time until someone dies?"

Arianne stared into his serious frown. "Of course not." Tears welled in her eyes. "I don't understand any of it. I wish I wasn't his daughter!"

Nathaniel crossed the room. "Perhaps Andre could escort her back to Los Angeles. It will move him out of harm's way and he can keep her safe there."

Reece's eyes moved to his friend. "Do you want to go?"

Andre walked across the room. "No, I don't. But if it's the only way to stop Dracula from waging war on us then I really don't have a choice. I want us all to be safe."

Charlotte appeared at the adjoining doorway. "You'll miss our wedding, Andre. You're the best man."

The PI spun around. "How much did you hear?"

"You mean the part about Arianne being Dracula's daughter? When was anyone going to fill me in on what's been happening? Don't I have a right to know?" She folded her arms and marched across the room to the standing group.

Reece rested a hand on her arm. "Sweetheart, you just got out of the hospital. I wanted to give you some time to adjust."

Charlotte frowned at him. "I'll be ok. Don't treat me like an invalid. I need to know what's going on. How do you expect me to keep myself safe if I have no idea what or who we're up against?"

Sarah walked over to her. "You need to rest and recuperate, Charlotte. You're safe. No one will harm you here. Don't be so eager to throw yourself back into the fight. Take the time you need to be one hundred percent well, for your son's sake."

Charlotte's gaze moved to the priest. "I appreciate your concern about Tommy, Sarah, but I'm fine. I want to know what the rest of you know. I am still a part of this team, aren't I?"

"No one's disputing that, sweetheart. Just take it easy for a couple of days. Enjoy the wedding preparations and relax." Reece didn't want her involved in any more of it.

Charlotte huffed out a frustrated breath, turned on her heal and marched into the adjoining room without another word.

"That went well," Sarah said, her eyes moving to the doorway.

"She'll get over it."

Sarah's right eyebrow rose. "Will she? She's been through a horrifying ordeal and is lucky to be alive. I can only imagine what's going through her mind right now."

"She needs time to adjust, that's all." Reece's intense gaze bored into hers.

Nathaniel turned and looked at the PI. "I do not think Charlotte is in a stable frame of mind. There is a lot of noise in her head. Something is troubling her."

Reece's eyes moved to the huge vampire. "What?"

"I cannot be certain. I only know she is not coping and will not tell you because she does not want you to be concerned about her while you are dealing with the situation at hand."

"But I'm already concerned about her. How could I not be?"

"Perhaps it would be wise to talk to her. You are the only one she will confide in."

Reece gave a heavy sigh, glanced around at the others then stalked into the adjoining room. Nothing had been resolved regarding Arianne. Could she be trusted? Or would she crumble under pressure and put all of their lives in danger?

CHAPTER FORTY SEVEN

Lozano was at his desk going over the report on the latest vampire victim. As it turned out, the young woman was a showgirl on her way home after work. Where her body had been discovered was the initial crime scene after all. The sheriff sat back in his comfortable, black leather office chair and studied the forensic photos. *Dracula did this. Unbelievable! Who'd believe it? He's meant to be a fictional character in a book.* How many more lives would be lost before they managed to take him down? Could they? He would be powerful after so many years. Did they have the capabilities to accomplish such a dangerous task?

The vampire had been roaming the earth undetected for hundreds of years. What made Reece think their small team could defeat a creature as old and as strong as he? Lozano let out a huge sigh. They needed more man power if they were to succeed in ridding the world of the most dangerous vampire ever to exist. He knew people who could help. People on the wrong side of the law who owed him a favor, but if he told them what they were up against they'd tell him he was loco.

His cell phone buzzed on his desk. He picked it up and checked the caller ID. "Hello, Reece, what can I do for you?"

"Nathaniel, Sarah and I are going back into the tunnels. Interested?"

Lozano frowned. "What about Andre and Arianne?"

"I'm sending them back to LA. Long story. One I'd prefer to tell you in person."

"I know some people…"

"What kind of people?"

"The kind that don't do things by the book."

"And?"

"I was thinking of contacting them. We could use the extra muscle down there."

Reece's jaw tightened. "Yeah, we could. Can they be trusted? Do they know about this kind of thing?"

"Trusted? Don't know about that. But they owe me, so they'll help without question. And no, they don't know about demons, vampires and the other monsters roaming the streets out there. They'd think I was crazy if I told them that."

Reece frowned. "So you're planning on asking for their help without telling them?"

"Yeah. They'll find out soon enough and then they'll believe it for themselves."

"How many?"

"Six. They lost a member last year and didn't want to find a replacement."

"How'd they lose him?"

"Her. In a gang war."

"I see. Well if you're prepared to contact their leader and get them to join us in the tunnels it would certainly help our cause. Are you planning to explain about the weapons and silver ammunition?"

"When they get there. What time are you going in?"

"We need to get inside before sundown. Dracula will be sleeping until then and we want to catch him off guard."

"What about the other vampires down there?"

"Sarah has it covered. I'll explain when I see you."

"Ok, so around four, four thirty?"

"Make it four, just to be safe. We still have to find another way in."

"Oh, yeah, the explosion."

"I've been going over the city's map and I think I've found one."

"Let me know where so I can tell the guys and we'll meet you there."

"Will do."

Reece slid his phone onto the table and looked at the others in the room. "All right. We're set for tonight. Lozano is bringing reinforcements. There'll be ten of us."

Andre and Arianne were at the door, luggage standing on the floor beside them. "Are you sure you don't want us to stay? Arianne asked. "Safety in numbers and twelve is better than ten."

Reece shook his head. "You two need to leave. I want you as far away from here as you can get. It's too dangerous. I'm sure your father knows about Andre and would use him to get to you... and to us. Go. And stay safe. Check in with me when you get back, Andre." Reece crossed the room and pulled his friend into a man hug. "Be careful."

"I will. You too." He opened the door and the pair left.

"Sarah, would you contact Ed and ask him to keep an eye on Andre and Arianne? I have a gut feeling something isn't right with her and I'm worried Andre won't sense it because of how he feels about her."

"I'm on it." Sarah disappeared through the adjoining doorway and into her and Charlotte's room. Sarah had also wondered about Arianne. What did they really know about her except that she was a half breed vampire with witch powers... and Dracula's long lost daughter?

Charlotte was sleeping when Sarah entered the room. She walked over to the bedside table, picked up her cell phone and took it back into Reece's room. "Hello, how are you? Yes, it's good to hear your voice too. I miss you. Reece asked me to call. Yes, everyone's ok. Andre and Arianne are on their way back to LA. Can you pick them up from LAX and drop them home? He'd also appreciate you keeping an eye on them. We've discovered some disturbing news about Arianne and he wants to know Andre's safe. Can I fill you later? Ok, my love, I'll let you know what time their flight arrives. Love you, too." She pressed the end button.

"How is he?" Reece asked.

"He's ok. He'd rather be here though."

"Yeah, I know, but what can he do? He has to make an appearance at the precinct or the hierarchy will start asking questions."

"He knows that." Sarah sat on Andre's bed. "But it doesn't make it any easier. He wants to help us."

"He will be by watching out for Andre. It's probably better he isn't here. Too dangerous. And he isn't getting any younger." The right corner of his mouth lifted.

Sarah gave him a half smile. "Mm. What does that say about me then?"

"You look great for your age?" Reece's left eyebrow rose. Sarah had explained to them that she had been attacked by a rogue vampire many years ago and rather than turning her or killing her it had prolonged her life, along with the regular injections of vampire blood. She was 149 years old and truly grateful because she still wanted to kill Dracula for what he'd done to her family. Now she'd have the chance.

"You sweet talker, you."

"I wonder if the men Lozano's bringing are reliable?"

"Did he tell you who they are?" Sarah folded her arms.

"Not exactly. He said they didn't do things by the book. And they're part of a gang."

"A gang? I'm not sure I like the sound of that."

"I was thinking the same thing. When we get there I'll ask him more about them and fill him in on Arianne, as well."

"Is Arianne's circumstances something we should be telling everyone?"

"Lozano is part of our team, while we're here. He has a right to know what we know."

"Ok. If you think it's best. Let's hope we can find Dracula and end him before he can do anymore damage."

"That's the plan."

CHAPTER FORTY EIGHT

Ed Borenko stood off to the side to wait for Andre and Arianne to enter the airport from the plane. His eyes moved around the passengers coming through the gate searching for Andre's dark mop of wavy, shoulder-length hair. When he spotted the couple he called out to them and they rushed over to him. Andre wrapped his arms around the older man and hugged him until Ed's discomfort kicked in and he eased out of Andre's man hug.

"It's good to see you, Ed."

"Yeah, yeah, good to see you too," Ed said, clearing his throat. "How was the flight?"

"Good. We made it here in record time. Less than an hour and ten."

"Must've had a tail wind." Ed gave him a crooked smile. His eyes moved to the young woman standing behind Andre. "How're you, Arianne. I hear it's been pretty tough in Vegas."

Arianne's eyes darted to Andre then returned to Ed. "Yes. A lot's happened."

Ed ran his gaze over the pair. "Well, let's collect your luggage and I'll drive you home."

Andre took Arianne's hand and followed Ed to the luggage carousel.

"Thanks for picking us up."

Ed waved it off. "No need to thank me. I took an extended lunch break for the rest of the afternoon. It's good to get outta the precinct sometimes."

"Just the same, I really appreciate you coming out here."

"What are teammates for?" He shrugged.

Andre snatched his and Arianne's bags off the carousel as they revolved past and followed the older man outside to the pickup point. He and Ed tossed the luggage into the trunk, then the three climbed into the Lieutenant's early model sedan.

"You might wanna call Reece and tell him you're here," Ed said over his shoulder. Andre had chosen to sit in the back with Arianne. He flipped the indicator on and eased out into the traffic. LAX was always chaotic.

"Yeah, I was just about to." He pulled his cell phone out of his jacket pocket, turned off the airplane mode and hit speed dial. "Hey, we're with Ed. He's driving us home. The flight got in earlier than expected, which was good. I'll be careful. You take care too. You're up against some pretty dangerous competition." He glanced at Arianne, remembering Dracula was her father. "I'll call you later tonight. Ok. Bye."

Ed glanced at Andre in the rearview mirror. "So, Dracula, huh?"

"Yep." He didn't want to talk about the vampire in front of Arianne.

"Ya think they'll be able to pull it off? Get rid of him, I mean."

Arianne turned her gaze to the window and Andre attempted to change the subject. "So how's work?"

"The same. Murder is murder no matter how you look at it. And I doubt people are ever gonna change."

"True. Miss having Reece around?"

"Yeah, but don't tell him I said that. Anyhow, we spend time together when I'm helping you guys with a case, so..."

"Ever thought about leaving the LAPD and working with us full time?"

Ed's earnest gaze met Andre's in the rearview mirror. "Hell, yeah, every day, but I don't know if I can, financially speaking I mean."

"I understand. The pay's not great. But the reward is."

"Yeah, it is. Do ya think Sarah will be able to close the rift? If she does, you guys might be out of a job."

"There will always be otherworldly creatures hovering between our world and theirs, Ed. They always manage to find a way out. It's the majority we have to worry about right now."

Ed drove along Sunset Boulevard to North Highland and made a right. He drove for about another half a mile and pulled into the curb outside Andre's apartment building, turned off the engine and leaned across the driver's seat. "Well here you are safe n sound." He gazed out the passenger window. "Like the new digs."

"It's in a good location and more secure than Adrian's property. And I needed a change of scene after..." Adrian, Andre's vampire mentor, had been savaged by werewolves while battling the Alpha at the old prison four months ago. A werewolf bite was lethal to vampires. It had been difficult for everyone to get over, but especially Andre because he felt guilty for not being able to save him.

Ed gave him a pained look. "Yeah, kid, I know."

"Thanks, again, for picking us up. I really appreciate it."

"Like I said, happy to do it." He gave Andre a crooked smile.

Andre opened the door, stepped out onto the sidewalk and walked around to the trunk to retrieve their luggage. Arianne slid across the seat and before getting out said, "Thank you, Ed. Maybe you can come over for dinner some time, as a thank you."

Ed's eyes moved to the young woman. "Thanks. That'd be nice."

Arianne gave him a smile then stepped out of the car and closed the door.

Ed watched the couple climb the front steps and go inside before driving away. He'd return later to do a surveillance of the building and Andre and Reece's apartment. He'd have to think up some excuse for why he came back.

CHAPTER FORTY NINE

The multiple entry points into the tunnels traveling underneath Dean Martin Drive and the I-15 freeway were directly behind Caesar's Palace. It was hard to believe this entrance into the subterranean world stood only a few feet away from a busy shopping mall parking lot. Medium-sized trees lined the perimeter of the embankment between the carpark and the entrance giving Reece and his team a certain amount of obscurity from curious eyes.

He'd calculated how long it would take for them to work their way back through the storm water drains to where they'd been the previous time they'd been down there. More than two hours. Time they didn't have. Time that made it dangerous for them to be underground.

Lozano arrived soon after they did but the group he'd asked to join them still hadn't shown up. The sheriff glanced at his watch, sighed, and gazed around the area hoping to see them crossing the parking lot or coming in from the unfinished gravel road. He hoped they'd show, but what could he do if they didn't? Arrest them? He had no proof of their activities, although he knew what they were capable of, and until he did he couldn't do squat.

Nathaniel helped Sarah organize the heavy-duty weapons they would take with them, while Reece and Lozano shrugged into flak jackets and slipped on infrared headsets. Sarah had in her possession an ultraviolet device which would exterminate the homeless vampire horde in one hit. She wished she could use it on Dracula, because she knew it would eliminate him once and for all. But it was essential to their task of locating him while he slept and killing him before he could orchestrate a plan to find Arianne and Andre and murder more innocents.

"Hey, hombre, we are here," a young male Latino voice called from behind them. They were a powerful looking group, strong young men in their mid to late twenties with an arrogant gait to their step. The leader, walking ahead of them, wore sunglasses, a black and gray checked shirt, white T-shirt, baggy jeans and a baseball cap turned backwards. His gang members were similarly dressed except two wore dark blue and white patterned bandanas around their shaved heads. They were all heavily inked too. The leader and one other member sported a SUR 13 tattoo on their forearm, a tribute to the Mexican mafia. The other members would have the same tattoo somewhere else on their bodies. They were tough wannabes.

Lozano stalked across to them. "You're late."

The leader of the group gave the sheriff an incredulous stare, then smirked. "We did not have to come at all. We are doing you a favor, amigo, not the other way around."

The sheriff knew what he said was true and nodded without saying another word. He had no intention of pissing them off and have them leave.

Reece crossed the gravel to the group.

Lozano introduced them. "This is Hector, Diego, Alonso, Tomás, Carlos and Javier. Hector and Javier are brothers."

The PI ran his gaze over the young men. "Thanks for coming. We appreciate your help."

Hector eyed him for a moment then raised his hand. "No worries, amigo."

Reece gripped the young man's extended hand and they moved together, shoulder to shoulder, in a gesture of comradery. "Let's go over to the car and I'll fill you in on why we're here."

Lozano shook his head.

"Why don't you go on ahead, Nathaniel and Sarah will fit you up with the gear. We'll be right there."

Hector moved his gaze from Reece to Lozano then back to the PI. "Sure." He waved his group on.

"You can't tell them what we're doing." Lozano spoke in a low tone, his eyes on the young men.

"I don't plan on telling them who we're up against, just that we're searching for a killer and we need to take him down."

"These kids *are* killers. Do you think they'll care?"

Reece stood with his hands on his hips. "Then what do you suggest? You don't want me to tell them about what's down there so what do you want me to say?"

Lozano gave a heavy sigh and shrugged. "I don't know."

"Then let me handle it. If the only way to get them to help us is to tell them, I will." He turned on his heel and headed over to the four wheel drive. Lozano followed.

The young leader's head turned as Reece approached. "You got some pretty powerful ammo here, my friend. Who are you chasing?" Hector asked, looking impressed with the array of weaponry.

Reece noticed he wore a medallion similar to Lozano's. "You believe in God?"

Hector pursed his lips, folded his arms and stared into the PI's eyes. "Why are you asking, hombre?"

"This mission... it requires an open mind... and some faith."

The leader of the group frowned. "Just say it like it is, man. What are we doing here?"

Reece exhaled a long breath through his nostrils and studied the tough young man standing in front of him. "If you believe in God do you also believe in Satan and his demons?"

Hector's eyes widened. "Why are you asking me about what I believe?"

"Because that's what we're chasing. A demon of sorts."

Hector's expression changed from shock to skepticism before a crooked smirk spread across his face. "Demon? Come on, man. Really? You expect us to believe that bullshit?"

Reece's stern gaze remained on him. The young man's smirk shrank into a frown. "You're serious?"

"You bet I am."

Hector swallowed hard and crossed himself. Watching the tough young guy with tattoos and an allegiance to the Mexican mafia make a gesture of faith seemed contradictory to Reece.

"So when you say *demon* what are you talking about exactly?"

Reece passed him an automatic rifle loaded with silver cartridges. The kid's eyes lit up as he inspected the weapon. "Dracula."

The members of Hector's gang chuckled and spoke in low tones among themselves. Just as Lozano had predicted they thought Reece was loco.

Sarah walked up to them. They wouldn't disrespect a priest. "I've seen him in the flesh. I've been chasing him for a long time. He murdered my family and he's killing again here. Haven't you seen the news about the bodies drained of blood?"

"Well, yeah, but... Dracula?" Javier said. "He's out of a book."

"That's what he wants you to think, but he's here in the tunnels and we have to find him before he kills again, with or without your help." Sarah turned around and strutted back to Nathaniel.

Hector's guys huddled in a close discussion then one stepped up behind him and whispered into his ear. Were they planning to leave?

Reece folded his arms and ran his gaze over the group. "Are you in or out?"

Hector turned around and eyed his crew. Each one gave a sharp nod. He turned back to Reece. "We're in."

"Ok. Gear up. We don't have much time."

∛∞∝

A chiming sound coming from Reece and Andre's room roused Charlotte from sleep. She gave a heavy sigh as she turned over, climbed out of bed and wandered barefoot through the adjoining doorway. She ran her gaze around the furniture trying to locate where the noise was coming from. Was it the alarm clock? It didn't seem to be. She frowned. Where were Reece, Andre and the others? She crossed the room to the table in the corner and noticed the laptop had a flashing symbol on the desktop. She moved the mouse over to it and clicked. A video popped up.

She pulled back one of the red patterned armchairs and sat down.

Reece appeared on the screen. "Hi, sweetheart. By the time you see this we'll be in the tunnels. Please don't worry about us. We have help. I'll call you as soon as we're done. I've ordered room service for you. It should arrive around six o'clock. Keep the doors to both rooms locked. I love you."

Charlotte gave a huffy sigh and snapped the notebook shut. *Why didn't he wake me?* She knew why. He wanted to protect her. She was still recovering and knew he didn't want her involved in any serious altercations with any more otherworldly creatures. She loved him for caring but hated the fact that he didn't trust her judgement. Maybe he was right not to. Right now she wasn't sure who she was or what to think about what happened. Was she still the same person?

She stood up and ran her eyes around the room once more before returning to hers to take a shower. As she stepped through the door her cell phone went off. Charlotte rushed over to the bedside table and snatched it up. Tommy. "Hello, honey, how are you?"

"I'm great, Mom. How's things? Having fun?"

"We're good. Yes, we're having loads of fun." Her eyes burned with tears and she raised her hand to her mouth and swallowed the lump forming in her throat before speaking again. "What have you been up to?"

"Jessie came over to hang out today. We had a great time playing Motorsport 4 on Xbox. I won every time." He gave a devious chuckle. "When are you coming home?"

"Not for another couple more weeks, honey. We'll bring you back something special. Maybe a new Xbox game. How does that sound?"

"Cool! Make sure you have a great time, Mom. Say hi to Reece for me. I'd better let you go. Will you call me in a couple of days?"

"Of course I will, sweetie. Stay safe. I love you."

"Love you too, Mom." He rang off.

Tears slid down Charlotte's cheeks and she sniffled. Her ten year old sounded so mature for his age. He was growing up so fast. She plucked two tissues from the box, wiped her eyes and blew her nose. It would be wonderful being back home with her son and Reece as a family. Their wedding was tomorrow night. She never thought she'd become Mrs. Charlotte Daniels at all, but her dream would finally come true.

₧₨

Ed Borenko swung by Andre's apartment to make sure everything was fine. Reece had spoken to him on the phone and asked him to do regular checks. The PI said his gut warned him not to trust Arianne and he wondered whether her dream was a foreshadowing of things to come. Would she turn on them and help her bloodthirsty father with his plan?

It was after 5.00 PM when the lieutenant made a U-turn and pulled into the curb about fifty feet up the road. He parked there in case Andre and

Arianne came out of the building and spotted his dark green sedan. These days, Andre meant as much to him as Reece did, they had all been through a lot together and he was determined to make sure nothing happened to him while under his watch.

Ed switched on the radio, eased back into the driver's seat and sighed. It could be a long wait but he'd keep them under surveillance for as long as Reece wanted him to. He opened the BLT deli sandwich he'd picked up earlier and took a large bit. At least it would keep him busy for all of ten minutes. He surveyed the street. He'd learned to be keenly observant over the years on the force. Taking in his surroundings and the people in them had always served him well while investigating crime. Something dark moved in the fuzzy edge of his peripheral vision. Ed peered through the windshield and frowned. Who was the obscure-looking male, dressed in black, standing against a lamp post outside Andre's apartment block?

CHAPTER FIFTY

Everyone had been fitted out and was ready to enter the pitch black tunnels. Not many knew about the storm water drains traveling 200 miles beneath Sin City, nor the inhabitants who lived in them. Reece had instructed the group to stay in the center of the passage, stick close, watch each other's backs and be ready for anything. The tunnels were infested with black widow spiders and scorpions, so they needed to be careful of those as well. He'd also informed Hector and his crew about the mob of starving vampires they would encounter on their way through the murky underground. It hadn't fazed the young men at all. They were eager to get in there and do what had to be done. The PI didn't want them going in all bravado and getting themselves killed or worse—turned.

The group needed to keep their wits about them while wandering through the dark. They could encounter unaffected homeless people down there and Reece didn't want to be the instigator of innocent deaths, if he could avoid it.

Hector stepped up alongside the PI. "How many vamps you think's in there?"

"At least fifty, but there could be more by now. There's around a thousand homeless living in these tunnels and who knows how many Dracula has fed from and initiated."

The young man nodded.

"We need to be careful not to pick off human homeless people too."

"How will we know the difference?"

"You'll know. The vampires are hungry and mean and they don't look human, so fire first ask question later."

The group followed Nathaniel and Reece in.

"Hey, man, these headsets are way cool," Alonso said, his voice echoing around the graffitied concrete walls.

"Glad you like them," Sarah said, "but you need to stop talking, we have to be as quiet as we can be in here."

Alonso glanced at Hector through the infrared viewer and saw him raise his finger to his mouth and glare at him. "Sorry."

"It's ok. Just be aware vampires have super-sensitive hearing. We don't want them finding us before we find them." Sarah moved back beside the sheriff.

They continued into the depths of the tunnel in silence, their anxiety levels palpable in the gloom.

After about an hour Reece and Nathaniel stopped and turned around. "We'll head off to the right. It should bring us out at the junction where we set off the explosives. Then we'll take the center tunnel. There's another way in from there." Reece turned around and the group kept moving.

The stale air around them became denser as they traveled further into the drains and made it difficult to breathe. Reece stopped again. "I think…"

A series of loud bangs echoed along the tunnel toward them. Everyone raised their weapons, took a step backwards and positioned themselves ready to fire.

"What was that?" Javier yelped, his voice echoing off the walls.

"Stay close." Reece pushed forward, the nerves in his stomach quivering above his leather belt. They were in vampire territory now and he still didn't like the fact that he may have to get up close and personal to finish off whoever remained. The others followed, their eyes darting behind them to make sure they weren't being pursued.

"Sarah, get the device ready," Reece ordered, his voice strained.

"Ready to go." Sarah held the orb in her hand. When Reece gave the word she'd set it and pass it to Nathaniel to hurl along the tunnel into the savage horde of ravenous vampires.

Nathaniel stretched his hand out to her. "Give me the device."

Sarah sat it in his hand. "It'll activate within seconds of throwing it so you'll need to get behind us quickly."

The huge black vampire tossed the orb like a baseball a hundred feet into the darkness then whipped around behind the group who shielded him from the effects of the device. It pinged, opened and emitted bright blue rays of ultraviolet light into the tunnel like the headlamp on a fast-approaching train.

Vampires on the ground burst into flames and crumbled to ash as the orb spun in midair, their high-pitched shrieks resonating around the cobwebbed walls. The ones crawling across the ceiling disintegrated and rained black soot down on the others. But not all of them succumbed. Some had dashed into a round opening in the wall on the left and waited out the glowing death of their cohorts. Once the metal device stopped spinning and dropped to the ground with a loud clang, six of them sprang from the hole and rushed toward Reece and his team.

Hector stepped between Reece and Nathaniel and fired continuous rounds from his automatic weapon. Spent silver casings rained out of the rifle in every direction. His crew followed him. Within minutes the vampires were a pile of black soot on the dirty concrete floor. "Take that motherfuckers!" Hector shouted, then turned and chest bumped his brother. "Yes!"

"Good work. You've certainly got what it takes." Reece told them.

Hector smiled. "Gracias, amigo."

"We'd better keep moving in case there are more of them." Reece's gaze met Nathaniel's and they continued heading further in. The others followed, weapons raised ready to shoot at anything that moved, which concerned Reece. "Just remember what I said about civilians. We don't want to shoot the innocent."

"Yeah, hombre, we know." Hector took up position between the PI and the vampire. "Let's go get the bloodsucking motherfucker!" He gave Nathaniel a sheepish glance and swallowed hard. He'd figured out what he was before they'd entered the drains. It wasn't difficult to tell he was something other than human. "No offence, brother."

"None taken."

Reece was impressed with the courage the young men displayed against the horde of vampires. He'd thought they might lose their shit and hightail it out of there. They stood their ground. Lozano had made the right decision asking them for help. Their resilience in this situation was extraordinary. He knew they had everyone's backs.

The group pressed onward.

A perpetual blanket of darkness wrapped itself around them as they continued to move deeper into the underground. Everyone was on high alert. They knew there were bound to be demons or more vampires up ahead. Dracula would have made sure their path to finding him was fraught with danger and death.

After twenty minutes without any further otherworldly conflict, they came to the junction. It seemed too easy to Reece and he wondered what was in store for them. The left tunnel's entrance had caved in due to the blast from the plastic explosives he had planted, the other two were clear. Reece checked the map on his cell phone again to be sure he was correct about which passageway to take. The last thing they needed was to get lost down here amongst flesh-eating demons, succubae, vampires and who knew what else. "It's this way. There's an opening about half a mile in for workmen to cut through to the other section." He pointed to the center tunnel.

Nathaniel and Hector moved ahead of them, Reece next, Lozano and Sarah, then the young man's crew. They kept checking the rear to make sure they weren't being followed.

The group came to the opening and Nathaniel's large form squeezed through the narrow space first. "It is safe." His voice echoed back to them.

Reece waved the young guys through then Lozano and Sarah and he went in last, making sure they were alone.

When Reece stepped out of the crevice Sarah asked, "Ok, which way now?" Her voice was tight with tension. Coming face to face with the vampire who had killed her family after all these years would be daunting for her, despite her determination to exact revenge.

"This way." Reece turned right and stalked along the tunnel. The others followed.

As they approached the opening to where Dracula was meant to be hiding, Reece noticed something. He raced along the drain and stopped. "It's Oriana's sisters." Both women had been drained of blood and their heads ripped from their bodies. All three succubae were dead.

"Let's go in quietly. Understood?" Reece's gaze moved to the gang. He was worried they might accidentally do something to tip the monster off.

Hector and his guys nodded. "Whatever you say, amigo, we will do what you want."

"Good. I want you to stand guard out here. Don't let anything get past you." Reece didn't want to risk their lives by taking them into Dracula's lair. He was hundreds of years old with capabilities beyond what they knew. The kids would be easy targets.

"Come on, man. Stand guard out here? What do you take me for?" Hector glowered at Reece.

"It's for your own safety. Trust me on that."

"I thought you needed our help to put the monster down." Hector crossed his arms, rifle in hand.

"What I need is for you to keep us safe while we eliminate the threat. If you come in there with us some of you won't make it out."

"We would rather go down fighting, amigo." Hector glanced at his crew then returned his serious gaze to the PI. "It's what we live for. Death before dishonor, and standing out here doing nothing is dishonorable."

Reece couldn't argue with that.

"Look, I need at least two of you out here."

"Ok." Hector turned around. "Tomás and Alonso you stay here."

Both young men groaned.

"Hey! Don't whine like little bitches. There could be other vampires or demons out here and you know what to do if there is. You're guarding our backs, mis hermanos."

The rest of the group followed Nathaniel and Reece in.

An elaborately carved wooden casket sat on a concrete slab in the center of the dark cavern.

Reece raised his arm and everyone stopped. "We'll circle the coffin and then Nathaniel will open it. Be ready to fire as soon as he does."

Sarah and Lozano moved around the coffin to the left side, Hector and Javier to the right and Carlos and Diego to the back. Reece and Nathaniel walked round to the front of the casket and Nathaniel stepped up to it.

Reece swallowed the lump of stinging nerves lodged in his throat, his racing heartbeat pulsing below his Adam's apple. "Ok, when you're ready."

Nathaniel reached out, snapped the solid metal lock and threw the lid open. Dracula was gone.

CHAPTER FIFTY ONE

Ed got out of his car and stepped onto the sidewalk. Was the guy waiting for someone or was he watching Andre's apartment? Ed wandered along to the next lamppost and stopped. He pulled his cell phone from his pants pocket and snapped a couple of photos. He'd run them through the precinct database later to see if he got a match, although he didn't think he would. The guy looked... otherworldly. Vampire? Maybe. The sun was low and beginning to sink into the horizon so it was possible.

The lieutenant sighed and moved to the next post. He wanted a closer look. He whipped his spectacles out of his shirt pocket and slid them on. No, he didn't recognize the guy. He was about to move again when he spotted Arianne coming down the front steps and walking over to the man in black. Ed squeezed his over-sized body behind the lamppost and peered around it. Reece had been dead right. Something was definitely suspicious about her. He snapped a couple more pics. As he did his heart sank. Poor Andre. Ed knew Andre was in love with her. How could he tell him about this?

Ed headed back to his sedan and climbed in. He pressed speed dial for Reece.

"Hey, can you talk? Ok, good. You were right about Arianne. I just got pictures of her talkin' to some guy on the street outside your apartment building. No, I don't know who he is but I think he could be a vamp." Ed moved his gaze to the lamppost where the guy had been standing. He wasn't there. "The guy's gone. Do you want me to see if I can tail him?

Sure. Ok. I'll stay put. Will let you know if there are any new developments. Yeah, you be careful too." He rang off.

He started the car and moved closer to the apartment block. He'd wait it out to see if the guy came back.

80C3

Reece and the others were standing at the four wheel drive when he got the call from Ed. When he finished talking to him he told Nathaniel and Sarah what his ex-boss had said. He wished his gut had been wrong about Arianne because he knew how much she meant to Andre. Was Andre safe with her or was she in league with her father? Had she been all along?

The PI shook hands with each of the young men who had risked their lives to help them. Even though they were a gang of street thugs they still had a moral code. "Thanks for your help. We couldn't have found Dracula's hiding place without you."

"No problem, hombre. I'm sorry you didn't get him."

"Yeah, me too."

"If you need our help in the future you know how to find us," Hector told him, raising his chin and motioning over to the sheriff standing at the vehicle.

"Thanks. Yeah, I do." Reece watched the young men strut across the dirt the way they had come. He turned and walked back to the others. "I wonder where Dracula is." His gut twisted into a tangle of twitching nerves and a look of awareness crossed his face. "He's gone after Andre and Arianne. Maybe that's who Ed saw her talking to."

The four jumped into the JEEP, wheels screeching and gravel spraying up as Reece spun the car around and headed for their hotel.

80C3

Reece threw open the door and charged into his hotel room. "Charlotte? Where are you?" Sarah, Nathaniel and Lozano followed him in. Reece rushed into the adjoining room. Charlotte wasn't there. He came through the doorway. "Charlotte's not here."

"Did you check the bathroom?" Sarah asked.

The PI gave her a blank look, turned on his heel and rushed back

213

through the doorway. He hurried over to the bathroom and breathed a sigh of relief when he heard the shower running.

Sarah came up behind him. "See, always good to check before jumping to conclusions."

He gave her a thin smile. "Yeah."

The pair walked back into the other room.

"We should pack," Nathaniel said. "If we are going to catch the next flight out."

Reece raised his hand. "Just let me explain it to Charlotte first. Ok? We're supposed to be getting married tomorrow night. Having to change our plans after everything that's happened isn't going to be easy for her to understand."

"What can I do to help?" Lozano asked.

"At this point I don't know. I appreciate everything you've done. You've gone above and beyond the call of duty."

"I was happy to do it. You've taught me a lot. Things I needed to know."

Charlotte came into the room wearing a hotel robe, her hair wrapped in a towel. "Hi. I thought you were going to call me before..."

Reece took her by the hand, led her over to his bed and sat her down. "I know I did, but things have taken a dramatic turn."

She gazed up at him. "What kind of dramatic turn?"

He gave a heavy sigh. "Dracula's disappeared." Charlotte's eyes widened. "And we think he's headed to LA."

"Why would he be heading to LA?"

"Because Andre and Arianne are there."

Charlotte frowned into his eyes. "They're not here?"

"No, sweetheart, I sent them back earlier today. For their own safety."

Her frown deepened into a scowl. "Why didn't you tell me before now?"

"You were asleep and I didn't want to wake you. Why do you think I made the video?"

Charlotte folded her arms. "I'm not an invalid, Reece. You should've woken me up and told me what was going on. I can handle it."

Reece could see the hurt in her eyes. "I'm sorry. You're right, I should have. And I don't doubt for a second you can handle it, you're the strongest woman I know." He glanced at Sarah. "Apart from Sarah.

The priest crossed the room. "We need to get back to LA as soon as we can."

Charlotte's head snapped up and her eyes met Sarah's. "When you say *we* you mean you and Nathaniel, right?"

"No…"

Reece stopped Sarah from continuing. "Sweetheart, Andre's in danger. Arianne isn't who she led us to believe she is. Apart from being Dracula's daughter, she's a half breed vampire with witch powers."

"We do not have time for this," Nathaniel said. "We must go."

"What about our wedding?" Tears stung the backs of Charlotte's eyes and she blinked them away before they could spill down her face.

"We'll get married as soon as we make sure Andre is safe. You wouldn't want anything to happen to him, would you?"

Charlotte gave him an affronted stare. "Of course not."

"Then we need to pack and get to the airport." He took her hand and helped her to her feet. "I promise we'll be Mr. and Mrs. Daniels as soon as things settle down."

"All right." Charlotte sighed, crossed the room and disappeared through the doorway.

Within fifteen minutes everyone was packed and in the lobby waiting for their rental car.

Lozano shook Reece's hand. "It's been eye-opening working with you. I hope we can do again some time."

"Thanks, so do I. But under different circumstances next time."

The sheriff nodded. "Yeah, you got that right."

The group wheeled their suitcases out to the valet parking lot, packed the luggage into the trunk and climbed into the car.

Sheriff Lozano waited until they drove away before heading back to headquarters. He hoped they made it back in time to save Andre.

Ed messaged a picture of the guy to Reece so he would know what he looked like and told him Andre was still inside the apartment.

Reece received the MMS while waiting to board their flight home. When the pic downloaded he got up and walked over to where Sarah was sitting, sat down beside her and passed her his cell phone.

"It's not him. Vampires don't show up on film or digital technology. Hence the reason why they've always commissioned artists to paint their portraits."

"I wonder who it is then."

"Maybe the guy from Arianne's dream?"

"Do you know how crazy that sounds?"

"Yes, I do, but her dream may have been a premonition of coming events." Sarah gazed at him sideways. "How can we discount it?"

"I already thought the same thing. What it does mean though is Dracula is in LA, somewhere. And we have to find him before he gets to Andre."

Reece's gut instincts were correct. The vampire had fled Las Vegas and traveled to Los Angeles in pursuit of Andre and Arianne. What did he plan to do now that he knew where they were?

CHAPTER FIFTY TWO

The flight to LA had been delayed, and by the time the plane landed an extra forty five minutes had elapsed. Reece's gut was wound so tightly bile rose up his throat and he thought he would vomit. He swallowed down the nausea, trying to ignore it, and followed the others to the luggage carousel. After collecting their suitcases, Reece, Charlotte, Nathaniel and Sarah headed for the pickup point out front of the baggage claim.

A black town car with tinted windows was idling behind Ed's sedan. Nathaniel said his goodbyes and the driver opened the back passenger door for him. "Call me when you need my assistance." Reece nodded. The large vampire climbed into the vehicle, the driver closed the door, got into his seat and eased the limousine into the sea of traffic.

Ed rushed over to help Sarah and Charlotte with their luggage. "Glad you're finally on the ground. I was gettin' worried."

"I hate delays at the best of times but today of all days when we needed to get here quickly there had to be issues." Reece tossed his bag into the trunk. "Andre and Arianne still at the apartment?"

"Yeah. I've got surveillance on the building while I'm here. Someone who owed me a favor. Didn't want to involve the PD, for obvious reasons." Ed climbed into the car. The ladies settled in the back.

"You seem to have a lot of markers, Chief." Reece eased into the front passenger seat and clipped in his seatbelt.

"Nothin' wrong with that. Good for times like this. A man can't be in two places at the same time, ya know." He gave the PI a crooked smile and pulled away from the curb into the traffic and shuttle bus chaos of the busy airport.

"You're right."

"Are we going to the apartment now? It might not be such a good idea to go charging in there, throwing accusations around we can't substantiate," Sarah said.

"No, we're not. I think we should stop by the office first. I'll call Andre from there and ask him to come over without Arianne."

"Do you think he'll do it?" Charlotte thought it was a bad idea. Andre was bound to be suspicious.

"If I tell him I need to talk to him alone he will."

"He's going to wonder why we've come back earlier than planned."

"Yeah, he might, but I have to make him aware of what's going on. His life is in danger. And whether he believes it or not Arianne can't be trusted."

"You don't want to say that to him, Reece. He won't believe you." Charlotte eased back against the seat and folded her arms.

"I'll show him the pictures. They should convince him."

"Charlotte's right. We need to tread carefully otherwise we could inadvertently get him killed." Sarah's gaze moved from Charlotte to Reece.

"What else can I do?" He turned around and peered between the front seats at the priest.

"Maybe we should let things run their course. Stay close but not intervene just yet."

Reece gave Sarah an incredulous stare. "You're kidding, right?"

"No. He's not in any immediate danger…"

"We don't know that for sure. He could be. Dracula's crony has been to the apartment building. He knows where we live. He's talked to Arianne and who knows what she told him. She could've given him a key. Andre's a sitting duck in that apartment alone."

"But he's not alone. Arianne is there."

"That's my point. Two against one."

"What if we've got it all wrong? What if Arianne isn't the bad guy? Yes, she talked to Dracula's crony or whoever he is, but what if she told him she didn't want any part of what he had to offer?" Charlotte said. "She's in love with Andre. Do you really think she'd betray him?"

Reece didn't know how to respond to her line of reasoning. From what he'd witnessed so far and what Ed had showed him it seemed as though Arianne was in league with her bloodsucking father.

𝔖𝔒𝔊

Ed pulled the car into the curb outside Reece's office building and turned off the engine. The PI was the first one out of the car, moving to the rear of the vehicle and pulling the luggage from the trunk. It could remain in the office until they figured out where they'd be staying. The lieutenant climbed out of his seat and walked around to him. "So what can I do to help?"

"Nothing at this point. Let's see how the situation with Andre plays out. If he won't listen to reason we might have to restrain him somewhere. That's where you come in."

"How so?" Ed frowned.

"We may have to lock him up for his own protection."

"Jesus, Daniels, I don't like the sound of that."

"Neither do I. But if he won't believe the facts what can we do? I'm not losing my best friend."

The women were waiting on the sidewalk. "I think it's a terrible plan," Charlotte told him. "You'd really lock your friend up like a criminal?"

Reece stared at his fiancée, his stern expression sincere. "You bet I would if it meant keeping him alive."

Charlotte shook her head in disbelief. "Remind me not to go against your unreasonable logic in future. I wouldn't want to piss you off and end up in a holding cell."

The PI sighed, picked up their suitcases and crossed the sidewalk.

"I think he's right," Sarah agreed. "If we don't do something to protect Andre he *will* die. Dracula never leaves anything unfinished. He'll pursue him until he's ended him. Make no mistake about it."

Charlotte climbed the five front steps and entered the building. Reece and the others followed. He wondered why she'd reacted the way she did. Normally, she would have agreed with him, especially when it meant the life of someone so close to them. She'd been different since she came out of hospital, moody and sleeping for long periods of time, and he was concerned she was hiding her post traumatic stress from him. Something they'd need to talk about once the new drama was over.

The four climbed the two flights of stairs and when they got to the landing outside the office they found the door ajar.

Reece set the luggage down and pulled his Glock. He motioned for everyone to stay put while he eased himself across the hallway without a sound. He pressed his back against the wall beside the office entrance, raised his weapon in both hands and darted into the center of the open doorway. No one. But the office had been completely turned upside down.

Ed, Sarah and Charlotte crossed the hall and peered into the room. "They did one hell of a job destroying the place, didn't they?" Ed said, standing next to Reece and surveying the room.

The PI stepped into the office. "Yeah. What were they looking for? And did they find it?"

"Dracula's guy probably did this. It must've been how he found your address." Sarah gazed around at the papers, files, books and broken furniture strewn across the deep blue carpet.

"Shit!" Reece rushed over to his desk, snatched up the drawer lying on the floor and turned it over. "The spare key to our apartment is gone. Now they have access." He picked up the phone on his desk. Dead. Reece pulled his cell phone from the pocket of his jeans and hit speed dial. "Come on, Andre, pick up." He paced. "Shit. He's not answering. We need to get over there *now!*"

“” ℰℭ

Reece jabbed at the elevator button but it still didn't make it arrive any faster. When the doors sprang open he and the others dashed inside and he pressed the button to his floor. The PI watched the numbers overhead light up and fade out as the lift moved slowly upward. "Come on, come on. Why is it going so slow?"

"It's ok, Reece, we're almost there," Charlotte said, reaching for his hand and giving it a tight squeeze.

The elevator stopped and when the doors opened Reece pulled free of Charlotte and ran along the hallway to their apartment door. He pushed the key into the lock and threw it open. "Andre?! Andre, are you here?"

Arianne appeared from the kitchen. "Reece?" She frowned. "Is... everything ok?"

"Where's Andre?"

"He went to pick up a pizza for me. It's only a short walk from here. Why?"

"How long has he been gone? He's not answering his phone." Reece wandered through the apartment taking in everything around him. Was anyone else there?

"About ten minutes." She shrugged. "I don't know why he's not answering."

Reece marched across the room to the coffee table, picked up Arianne's cell phone and pushed it at her. "You call him. See if he picks up."

She gave him a curious look. "What's going on? Why are you back so soon?"

"Just call him." Reece glowered at her.

Sarah, Ed and Charlotte entered the apartment and Ed closed the door.

"Andre, it's me. Are you on your way back?"

Reece snatched the phone from her hand. "Andre? Why didn't you answer my call earlier?"

"Sorry, Reece, I didn't hear it. The music in the pizzeria was pretty loud."

"You have immortal hearing, remember."

"Why are you in LA? What about your wedding?"

"Don't change the subject."

"Look, I'll be upstairs in less than five minutes. We can talk then." He rang off.

Reece gave Arianne a severe stare as he passed her phone back. "Someone needs to tell me what's going on."

The door opened and Andre walked in. "Is something wrong? Why are you back so soon?"

"Yeah, something's wrong. We have to talk. Alone." The PI's eyes moved to Arianne then back to his friend.

Andre frowned. "Whatever you have to say you can say in front of Arianne."

Reece swallowed his anger. "All right, if that's how you want to do this."

"Do what?" Andre folded his arms.

"Arianne is hiding things from you."

Andre glanced at her then scowled at Reece. "What are you talking about?"

Reece's serious gaze moved to Arianne. "Are you going to tell him or am I?"

Ed charged over. "Let's cut the crap. Arianne's been talking to some guy. He could be one of Dracula's cronies."

"He's not!" Arianne rushed across to Andre. "You believe me, don't you?"

Andre frowned into her eyes. "Who is he?"

Arianne's disgruntled gaze fell on Reece. "He's my half-brother, Nicolae. He's Vlad's bastard son by a human lover so he's like me."

"How did he find you? And why is he here?" Andre asked.

"I can't tell you." She gave him a sheepish glance. "He asked me not to."

Reece folded his arms. "Is he with your father?"

Arianne looked at him sideways, anger flashing in her eyes. "I don't know. Are you going to kill him too?"

"Someone broke into our office and ransacked it looking for a key to this place and they found it, so if your brother had anything to do with it it means he's working with him. Your father came here looking for you and Andre with one purpose in mind, to kill one or both of you. If you're not helping him then you need to be honest with us."

"I'm *not* helping him!" Arianne stood with her hands on her hips. "Why would you think such a thing? I came here with Andre to get away from him."

"Or you came back to LA to make sure you knew where Andre was." Ed stepped up alongside Reece.

"No." Arianne looked at Andre. "You don't believe them, do you? I – I love you, Andre."

"I don't know what I believe. You need to tell us everything you know."

"But…"

"Arianne," Sarah said, "You have to tell us."

CHAPTER FIFTY THREE

The Roosevelt Hotel had a welcoming old world charm to it. Entering the art deco lobby with its subdued lighting, decorative ceiling, and central fountain was like stepping back in time to a bygone era, where socialites and A-listers of 1950s Hollywood rubbed shoulders at lavish functions arranged only for them that ran on until the early hours of the morning.

Reece, Andre and Arianne wandered casually through the extensive, luxurious foyer to the elevator bank and waited for one of the six lifts to arrive. They had come to see Nicolae to find out what he knew and if he planned to help them. When the elevator door glided open the trio stepped inside. "Which floor?" Reece asked, his right index finger poised ready to poke the gold button for whichever level Arianne's brother was on.

"Nine." Arianne leaned against the back of the cubicle and sighed. Her brother wouldn't be pleased with her for telling them where he was.

Andre settled back next to her. "You're doing the right thing. We have to know what's going on so we can prepare for whatever's coming. What if your father plans to kill us all?"

Arianne's serious gaze moved to him. "He's an immortal psychopath. What else would you expect?" A quiver rippled through her solar plexus and flipped over into a sickening wave at the thought of coming face to face with the infamous Dracula... her long lost father. She hated the fact that his blood ran through her veins. She eased her hand into Andre's. "I hope you believe I'm not a part of his demented plan. I meant what I said earlier. I love you."

"I don't doubt you love me. I love you too. But..." He gave her a wry smile. It had been three years since Beth walked out of his life and it felt good to actually feel something for someone again.

"You still think I'm involved in some way?" She pulled her hand free.

The elevator stopped and the door slid open.

"Here we are." Reece stepped into the hallway, the wall opposite the elevator lined with black framed photographs of famous Hollywood icons. "Which room?"

"Nine twenty eight. It seems he has a propensity for the macabre."

The group walked along the hall checking room numbers.

"What do you mean?" Reece eyed her sideways.

"Surely you've heard about room nine twenty eight?"

"No, I haven't. What about it?"

"The hotel is renowned for having its fair share of supernatural residents. Marilyn Monroe and Clark Gable, among others, have been seen walking the hallways late at night. The room my brother is occupying is meant to accommodate the ghost of fifties actor Montgomery Clift. Guests who've stayed in the room have seen and heard things: TVs turning on and off, lights flickering, music playing."

"And it doesn't bother you that your brother's tastes are... peculiar?"

Arianne turned her head and glowered at Reece. "Why do you think I didn't want to come here?"

Nine twenty eight stood at the end of the hall angled in an L shape beside another room. The trio stopped outside the nondescript white door.

"Now what?" Andre said, his tone low.

"We knock. What else?" Reece raised his hand but the door moved out of his reach before his knuckles met the wood.

"To what do I owe the pleasure, Detectives?" Nicolae's gaze moved to his sister. "Arianne." He gestured for the trio to enter.

Reece stepped inside first, followed by Andre. Arianne held back.

Nicolae gave her an inquisitive frown. "Coming in, sister?" A self-satisfied smirk turned the left corner of his mouth up.

Arianne swallowed her nerves and stepped into the room. She jumped when her brother closed the door with a swift bang.

"Please make yourselves comfortable." Nicolae crossed the room, took a seat in a high-backed brown leather arm chair by the window and crossed one leg over the other, resting his hands in his lap.

Reece, Andre and Arianne remained on their feet.

"Why are you in LA?" Reece folded his arms.

"I came here to reunite with my long lost sibling." Nicolae's gaze rested on the PI and a smug smile slid across his pale, handsome face.

"It seems too much of a coincidence that you're here at the same time as your father."

The young man's right eyebrow rose and the expression on his face changed to one of surprise. "I wasn't aware."

Reece could see Nicolae was telling the truth by his reaction. Did he fear his father as much as Arianne? As much as they all did?

"We need your help to locate him."

Nicolae sprang from his seat. "I would prefer to remain anonymous as far as my father is concerned. I didn't know he was here and I hope he doesn't know I am."

"We have to find him before he finds us," Arianne told him. "He will kill Andre to get to me. I think he wants me to join with him and our brothers."

Her brother's eyes widened. "So you had the dream too. It's the reason I came to find you."

Arianne crossed the room to Nicolae. "Then help us."

He shook his head. "I cannot. I'm sorry. I came to take you away from here before he found you, not get involved in a war that cannot be won. Our father is a *fiend*. There is no way to stop him."

"We have to try, Nicolae," Reece said. "If we don't we're all doomed to die. You included."

The young man swallowed the tight wad of fear lodged in his throat, looked into Arianne's eyes and sighed. "All right. I know someone who can find out where he is. Give me some time and I will contact you. But that is all I can do."

"Time is something we don't have. He has a key to our apartment." Reece realized it was Dracula who had caused the damage in their office. Perhaps not directly, but one of his cronies had, which meant he was one step ahead of them once again and would stop at nothing to get what he wanted.

"Then I suggest you not go back there. Find somewhere else to hide."

Reece knew the perfect place where they could stay. Decadent Desire, Nathaniel's night club.

CHAPTER FIFTY FOUR

Nathaniel had put out feelers to try to find Vlad too, before the vampire found them. His contact had called with information about him having a suite at the Millennium Biltmore Hotel which stood across from the Los Angeles Central Library. He had used the alias Vladimir Fieraru. The guy had chuckled as he told Nathaniel the name and when Nathaniel had asked why he'd said the surname Fieraru meant blacksmith with variations attributing to the surname Smith. He had signed in as Vladimir Smith.

How ironic.

When Reece, Andre and Arianne arrived at the night club they sat down to devise a plan. Now that they knew where the monster was holed up they needed to strike first—and fast. He had to be lured out of his comfortable surroundings somehow. Sarah, Charlotte and Ed came to the club after the chief finished at the precinct. Sarah knew more about Dracula than anyone else on their team, so perhaps she could shed some light on any other vulnerabilities he might possess.

"Are his weaknesses the same as any vampire?" Reece asked, rubbing the dark blonde stubble on his chin.

Sarah's eyes met his in a serious stare. "Yes, as far as I'm aware. He may have found ways to protect himself from some of them though. He's had centuries to do so. What you need to be aware of is he's incredibly powerful and super-fast. His strength and agility comes from centuries of murdering his victims, human, werewolf, and vampire alike and drinking them dry."

"Wait. I thought werewolf blood would kill a vampire," Reece said.

She shook her head. "A bite or scratch will but their blood increases a vampire's strength. And before you ask, I have no idea why. Experts in the field who have researched this phenomenon don't even know why."

"Maybe we can poison him with … what was it, oh yeah, Belladonna," Ed offered.

"I wish it were that simple." Sarah gave him a thin loving smile. "He's immune to those kinds of methods, unfortunately."

"Is there anything apart from the obvious we can try?" Reece folded his arms and sighed.

"What we need to do is make a move while he's sleeping, when he's at his *most* vulnerable."

"We tried that in the tunnels and look where it got us. If he figures out we're on to him he'll disappear again." Reece paced. "We have to use the element of surprise."

"May I make a suggestion?" Nathaniel joined the group sitting at the tables on the perimeter of the dance floor.

"Sure," Reece said.

"If Arianne is willing," he said, his eyes moving to her, "perhaps we can draw him out by setting up a meeting between them."

Andre glowered at him. "You can't be serious. He'll take her and we'll never find her."

"Not if we have a flawless plan." Nathaniel's eyes moved to Reece. "If Arianne makes contact and asks him to meet her out in the alley behind the night club tonight we can be ready to dispatch him. We will have time to implement a booby-trap."

"How?" Ed asked.

"Motion sensored ultraviolet lighting."

"That's not a half-bad idea," Sarah said. "It will finish him in seconds."

Reece studied Arianne's reaction. She could still be part of his plan. "Do you want to do it?"

Arianne's eyes moved around everyone in the group then back to the PI. "I don't have a choice. If I don't, it will be only a matter of time before he kills us all."

"You don't have to. We'll find another way." Andre took her hand.

"I want to prove I'm not involved with him in any way. What about Nicolae?"

"Do you want him to come here?" Reece asked.

"It's better than him being alone. What if Vlad knows he's in LA?"

The PI ran the thought around his brain. "Ok. Call him."

"Thank you." She gave him a grateful smile.

"Let's get things set up, then Arianne can make the call to the hotel."

Dusk had set in by the time the group finished installing the lethal lighting in the alley and testing it to make sure it worked. Arianne would wait mid-center and when her father reached the activation point the lights would flash on. The monster would turn to ash and the world would be rid of an historical, demented serial killer.

The element of surprise.

Arianne had called the Millennium Biltmore Hotel and left a message that she was tired of running and wanted to meet with him. She didn't want to speak to him personally, not yet, and he had replied with a text message saying he would see her at midnight. She'd also tried to contact her brother but his phone kept going straight to voicemail. Where was he?

Inside Decadent Desire, everyone went over the plan. In case the lights failed they would be ready to open fire with sanctified silver bullets. The one thing they knew for sure, Dracula wasn't getting away this time.

Arianne's mind was somewhere else. She was worried about Nicolae. Had something happened to him? Or was he working with her father like Reece had suspected about her? For some reason she was wary of her brother. She wasn't sure why. He had a pretentious streak in him inherited from their father and it bothered her. Nevertheless, she hoped he'd turn up at the night club.

Reece crossed the expansive room to where Arianne was sitting. "You're sure you're ok with this?"

She gazed up at him. "If it'll prove to you I'm not working with Vlad, then yes."

"Nothing's foolproof. Something could go wrong. He could be stronger than any of us suspect."

"I'm aware. But if it's the only way to stop him then we have to go through with it. I'll be fine. I can take care of myself." Deep down, she wasn't sure she could. Not because he was her father but because of who he was and what he was capable of.

Sarah and Ed were checking weapons, Nathaniel organized three members of his vampire team as backup, and Charlotte sat alone by the spiral stairs.

Reece walked over to her. "Everything ok?"

She glanced up at him, tears glistening in her eyes. "I'm not sure. I don't feel like me anymore."

He sat down beside her and pulled her into his arms. "Why didn't you tell me? We could've seen someone who could help you."

Charlotte jerked out of his embrace. "I don't want to see anyone. I just need some time."

"Sweetheart, your mood swings are not normal. You sleep all the time, you're edgy..."

"You think I don't know that?" She gave a heavy sigh. "I'll be fine, as long as I have you."

"Charlotte, you have me heart and soul. Once this is all over we'll fly back to Vegas and have the wedding you wanted. Ok?" He lifted her chin so her eyes met his. "Ok?"

A tear slid down her cheek and she nodded. "Ok."

"I want you to sit this one out. I don't think you're ready for a confrontation with Dracula."

"You're right." She gave a thin smile. "I'm happy to stay right here."

Andre came across to them. "We're ready. There's forty five minutes to go before he arrives."

"Good. Let's go over what we have to do." As he walked away from Charlotte, Reece glanced over his shoulder. He was worried about her state of mind.

CHAPTER FIFTY FIVE

Vlad stepped out of the hotel room and followed his driver along the hallway to the elevator bank. Tonight he would reunite with his daughter. He smiled as he entered the lift and tipped his hat at the woman standing in the corner, his mesmerizing gaze resting on hers. She gave him a captivated smile then returned her eyes to the bright pink, digital floor numbers on the button panel. He couldn't allow her to see that he had no reflection in the framed mirrors lining the walls.

When the elevator reached the lobby and the door opened, Vlad motioned for the woman to step out ahead of him and his driver. Again, she gave him an enchanted smile and scooted past them with a nod of her head. "Thank you, you're a true gentleman." Little did she know who she was speaking to. Dracula was a striking, charismatic figure, smooth when it came to women, and yet he had never truly been in love with any. They had only been a means of bearing his offspring.

He stepped through the double glass doors, under the domed and columned 1920s entrance out to the street, and gazed up and down the busy road. LA was a bustling city and he did not care for it. The sidewalk was relatively quiet with only a handful of pedestrians making their way to wherever they were going. Vlad crossed the concrete walkway and climbed into the black town car. When it pulled away from the curb, heading for the night club, another dark colored prestige sedan followed.

Decadent Desire? He hadn't heard of it before now. Checking the internet earlier, he found the venue was situated in an obscure location not far from the port of Los Angeles. He wondered why Arianne would choose a back alley far from anywhere for their first meeting, a meeting of her choosing. He didn't trust anyone, not even his children, and was well prepared.

As the car traveled closer to the club, Vlad sensed danger. His daughter and the PI's team were awaiting his arrival. She had betrayed him just as he had suspected. A conceited smirk spread across his face. Did they really believe he would walk blindly into a trap? They were the ones who were in for a rude awakening.

The limousine pulled up at the entrance to the alleyway. The driver got out, rounded the car and opened the rear left-hand door. His passenger emerged from the back seat and gazed at his gloomy surroundings, the port's lights glimmering in the distance. A single lamppost stood sentinel about half way along the alley and under it stood a young woman dressed like a warrior in dark pants, jacket and hood. He recognized her immediately and made his way toward her.

She took an uneasy step backwards as he approached. She couldn't see his face; it was shrouded beneath a hood too. He had a purposeful stride which unnerved her but she stood her ground.

When he reached the activation point, the stark burst of blue ultraviolet light lit up the dark alley like fireworks in the night sky, still he kept coming. He drew a large iron sword from under his long coat and raised it in gloved hands. Arianne whipped her samurai sword from its sheath on her back and took an aggressive stance, her fingers wrapped tightly around the handle of the weapon ready to fight, her knuckles white. "Stop!" she yelled, her voice echoing along the brick wall of the night club and neighboring buildings.

He continued toward her.

Reece darted to the open doorway ready to race into the alley and fire his Glock but Nathaniel grabbed the back of his jacket.

"Do not intervene," the vampire warned.

"She's in trouble."

"She is not."

Ed and Sarah were positioned on the roof of the night club and were given the order to stand down. Sarah frowned as she lowered her weapon and stepped silently away from the edge. Her eyes met Ed's but neither of them spoke otherwise they'd be heard by the monster below.

"Stay where you are and remove your hood," Arianne shouted, her long sword aimed at the oncoming figure.

He stopped, raised the heavy sword and thrust it into the air. It rocketed toward her in a blur and she only just managed to jump clear.

Reece gave the order and everyone opened fire on the figure.

His body jerked back and forth as blood and fibers from his black hooded jacket showered him and the alley.

He remained on his feet despite the onslaught of bullets.

Arianne charged at him and thrust her sword deep into his chest.

His knees buckled and he fell backwards onto the ground, his arms splayed on the damp cobblestones.

Reece, Nathaniel and Andre raced out of the back exit and along the alley. Arianne stalked up to the figure lying unmoving on the ground and snatched the hood from over his face. "Nooo!"

Sarah and Ed came rushing up behind them. "Who's that?" Sarah asked.

"Arianne's brother." Reece shook his head and swore under his breath.

Nicolae's dead eyes stared up at them, his mouth covered with duct tape.

Arianne dropped to her knees and pressed her ear to his chest. Nothing. "No, no, no!" Tears spilled down her face as she pumped his chest. "That monster compelled him to kill me." She listened again. Still no heartbeat.

"To force you into killing him," Nathaniel said.

The second black limousine idling at the other end of the alley drove away.

Reece spotted it and raced to the street but by the time he reached it the red taillights were disappearing into the distance.

"Why? Why would he kill his own son?" Arianne asked through tears.

Andre kneeled beside her. "Because he's a psychopath, just as you said." He helped her to her feet. "Let's get you inside."

"He's going to kill us all." Arianne's tears turned to sobs.

"Not if we can help it," Reece told her, a mark of determination in his voice.

Sarah and Ed walked with Andre and Arianne back to the door.

Nathaniel scooped the body into his large arms as though it had no weight and carried it inside. Reece collected the swords and followed him in.

After laying Nicolae's body in the freezer room, Nathaniel climbed the cellar stairs and entered the night club. Charlotte and Sarah were with Arianne doing their best to console her while Reece, Andre and Ed sat at the bar discussing their next move. What move? Dracula had been one step ahead of them once again. He'd figured out their plan and implemented one of his own.

Nathaniel stepped behind the bar and poured whiskey for each of them. "Vlad is very shrewd and well prepared. I do not understand why he allowed his son to die at the hands of his daughter."

"Because he's a maniac, that's why," Ed told him, slapping his hand on the counter top. "Hit me."

"It's a message." Reece swallowed his shot of whiskey in one go and coughed as the heat slid into his stomach. "He's warning us no one is safe. Not even his children."

Sarah crossed the night club and climbed onto the stool next to Ed. "As I said before we need to go in while he's sleeping. It's the only way we can finish him."

Reece frowned at her. "Ok, but how are we going to do that at the hotel?"

"We wait until sunrise. There'll be a skeleton crew on then and we won't be noticed if we're careful. We'll go up to his floor, break into his room and end his undead life."

"I like your way of thinking, sweetheart," Ed said, giving Sarah a crooked half smile and squeezing her hand.

"Why sunrise?" Reece asked.

"Because it's the beginning of his sleep cycle and he'll be completely out of it," she told him. There's a window of opportunity for a few hours, after that his subconscious will be alert even while he sleeps."

"It sounds too easy. He'd have a body guard... or three. He wouldn't risk being alone while he's vulnerable." Reece smacked the bar for another shot of whiskey. Nathaniel poured the amber liquid into his glass.

"But if it works who cares." Ed shrugged.

Reece's eyes moved around his team. "It has to be foolproof, not like tonight. We have to be one hundred percent sure it'll work or we're not going in. It's too dangerous."

"His minders would be human so we can tranquilize them like we did Jacques' adherents. Should be easy if there are only a couple of them." Sarah grabbed a paper napkin and a pen and drew the layout of the floor.

"I've had a look at the floorplan for the hotel. From what Arianne found out when she called, Dracula's room is here. The elevators are here. I'd say his cronies would either be in this room or this one. Something we'd need to confirm. There's a service elevator here—she pointed to it on the floor plans—we can use it to get out of the hotel once we're done. No one will be able to say they saw anything. Anyhow, there won't be much left of him except a pile of ashes. And what could his cronies say? He was a vampire?"

"You don't think hotel management won't wonder where he's gone?" Andre asked.

"Why would they? Guests arrive and leave at all hours of the day and night."

"Maybe I should book a room on the same floor for Andre and me. At least then we're already inside," Reece suggested, his eyes running over the floor plan.

"Good idea. The rest of us can join you there and wait until it's time to move in." Sarah scribbled down some notes. "Perfect."

Arianne and Charlotte came over to the bar. "I want to make sure he's dead this time," Arianne told them. "Very dead."

Sarah gave her a confident smile. "Oh, he will be. He's defenseless while he's sleeping. As we know, vampires are dead while in repose so this time we'll finish the job."

"What if something goes wrong?" Charlotte asked.

"Nothing will go wrong," Sarah assured. "Dracula will be dispatched from this world *for good!*"

CHAPTER FIFTY SIX

Vlad paced his hotel suite, hands clasped behind his back. He stopped from time to time to gaze out of the window, the light behind him casting no reflection against the pane of glass. His plan to reunite with his daughter and turn her into a full-blood vampire had been thwarted. But it wouldn't stop him. It only made him more determined to have what he wanted. His sons were close by in the adjacent room, and two of his men were in the one behind him. If the PI and his team made another attempt on his life he was prepared.

A knock on the door brought his thoughts back to the present. He turned on his heel, crossed his suite and opened it. "Father, I've had word the humans are going to try again. Do you not think it would be wise to change rooms?"

Vlad rested his hand on his son's shoulder and smiled. "No, Mihnea, I want them to come. It's all part of my plan."

"We will be ready for them." Mihnea crossed the hall and returned to his room.

"Yes, we will." Vlad smirked, closed the door and walked back to the window. Two things would happen this time. First, he would rid himself of the priest. She had been pursuing him for far too long and meddling in his affairs. And second, he would eliminate Reece Daniels and his team and take what belonged to him. Arianne.

The thought gave him a sense of satisfaction. He would be the victor… as always.

CHAPTER FIFTY SEVEN

Reece and Andre arrived at the Millennium Biltmore around 10.00 PM, checked in and traveled up to the tenth floor. Their room was on the same side as Dracula's and only three doors down. The perfect vantage point. Andre had compelled the reception desk clerk who had informed them Vlad Fieraru's entourage was in the adjacent room and the one behind his. The two guests in the room opposite were his sons. That changed the game plan dramatically. Andre had also requested a plastic master key card, which the clerk was happy to provide and told them to enjoy their stay. Once they walked away from the counter he would have no recollection of their conversation.

As soon as they were inside their room, Reece called Sarah and told her about the sons. They would need a new strategy to take them out before attempting anything else. Sarah informed him she had a similar, smaller device like the one they'd used in the tunnel which would be perfect for the task of eliminating Dracula's sons. She told him to get a good night's sleep and that she and the others would be there before sunup.

Reece couldn't sleep. He paced the room, stopping at the window occasionally to look out at the street below. Andre was out of it, lying on the second bed, hovering somewhere between reality and the otherworld. The PI's mind was overflowing. Could they pull it off this time? Would they finally be rid of Dracula once and for all? Before he realized it was already after 2.00 AM. He slid under the covers, still dressed, and closed his eyes. The others would arrive in a couple of hours.

So as not to draw attention to themselves, Sarah, Arianne and Charlotte went into the hotel first. They made their way through the lobby, which had once been the reception area, and on to the guest elevator bank. When the lift arrived they stepped inside, pressed the tenth floor button and headed up to Reece and Andre's room. Nathaniel and Ed entered the building ten minutes later, walked to the elevators and headed upstairs.

Once inside the room, they made preparations for the attack.

Sarah would activate the device outside the sons' suite and Nathaniel would open the door with the master key and toss it into the room. When the device deactivated they would enter and make sure the sons were dead. If not, Nathaniel would finish them.

Ed and Andre had the task of tranquilizing the human cronies. Nathaniel would pass them the master key on their way past, they'd enter the room and Ed would knock out the pair in a matter of seconds then he and Andre would tie them up and move them to the bathroom.

With his protectors out of the way it would be easy to take down the monster.

Reece checked his watch. 4.35 AM. "Everyone know what they have to do?"

Each member of the group nodded, all except Charlotte. "What am I doing?"

"I think it would be better if you stayed here…"

Charlotte jumped to her feet. "But I want to help."

Reece rested a hand on her arm and eased her back down onto the foot of the queen-sized bed. "I know you do, sweetheart, and under any other circumstances it wouldn't be a problem, but you've only been out of the hospital a few days. Give it some time."

Tears stung the backs of her eyes. "I'm fine. Let me help you."

Andre sat beside her. "You've been through a lot, Charlotte. As a doctor I can see the stress you're still under from the ordeal. Please listen to Reece and stay here. It's for your own safety."

Charlotte's tear-filled eyes met his. "All right." She hated being treated like an invalid.

"Ok, let's get ready," Reece said, checking his watch again. 4.38 AM.

Nathaniel opened the door and glanced up and down the hallway. No one. Most guests would still be asleep. Sarah stepped into the hall and waited for Nathaniel.

"Remember what I said, don't take any unnecessary risks. Just get it done and be ready for the next phase of our plan. Ok?" Reece reminded.

The pair nodded and headed along the passage.

Reece turned around and eyed his friend and ex-boss. "Ready?"

Both men nodded and headed to the door, Ed carrying the tranquilizer gun that resembled a larger version of Reece's Glock. It would be easy to hide under his jacket if they ran into any guests along the hall.

Sarah and Nathaniel stood outside the suite, their watches synchronized. In two minutes, they would begin a chain of events that would finally destroy Dracula.

The PI stood at the room door, eyes on his watch. Once the others had completed their arduous tasks, he would join them outside Vlad's suite. It shouldn't take more than five minutes, unless something went wrong.

4.40 AM.

Nathaniel slid the key card into the lock, held the door ajar and tossed the activated device into the room. A high-pitched ping erupted and the orb emitted ultraviolet rays that spanned the width of the suite. Ed and Andre came along the hallway and Nathaniel passed Ed the master key. They continued to the second room, unlocked the door and stormed in.

When the device deactivated, Sarah entered the suite first in case there was any residual contamination which would be deadly for Nathaniel. She called him in and both surveyed the room. No ashes. At that moment, the bathroom door swung open and Vlad's sons charged into the room.

Andre and Ed gazed around the empty space. Where were Dracula's cronies?

Ed motioned with his head toward the bathroom and both men moved silently across the room to the door. Andre stood on the left and Ed on the right of the closed doorway, weapons raised. Andre had Reece's Glock.

His frowning gaze met Ed's and the older man moved for the handle. He gripped the knob, twisted it and threw the door open. No one.

"What the hell's goin' on?" he whispered.

"They were prepared for us. Let's get back to Sarah and Nathaniel now!" The pair raced out of the room and could hear the crashing and banging before they reached the open doorway. Andre flew into the fray while Ed rushed back to tell Reece.

Vlad's sons were fast and strong and Nathaniel couldn't hold them at bay. Sarah raised her automatic and fired several shots off but missed them every time. Reece and Ed leaped into the assault taking on the brothers alongside Andre and Nathaniel. The pair of vampires fought, clawed and attacked with fangs as the four tried to fend them off, blood spraying into the air and spattering the cream colored walls.

Sarah scrambled for the doorway between the fighting men. She had to get her crossbow. She flew down the hall and into the room. Charlotte was gone. Sarah couldn't worry about that now she had to get back to help the others.

She loaded her high-powered, double chamber crossbow with silver shafts and raced back along the hall. She fired off an arrow and it hit one son between the shoulder blades. He went down and Andre and Ed were on top of him. She quickly let the other arrow fly and it hit the second son in the middle of his chest. His body swelled and exploded into a spray of black soot.

Ed was hurtled across the room, hitting the wall with a loud thud. Sarah rushed over and helped him to his feet. Bloody bite marks dotted both of his arms, his shirt was covered in splashes of red and his breathing was short and sharp.

"Ed, look at me," Sarah said, her voice anxious, "Are you all right?" He had been attacked by werewolves once and had almost turned on the full moon. Could there be a risk to him now being bitten by vampires? Sarah turned his face to hers. "Ed? Ed, look at me."

"Yeah, yeah, I'm ok. I think." He slumped to the floor, his breathing becoming more labored.

The fight was over. Both of Vlad's sons were gone.

"Reece, Ed needs help." Sarah's shocked expression caused his heart to lurch.

He raced across the room and got down on his knees. "Chief, can you hear me?"

"Yeah. I don't feel so good."

"Andre!"

Both Andre and Nathaniel whipped across the room.

"He needs my blood." Andre bit into the vein in his wrist and pressed it to the older man's mouth.

Ed turned his face away from the trickle of blood running down Andre's arm. "I – I don't need it."

"Yes, you do." Andre held his wrist out to him.

The older man gripped Andre's arm and brought it to his mouth.

Reece climbed to his feet and raced out of the room. He eased himself across the hallway and slid the key card into the lock of Vlad's suite and threw the door open. The vampire stood in the center of the room holding Charlotte in front of him.

Reece's intense stare locked onto the vampire and his jaw clenched. What he wanted to do right now was race across the room and thrust a wooden stake into the heart of the monster. But he couldn't. The monster had Charlotte. Andre and Nathaniel appeared at the door.

"I would stay there if I were you otherwise this young woman might lose her humanity." He gripped her chin from behind and raised it so her throat was exposed.

"What do you want?" Reece asked, his voice tight. He kept his eyes focused on Dracula.

"What any father wants, to be reunited with my daughter." He stepped backwards, closing the distance between him and the window. Daylight had only just broken, the sun not yet above the high rise buildings.

Arianne arrived at the door and Andre raised his arm to prevent her from entering the room.

"Ah, there you are my sweet. So nice of you to join us."

"Let Charlotte go." Arianne pushed Andre's arm aside and stepped into the room.

"Why should I?"

"Because if you do I'll stay with you."

Andre rushed forward. "No! Arianne, you can't."

She turned and gave him a wry smile. The love she had for him evident in her eyes. "I don't have a choice."

"A wise decision, my daughter." He pushed Charlotte forward and Reece grabbed her as she stumbled. "Now go. Before I change my mind and kill you all."

Sarah appeared at the doorway and without hesitation she fired off both silver arrows. They rocketed across the room hitting Dracula in the left shoulder. "Ahhh!" He threw himself backwards and crashed through the closed window, shards of glass spraying everywhere.

"Dammit! I can't believe I missed." Sarah crossed the suite with the others and they peered out of the broken window pane.

Dracula was gone.

Nathaniel and Ed appeared at the door. "What happened? Did you get him?" Ed asked.

"No, he got away. Again." Reece's face was taut with frustration.

"We need to go before security gets up here. Someone's bound to have called downstairs." Sarah crossed the suite to the door. "Come on."

The group followed her out of the room and Nathaniel put the DO NOT DISTURB sign on the door and closed it. He did the same to the adjacent room. It would buy them a little time as no one would know where the noise had come from.

After collecting their things, they headed to the service elevator and traveled to basement two. Once out in the street the group split up and drove back to the night club in separate cars.

On the drive back, Reece's mind was reeling. The monster had managed to escape them again. Where would he go? And how could they find him?

CHAPTER FIFTY EIGHT

By the time Reece and his team arrived back at Decadent Desire it was 5.35 AM. The scenario had played out very differently to what they'd envisioned. Why? How could Dracula have known their plans unless someone told him? His thoughts returned to Arianne. Could she be acting as a double agent? Was she the one who had warned him of their plan to finish him while he slept? Reece pulled the keys from the ignition and climbed out of his convertible. Charlotte, Andre and Nathaniel had already gotten out of the passenger side of the car and were waiting for him by the back door.

As they were about to go in, Ed pulled into the alley behind Reece's midnight blue Mustang, turned off the engine and moved around the car to open the doors for Sarah and Arianne.

The seven members of the group made their way into the club. The place was deserted as it was Sunday and the night club's operating hours were Monday through Saturday. Nathaniel flicked on the auxiliary lighting and crossed the dance floor to the bar. "Would anyone like a nightcap?"

"Yeah, great idea," Ed said, climbing onto a black metal swivel stool at the counter and groaning from the pain of the injuries he'd sustained fighting Dracula's sons. His bruised shoulder and knee ached like a bitch.

"Make mine a double," Reece told him, sliding onto a seat next to his ex-boss. "You ok?"

"Yeah, I'll be fine. Just gettin' old."

"Nothing for me," Charlotte said. "I think I'll head up to bed."

Reece got off the stool and walked over to her. "Everything all right?" he said, frowning into her eyes.

Her right eyebrow rose. "After Dracula threatening to turn me into a vampire you mean? And almost being killed by him and his demons before that? Sure, everything's great."

He rubbed her arm affectionately. "Sweetheart, I didn't mean…"

Charlotte sighed. "I know. You never do." She turned on her heel and headed to the spiral staircase.

Ed frowned at Reece. "What was that all about?"

The PI returned to his stool, swallowed a large mouthful of whiskey and gave a heavy sigh. "She's not coping. I'd like to send her to stay with Mrs. Jenkins and Tommy but I can't. If Dracula found out where they were it would be catastrophic. Can you imagine the leverage it would give him?"

"Yeah, I can." Ed gulped down the last of his drink. "I wonder where he disappeared to."

"Good question. He could be anywhere by now." Reece checked his watch. 6.07 AM. "I'm heading up. Better try and get a couple hours' sleep."

"You're right." Ed looked at Sarah. "Coming up?"

Sarah nodded and slid from her stool. "I'm exhausted."

Andre, Nathaniel and Arianne remained at the bar. As immortals and a half immortal they didn't need as much rest. "We'll see you later," Andre said. "Sleep well."

Ed took Sarah's hand and led her across the night club. "Want me to tuck you in?" He gave her a cheeky wink.

"Don't tempt me," Sarah joked. She knew he was playing with her.

"See you in a couple of hours," Reece said and followed them over to the staircase.

When everyone was gone Andre turned to Arianne and Nathaniel and said, "Ok what's the plan?"

"I think I know where he has gone," Nathaniel told him.

"Where?" Andre and Arianne said together. They glanced at each other and smiled.

"To Nicolae's hotel room. It is obvious Vlad knew where he was staying so why not make use of it?"

"Why would he? It's too close." Andre frowned.

"And you do not believe he wants to be close? Think about it. He would not contemplate that we would consider Nicolae's accommodations as his place of refuge after what he has done. He would think we would reason he had fled Los Angeles."

"Nathaniel could be right," Arianne said. "Although I don't know much about my father, except he's a bloodthirsty psychopath, it seems like something he would do to trick us into thinking he was gone."

"So what do you want to do? Go there and check it out?" Andre slid from his stool.

"It would be wise to formulate a plan before going there. Do you not agree?"

"We can't make any more mistakes where he's concerned. He's going to be hell bent on taking revenge for the deaths of his sons." A look of awareness crossed Andre's face. "You're right. He'll be laying low planning his next attack on us."

"Perhaps it is time for us to do something without the others." Nathaniel's left eyebrow arched over his intense gaze.

"What do you have in mind?" Andre asked.

"He would expect us to use Arianne to lure him out again. So it is not an option."

Arianne sighed. "I wish it had worked the first time. It should have been him and not Nicolae who died."

"He is cunning and well prepared. He knows how to use the people we love to manipulate and weaken us." Nathaniel came around the bar. "I think it is time to make it work to our advantage."

"How?" Both Andre and Arianne said together and gave each other another smile.

"By using me as bait." Sarah came up behind them.

"No. We're not doing that." Andre shook his head.

"It's the only way. He won't suspect it's a ruse to lure him to the night club so we can finish him once and for all." Sarah slid onto the stool to Andre's left.

"Ok. I'm listening." Andre rested an elbow on the counter.

"You have to go to his hotel and pretend you want to make a trade. Arianne for me…"

"It won't work and it'll put us all in danger. We don't know how many he has working for him. Just because we've seen two of his men doesn't mean there isn't more. He won't come alone, not after what happened here.

He wouldn't put himself at that kind of risk again. We all know that."

"Yes, we do. But he craves me more and his hunger for wanting me dead will be his undoing. He will come."

"What about Reece, Charlotte and Ed?" Andre knew they wouldn't buy it.

"We'll explain everything to them when they wake up. They don't have to be here. They can leave and we," Sarah said, glancing at the huge black vampire, "and Nathaniel's team can finish what we started."

"Reece won't go for it. He'll want to be here." Andre slid from his stool and paced.

"Maybe you can convince him to take Charlotte and Ed and go to Mrs. Jenkins' house."

Andre turned around. "He said he wouldn't do it because we don't know if we're being watched and it would be too risky."

Reece came down the spiral staircase. "What's going on?" he asked, padding across the night club in bare feet and joining everyone at the bar.

"Couldn't sleep?" Andre's gaze moved to his friend.

"No. Charlotte's sleeping though, which is a good thing." He folded his arms. "What did I interrupt?"

"Nothing. We're just…"

"Working on a plan to take down Dracula without me?" His left eyebrow rose and his gaze ran around the guilty faces.

Sarah sighed. "You got us. We've come up with an idea I think will work."

"Ok, fill me in?"

"Andre can set up a meeting in the lobby of the hotel, he'll be safe there. He can tell Vlad he wants to make a trade. Me for Arianne."

Reece frowned into the priest's eyes. "And you think that'll work? Are you nuts? It isn't safe and he'll know right away we're trying to con him."

"I don't think so. He's wanted my scalp for a long time. If Andre tells him he's in love with Arianne and he's prepared to hand me over in her place I know he'll buy it. He wants us to turn on each other. He gets pleasure from ruining people's lives. Strength in numbers, remember? If he believes he's breaking down the bond between us he'll think he's won."

"And once Andre does, what then?"

"He'll set up a meeting here at Decadent Desire at sunset and we'll be ready for him, inside this time. It'll be far more difficult for him to get away. Nathaniel's team will help us so there will be plenty of back up," Sarah told him. "It's our only chance."

"It is the best opportunity we have," Nathaniel said. "There are already certain measures in place here."

Reece's jaw tightened and his serious gaze moved to the vampire. "Like what?"

"Ultraviolet lighting that covers the center of the club." He raised his huge muscled arm and pointed to each corner of the ceiling. "There, there, there... and there. We also fitted a sanctified silver net." He pointed to the center of the matt black ceiling above the blue and pink disco lights. "There."

"You have been busy." Reece's gaze moved around the devices. "As long as you, Andre or any of your team don't get trapped under it in the process it could work."

"After what happened with MacKinnon and his men I thought it wise to take some necessary precautions."

"So what do you think?" Sarah asked.

"Where were you thinking of sending us while all of this took place?"

Nathaniel moved behind the bar, pulled four shot glasses from the shelf and poured whiskey into each. "I suggested Andre ask you to take Charlotte and Ed to Mrs. Jenkins'."

"No can do."

"Yes, Andre explained why." Nathaniel thought it was the best place for them but understood the PI's reasons for not wanting to risk it.

"Ed could take Charlotte to St. Joseph's," Sarah offered. "It would be safe there."

"I don't think either of them will want to go." Reece raised the shot glass to his lips and swallowed the amber fluid in one gulp. "We're all in this together, like it or not."

CHAPTER FIFTY NINE

Andre sat in the lobby of the Roosevelt Hotel strumming his fingers on the arm of the brown leather chair. He was anxious. Coming face to face with Dracula in such close proximity caused a fist of dread to tighten around his gut. Would the most notorious vampire of all time buy what he was selling? He hoped Sarah was right. He swallowed the fear and stood as Vlad approached him, extending his hand.

Their meeting had to appear cordial so he took the monster's hand and gave it a firm shake.

"How did you know where to find me?" Vlad asked, pulling his knee-length Baroque style, gold and black patterned coat around his tall, well-built frame, taking a seat opposite Andre and crossing one leg over the other. The conversation was all very civilized.

"It wasn't difficult to figure out. I knew you wouldn't leave LA without Arianne so…"

Vlad eyed Andre sternly. "You thought you would approach me and what?"

"I – I'm in love with your daughter. I want her to stay here with me and I'm prepared to offer you a trade."

The vampire's right eyebrow arched. "A trade?" A smirk spread across his serious features. It amused him that this vampire would betray his people in such a way, and it pleased him. "Whom do you plan to offer as a replacement?"

"I know you want the priest. I don't care why. I'm offering her to you."

Andre shifted uncomfortably in his seat. He hated the pretense of doing something like this.

Vlad sat in silence summing up the immortal sitting opposite him. Was he telling the truth? "Are you prepared to marry my daughter to keep her with you?"

Andre wasn't expecting such a question. He swallowed hard, his Adam's apple bobbing. "Yes, I am. I love her that much."

"Mm." Vlad leaned forward. "Where do you want to make this *trade*?"

"Sunday at Decadent Desire after sundown. The night club is closed so no one will be there. You can enter through the alley unseen and I'll be waiting inside with Sarah."

"How do you plan to get her there?"

"I'll tranquilize her. Shouldn't be difficult."

A satisfied smile spread across Vlad's clean shaven face. At last he would rid himself of the one person who knew as much about him as he did himself. She had been a thorn in his side for far too long and it would be a pleasure to dispatch her from this world to the next.

He pursed his lips, his dark gaze remaining on Andre.

Those steel fingers in Andre's gut squeezed tighter and he did his best to remain composed. He couldn't allow the vampire to sense his discomfort. Would Dracula take the bait?

CHAPTER SIXTY

Sunday evening, everything was in place to take down the monster once and for all. Reece, Charlotte and Ed dressed in Kevlar jackets, pushed intricate earpieces into their ears and checked their weapons. Communication between them was vital in order to stay alive. Reece had given in to his fiancée. He hoped it would give her some closure.

Nathaniel briefed his team of four and they dissolved into the shadows. They didn't need weapons.

Andre and Sarah waited on a deep purple, two seat sofa wedged against a mirrored wall on the left-hand side of the dance floor and Arianne crouched behind the bar gripping Sarah's crossbow in nervous, sweaty hands. Nathaniel had hunkered down at the other end with an automatic rifle. Everyone was situated in the perfect vantage point to end Vlad's life. Now the waiting game began.

The tension in the room was as thick as molasses.

They had no idea what plans the vampire had implemented to protect himself. How many men, immortal and human, he would bring with him tonight.

Nathaniel could communicate with Andre telepathically but wasn't sure if Dracula could hear their thoughts so he would only use that method if absolutely necessary.

The hinges squeaked as the heavy, red leather padded door drew back and Vlad entered the night club.

Sarah closed her eyes and went limp on the sofa before his discerning gaze moved in their direction and Andre stood up. "I wasn't sure you'd come."

"I always keep my word, no matter what I have promised." He strutted across the floor. "I see you have kept yours."

"I always keep my promises too." Andre's eyes moved to the doorway. Standing in the shadows were two men dressed in black. Humans. He could smell the sour stench of fear in their sweat. They had weapons. "You didn't trust me?"

"I trust no one." A lopsided smirk spread across his face and he gazed around the room. "Where is Arianne?"

"I didn't think it was necessary to bring her. We agreed on Sarah for Arianne."

Vlad waved the comment away. "Yes, yes, I am aware of our agreement. But there has been a change of plan."

"Wait. You said you always keep your word. What kind of change?" Andre took a step back to be closer to Sarah who had a weapon for him underneath her cushion. "You said you wanted Sarah." He motioned toward the priest. "Well here she is."

"I know what I said." He stopped and turned around, his gaze moving around the dimly lit night club again. "But plans can always be altered. As you well know." His eyes returned to Andre.

Reece's finger was itchy on the trigger of his Glock. He wanted to leap out of his hiding place and shoot the monster right between the eyes. Andre was in danger.

"Arianne? I know you are here. I can smell your scent," Vlad called, his eyes moving to the bar. "Come out where I can see you." It was not a request but an order.

The young woman swallowed hard and frowned at Nathaniel. He nodded.

Arianne lowered her weapon onto the floor and reluctantly climbed to her feet.

"Ah. There you are." He motioned for her to come to him.

She didn't move. Fear pinned her to the spot.

"I asked you to come here." Her father's words were harsh.

Arianne tried to move but her legs wouldn't cooperate.

Dracula's hand moved so fast no one saw it. He dug his claws into the flesh of Andre's breast over his heart, blood seeping around his fingers into the black and white check shirt Andre had on. "If you do not move now I will rip out your lover's heart."

Arianne pushed herself forward, her shallow breathing ragged. Their plan had failed yet again.

"That is more like it. Come." He waved her over and retrieved his hand from Andre's chest. Andre slumped to the floor, holding his heaving chest, blood spreading across the front of his shirt.

"What is it you want?" She attempted to steady her wavering voice. "You made a deal and you should honor it."

Her father gave her a satisfied smirk. "And I will, but only if you give me a few minutes of your time."

"Why?"

"You are my daughter. It has been many years…"

Right at that moment all hell broke loose. Everyone in the room sprang from their positions and opened fire on Dracula. Sprays of cartridges and smoke filled the room, the acrid smell of gunpowder hovering in the air.

Reece rushed forward and dragged Andre out of the monster's grasp. Ed and Charlotte continued to fire off silver bullets at the vampire. Sarah sprang from the sofa, raced across to the bar, snatched up her crossbow and fired. He was too fast. Every round of ammunition missed him. He grabbed Arianne and whisked her through the open doorway. His men slammed the door behind him and locked it.

Nathaniel, Reece and Ed shot out of the front entrance and around to the alley.

Arianne's arms and legs flailed as she fought to free herself.

"Do not struggle, my dear. I would not want to hurt you." He tugged her over to the waiting limousine, threw her into the back seat and climbed in. The car sped away before the others could reach it. Reece stood in the center of the alleyway firing continuous rounds at the swiftly moving vehicle hoping to take out a tire. It disappeared into the dark.

"Now what?" Ed asked, panting. He was getting too old for this shit.

Reece turned around and gave a heavy sigh. "I don't know."

"We have to go after them." Andre stalked up to his friend, fully recovered.

"Do you know where they're going because I sure as hell don't?" Reece stood with his hands on his hips. "He won't go back to the hotel. That's a given."

"We can't let him take her."

Reece scowled. "He already has, Andre."

Sarah and Charlotte raced around the corner and into the alley. "What happened?" Charlotte asked.

"He got away."

"Well let's follow him," Sarah said.

Reece folded his arms. "He's long gone. Where do you suggest we look?"

"Let's see if we can catch up to them." Sarah frowned into the PI's eyes. "We have to try."

He sighed. "All right, but I think it's a waste of time."

The group headed for the night club's van. Nathaniel screeched out into the alley and hurtled the vehicle in the direction of the limousine.

CHAPTER SIXTY ONE

The limousine traveled along the highway at breakneck speed, heading toward Los Angeles. Vlad had rented a property in the Hollywood Hills and knew the PI and his team would not be able to find him. He would make them pay for the demise of his sons. He glanced at his daughter pressed into the corner of the back seat. She would make up for that loss. Once they were in his villa he would turn her before anything else could interfere with his plans.

Arianne's eyes moved surreptitiously to him. Her heart thumped in her chest as she wondered if she could throw the door open and leap from the fast-moving vehicle before he could stop her. She eased her hand across to the handle, wrapped clammy fingers around the shiny metal lever and pulled. The door didn't release.

"No point in trying to escape, my dear. The doors are quite secure," he told her, keeping his gaze forward.

Tears stung the backs of her eyes. "Why are you doing this? You made a deal with Andre... Sarah for me."

"Yes, but I knew Andre would not allow me to take the priest. I was aware there were humans and vampires in the night club." He turned his severe gaze to her. "Did you all believe me to be that foolish? I am always prepared for the unexpected. It has kept me alive for centuries and will continue to do so."

"They'll be looking for me." She knew it sounded desperate but she didn't care.

"I hope so."

"You're planning to kill them, aren't you?" Her eyes widened and a single tear slid down her right cheek.

"Eliminate the competition, as I have always done." He gave her a satisfied smile.

"Why did you take Charlotte? Why didn't you go after Sarah?"

Her father shifted in his seat and faced her. "I knew Andre's brother, Jacques. And I had heard on the immortal grapevine what they did to him. We had had many a blood ravaging adventure together while in Europe. I considered him a trustworthy comrade."

"Did you plan on killing her?" Arianne's body stiffened.

"Of course, but that wench Oriana rescued her while I slept."

Arianne swallowed the lump of nerves threatening to choke her. She had to get out of the car somehow. "Who's next?"

"I do not have a set list. Whoever crosses my path first, I would expect."

"Would you let them live if I promise to stay with you?"

He gave her a peculiar smile. "No. I will exact revenge for my sons' and Jacques' untimely deaths."

"But you don't have to. Please let them go. Please!" The high pitch strain in her nervous voice echoed in her ears.

"Arianne, do not beg. It is unbecoming of a countess."

"I am not a countess. I'm me. I will never be like you." She squeezed herself further away from him.

"But my dear, you are like me. My blood runs in your veins. You *are* mine."

"I am no one's." She folded her arms.

"Not even Andre's?"

She gave him a dark sideward glance and didn't answer.

80C3

Nathaniel whipped the van up the on ramp and onto the 110 highway heading north. He could sense the vampire was not too far ahead. He pushed the accelerator to the floor and weaved in and out of the speeding lanes of traffic. "I can sense him. The car is up ahead."

"Then step on it," Reece ordered, his voice tense. "We need to stay close and make sure they don't get off the freeway before we catch up to them."

"Very well. Hold on." Nathaniel swung the van out into the left lane of traffic, car horns blaring behind him, and hurtled along the multilane carriageway. He spotted the limousine a few cars in front and edged in and out of the vehicles until they were one car behind. Vlad nor his driver would recognize the van so he wouldn't suspect they were on his tail.

"Don't let him slip away, Nathaniel." Reece gripped the dash and peered through the windshield.

"I will not."

The limousine slid across the lanes toward the next exit ramp. Nathaniel squeezed the van into the rows of cars and remained in hot pursuit.

Andre leaned between the front seats. "They're getting off the freeway."

"We're on it," Reece said, tension resonating in his voice.

"He's heading for Hollywood."

Reece frowned. "Yeah. I wonder where he's going."

The tinted windows on the van would afford them some anonymity. They continued to follow the prestige, black sedan at a distance as it traveled along Sunset Boulevard.

"Perhaps he's using another hotel," Sarah suggested.

"Maybe," Reece answered vaguely, his mind sifting through all the places the monster could hide.

The limousine's right indicator flashed on.

"They're turning into the hills." Andre sat back and stared out of the passenger window.

"He must have found a place up there." *Smart move.* "He knew we'd check hotels for new reservations, so he leased a property," Reece deduced.

Nathaniel was about to turn into the narrow uphill street when Reece gripped his arm. "Wait. Give them a few seconds then follow."

"We need to keep close, Reece. Those streets twist and turn. We could lose them if we don't stay on them." Andre's stomach clenched.

"He's right. They could drive into a garage and we'd miss them." Sarah peered out of her window.

"Ok, ok, keep on them, Nathaniel." Reece jabbed at the air. "They're making a left."

"I see that." Nathaniel slowed the van and waited until the limousine was just out of sight. He followed.

The black car kept traveling higher.

"The house must be right up top," Reece said.

"You don't think they know we're following them, do you?" Sarah asked. "I mean, why would a van like this be up here?"

"Catering?"

She frowned at him.

The limousine slowed and pulled into the driveway of a modern, concrete two story house with high fence line.

"Stop!" Reece said. "Don't get too close. We can't afford to be seen."

The automatic double garage door glided upward and the driver eased the vehicle into the large space, the gray metal door rolling down again once the car was inside.

"It's like a fortress." Sarah observed the six feet concrete wall surrounding the property and solid, black metal double gates. "How are we going to get in there to rescue Arianne?"

CHAPTER SIXTY TWO

Vlad exited the vehicle and leaned into the open doorway. "Coming?" he asked, gazing at the young woman pressed against the other passenger door. "You will be more comfortable inside the house than out here. There is no way for you to escape, Arianne. The garage door is automatic and my driver and I are the only ones with remote controls, so you might as well take advantage of the luxurious surroundings while you are here."

The door swung away from her and she almost fell out of the limousine. The driver gripped her arm to prevent her from landing on the concrete floor. Arianne shrugged out of his grasp. "Don't touch me."

"We can do this the easy way or the hard way, the choice is yours." Vlad moved around the trunk of the car and stood at the open doorway. "Well?"

Arianne's gaze met his. "All right. I'll come inside. But it doesn't mean I'm doing what you want. It's my decision." She eyed him darkly as she stepped out of the vehicle.

"Have it your way." He knew she would do exactly what he wanted. He gestured for her to move ahead of him. She had a fighting spirit which would serve him well once she was a full-blood. And he would use it to his advantage.

The home was opulent with a large galley kitchen, formal living room, a white grand piano standing in front of the floor to ceiling windows framing the large fireplace, and plush cream carpeting throughout.

Vlad removed his black leather gloves and sat his elaborate walking cane with the etched gold handle by the coffee colored sofa. "Show my daughter to her room," he ordered.

The driver grasped Arianne by her forearm and marched her to the cascading staircase. She tried to pull free but his grip was too strong. She sighed and allowed him to escort her to one of the many bedrooms on the top floor. What else could she do? As they walked the wide lengthy hallway, Arianne's eyes took in every detail of her surroundings. Was there a way to escape?

Vlad's manservant opened the door and pushed her into the room. "Don't try anything. There is surveillance throughout the entire house so we'll be watching you." He closed the door and locked it.

Arianne plonked herself onto the king sized bed with a huff. *How can I get out of here?* Her eyes moved around the ceiling. A camera in the right-hand corner. She got up and wandered into the bathroom. One in the left-hand corner. She moved back into the bedroom and walked over to the window. Were Andre and the others out there somewhere? Would they attempt to rescue her or did they think she was where she wanted to be?

"I can fly over the wall," Nathaniel told them. "They would not see me in the dark and I could check the upstairs rooms for Arianne."

"I know you could, but we all need to get in there at the same time," Reece said. "We don't know how many there are inside and you couldn't handle them all on your own."

"He's right," Ed agreed. "It's too risky."

Reece's eyes moved to the garage. "Could you lift up the door long enough for us to climb underneath?"

"Yes. But what if it is alarmed?" Nathaniel's gaze moved to the double metal door.

"Mm. Good point."

"We have to get in there, Reece. Who knows what he's doing to her. He could've turned her already." Andre's worried gaze met his friend's.

"Look, Andre, we have to be prepared. So far our efforts to take him down have failed. We need to get in there and make sure we do it right this time."

"I can't sit around and wait for you to come up with a plan." Andre slid back the side door on the van and jumped out.

"Andre, come back here!" Reece whispered loudly.

His friend kept moving.

Nathaniel stepped out of the van. "I will go with him and make sure he doesn't do anything stupid."

Reece nodded. "Thanks."

"We have to get inside," Sarah said. "We can't leave those two to deal with Dracula alone."

"I know." Reece's eyes rested on the boxes of wine in the back of the van. He remembered taking out Jacques' vamps with Molotov cocktails. Maybe they could do the same now. Or at least set a fire in the yard to draw them out.

"I have an idea."

"What?" Ed folded his arms and stared at the PI.

"Molotov cocktails." He pointed to the unopened boxes sitting at the back of the van. "What if we create a diversion?"

"It still doesn't solve the problem of getting inside," Sarah told him.

"While Vlad's guys are dealing with the fire Nathaniel can open the small gate beside the garage."

"Good idea," Ed said. "Let's get to work."

"I'll send Nathaniel a text." Reece pulled his cell phone from the back pocket of his jeans.

Nathaniel would be ready to let them in the moment the fire was out of control.

Arianne noticed a dark shadow under the trees. *Nathaniel?* She breathed a relieved sigh. They had come for her. She wondered how the others were going to get into the yard. Perhaps she should cause some kind of diversion. She pounded on the bedroom door. "Vlad? Vlad, I want to talk to you."

An explosion of bright orange light lit up her room and she rushed to the full length window and pressed her face against the huge pane. The bushes and trees in the yard were on fire, the flames spreading rapidly.

She spotted Nathaniel and Andre. Her heartbeat thundered in her chest. She loved Andre so much.

When he glanced up and saw her he gave her a reassuring smile. They were coming for her.

Nathaniel flew across the yard and unlocked the latched gate.

Reece and the others entered the yard, keeping to the shadows.

No one had come outside.

Arianne pressed her hands against the window pane and smiled at Andre. Just as she was about to turn around, Vlad stepped up and punched her in the face, catching her as her unconscious body slumped into his arms.

Andre's face contorted in pain as he watched the vampire carry Arianne out of the room. "We have to go in now!" he yelled. "He's moving her."

Nathaniel raised his massive, muscular leg and hefted his booted, size fifteen foot at the elegant, double white front doors. They flew open and the group surged into the mansion, weapons raised.

The driver hurtled himself at them, fangs bared, but Nathaniel swatted him like a fly and once subdued on the ground twisted his neck. There didn't seem to be anyone else in the mansion apart from Dracula and Arianne.

They poured through the lower level of the extensive property. No one.

As they were about to climb the staircase, Vlad appeared on the landing clutching Arianne to him, his hand around her throat. "Toss your weapons over there and step back or I will end her."

The group did as he asked. Reece's jaw clenched, his intense gaze remaining on the monster. He had another gun on his ankle under his jeans. Could he reach it and take a shot without jeopardizing Arianne's safety? He let the idea circle his mind, imagining the various scenarios. Was it worth the risk? He decided against it. For the moment.

"Now, step back into the living room. And don't make any sudden moves." Vlad pushed Arianne forward and they descended the stairs.

Sirens rang out in the distance. The fire department was on its way.

Vlad turned his head toward the distant sound and Reece pulled his weapon and fired. The bullet whisked past the vampire's ear and was enough to distract him. Arianne tugged free and flew down the staircase.

Everyone grappled for their weapons but when they looked up Dracula was gone.

He's still here somewhere. Spread out. We have to find him!" Reece ordered, his voice tight.

The group split up and moved through the property.

CHAPTER SIXTY THREE

The tension in the mansion was palpable as they cautiously made their way through the extensive home: Reece and Charlotte upstairs, Nathaniel, Arianne and Andre downstairs in the basement and Sarah and Ed on the ground floor. As the groups moved through the numerous rooms, keeping their eyes and ears alert, the lights snapped off. They were in the dark except for the orange glow of the fire through various windows in the house. The sirens of the fire trucks were getting closer. They would converge on the mansion within minutes. They had to find Dracula, finish him and get out before they arrived.

Everyone wore earpieces to communicate with each other.

"Anything?" Reece asked.

"No, nothing," Nathaniel replied.

"Same, nothing," Ed said. "What now?"

"We keep looking. He has to be here."

"What if he got out?" Sarah offered.

"I don't think he did. He likes to play games with people. And who turned out the lights?"

"Yeah, you're right." Ed and Sarah continued through the lower level to the library.

Reece and Charlotte moved along the upper hallway, guns in hand. Vlad had been midway on the stairs so he could've gone up or down. Vampires moved too fast to see, which gave them the advantage.

The pair stepped up to the first closed door and Reece gripped the handle. He gave her hand signals similar to a baseball catcher, counted to three with his fingers, threw the door open and swept the room with the beam of his flashlight and weapon. Both entered and eased themselves across to the bathroom. The door was closed. Again, they went through the same motions and Reece threw open the door. Still nothing.

He gave a frustrated sigh. "Let's move to the next room. He's here. I know it."

Nathaniel, Arianne and Andre stepped into the huge underground basement which ran the length of the building. Andre could sense something, but wasn't sure what it was. Maybe Dracula had other immortals with him lying in wait down here.

Arianne turned to him. "There's something down here."

Nathaniel stopped. "Yes, I sense it too."

"Vampire." Andre's immortal vision scanned the underground room.

"Most assuredly," Nathaniel agreed.

"Then why aren't they attacking?"

The large vampire moved ahead of the pair. "Stay behind me."

Ed and Sarah ran the beam of their flashlights around the massive library. Solid wood shelves stacked with books lined the walls from ceiling to floor. Sarah noticed something about the bookshelf across from them and walked over to it. "Ed, can you shine your light on here for a minute?"

He wandered over to her and directed the bright circle of light to where she was pointing.

Sarah pocketed her flashlight. "Looks like a doorway to me. What do you think?" She ran her fingers down the crease in the shelves.

"You could be right," Ed said. "Wonder how it opens."

"There has to be a lever here somewhere." Sarah felt along the shelves, moving books. Nothing.

Ed frowned at the crease between the shelves. He poked his podgy finger into it and moved it up and down. "I feel somethin'," he said.

A metallic click echoed into the room and the shelf swung inward.

After checking all the rooms on the top floor, confident Dracula wasn't up there, Reece and Charlotte headed downstairs to Ed and Sarah. They wandered through the living room, dining room, study and on to the library. Sarah and Ed weren't there.

"Chief, where are you?" Reece asked, knowing his ex-boss could hear him through the earpiece.

No answer.

Reece frowned at Charlotte. "They were in here before we came downstairs. Where could they have gone?"

"Maybe they're checking the kitchen and laundry. Or the garage."

A sharp click echoed into the room and Reece and Charlotte spun around, weapons ready to fire.

Ed stepped out of the shelf door into the library, Sarah following him. "You gonna shoot me, are ya?" He raised his hands to his eyes to stifle the glare from the pair's flashlights.

Reece and Charlotte lowered their lights and weapons. "What's in there?" Reece asked.

"Come and see for yourself." Ed waved them over and stepped aside.

"A panic room."

"Yeah, pretty nifty, huh?" Ed followed them in.

Reece walked over to inspect the solid metal door in the opposite wall. "Did you check where this goes?"

"We couldn't open it," Sarah told him. "But my guess would be the basement."

"So Dracula could've gone through here and be laying wait downstairs." Reece spun around. "Let's get down there now!"

CHAPTER SIXTY FOUR

Vlad could hear his daughter's ragged, nervous breathing. They had no idea how close he was. A sly smile spread across his face. Andre was in for a shock, one he would never have expected and was not prepared for. The vampire remained in the shadows. It would not be long before they found the gift he had left for him.

Nathaniel sensed a hostile presence ahead. He stopped and turned around. "I sense an aggressive immortal. She is ravenous. If she is free she will attack."

Andre's right eyebrow rose. "She?"

"Yes."

"Do you know who it is?" Arianne stepped up beside Andre.

Nathaniel didn't answer.

"Who is it, Nathaniel?" Andre's intense gaze rested on the vampire.

"Let us continue." Nathaniel led the way through the maze of boxes, covered furniture and other items.

Andre's skin prickled, his anxiety getting the better of him. *She? Who is it?*

They came to a closed wood-planked door containing a huge, steel lock.

Nathaniel gripped the lock in his large fist and gave it a firm yank. The body fell away from the loop and he unbolted the door. "You must be prepared for what is inside, Andre. You cannot allow it to hinder our mission."

"What's in there?" Andre's gut tightened.

"The question you may want to consider is *who* is in there."

The trio stepped into the dark space.

A vicious, hungry growl emanated from a covered cage.

"I believe he left this for you to find." Nathaniel stepped aside making room for Andre to move closer to the container.

Andre swallowed hard. His gut churned.

Arianne shone her flashlight at the metal crate covered with a canvas tarp. "Don't, Andre, please." She was afraid for him. Her heartbeat raced and her hand wavered. She moved her left hand to the flashlight to steady it.

Andre reached out and lifted the hem of the cover.

Reece and the others rushed into the room. "Andre, don't!" he shouted. "Step away from the cage."

"No, Reece, I have to know who's under here." He threw back the cover.

Dracula edged his way closer through the shadows. He wanted to see Andre's reaction.

"Beth!" He stared at her in disbelief, tears stinging the backs of his eyes. How could this have happened?

Reece rushed forward and pulled his friend backwards. "She's not Beth anymore. She's dangerous."

The ravenous vampire clawed at him and the others through the bars, fangs bared, growling like an animal.

"She needs to be put out of her misery." Reece raised his Glock, aiming for her heart.

Andre knocked the gun aside. "No!"

"It's the only humane thing to do," Sarah said. "She'll never be the same Beth you knew, Andre."

He turned his intense gaze toward the priest. "You're not shooting her."

A metallic snap echoed around the room and the cage sprang open. Beth lunged at the door and it swung back with a loud clang as it hit the brick wall.

"Get out of here!" Reece shouted, stepping back. "Andre, come on."

The group made a dash for the door but it slammed shut.

"Holy crap," Ed said, spinning around, his weapon raised, his breathing ragged. "What do we do now?"

Beth rushed at them, mouth open, snarling like a beast.

A loud boom and a bright flash lit up the room.

The vampire hit the ground and disintegrated into ash.

Charlotte stood off to the side, her weapon still raised.

Andre rushed over to the pile of smoldering ash. "Why?"

"Because she would've killed you." Charlotte holstered her 9mm. "I did what was necessary."

"How're we gonna get outta here?" Ed asked, staring at the solid wood door.

"Move." Nathaniel stalked up to him.

Ed eyeballed the black vampire with a scowl.

Nathaniel gripped the knob and tugged at it. The door didn't budge. He tried again. Still nothing.

"What now?" Reece said.

"I will get it open," Nathaniel reassured, stepping back to shoulder the door. It didn't move.

"Must be reinforced," Charlotte offered.

"We need something to lever it with." Reece shone his flashlight around the tight space. "There."

In the corner sat a tire iron on top of a set of old tires. He rushed over and picked it up. "This should do the trick." He handed it to Nathaniel.

The vampire wedged the iron rod into the crease of the door and pulled. A huge crack boomed in the room and the door swung outward.

The group spilled into the cellar. When Reece turned around Andre was still kneeling on the floor beside the pile of ash. The PI stalked back into the room. "I'm sorry, Andre, but Charlotte was right. It had to be done." He glanced over his shoulder. "We need to go."

Andre's blood-teared eyes gazed up at him. "I loved her."

"I know you did." He reached out his hand. "Let's get back upstairs. It's not safe down here."

His friend took his hand and climbed to his feet, wiping the tears from his face. "I'm going to *kill* him." Andre stormed out of the room and disappeared along the dark basement in a blur.

By the time Reece and the others made it back upstairs Andre was nowhere to be found. They checked every room in the mansion. He was gone. Arianne's heart ached for him. She wasn't angry because he still loved

Beth. She knew Beth had been an important part of his life at one time. All she was concerned about now was what would happen when Andre found her father?

"How are we going to locate Andre?" Sarah asked.

"I think he'll head back to our place before doing anything else. We have some weapons of our own stashed in the apartment he'll want to make use of."

"I can go ahead through the air and prevent him from leaving, if you want me to," Nathaniel offered.

"Thanks. Keep him there any way you can."

Nathaniel left the mansion and took to the air.

The rest of the team exited the house through the garage side door, noticing the limousine was missing. Dracula had used it to escape. The fire department was on top of the fire and Reece didn't want the group to be seen. They made their way back to the van and the PI stepped up into the driver's seat. "I hope Nathaniel catches Andre before he gets away, otherwise we'll have no idea where he is either. It's too dangerous for him to be chasing Dracula alone."

"Check the tablet, Reece," Arianne said, pointing to the electronic device lying on the dashboard.

"Why?"

"I slipped something into Vlad's pocket." She smiled.

Reece picked up the iPad and clicked on the tracking program. A red dot beeped on the screen. He turned around and peered between the front seats. "Good thinking."

"Thanks."

The PI passed the tablet to his ex-boss, started the engine and eased the van away from the curb, squeezing past the fire trucks parked in the middle of the narrow road, Reece headed in the direction of the red dot.

CHAPTER SIXTY FIVE

Nathaniel stepped out of the elevator and stalked along the hallway to Andre and Reece's apartment. The door was ajar. Reece had been right. The vampire stepped up to threshold and ran his eyes around the room. No sign of Andre. But he knew he was still here. He moved into the apartment, closed the door quietly and walked down the short hall to the bedrooms.

Andre was sitting on the bed, a photo of Beth in his hands, bloody tears running down his face. His head snapped up. "What are you doing here?"

"I came to make sure you are all right." The huge vampire filled the doorway.

"No, I'm not all right. I had always hoped I would see her again one day. Talk to her. Make sense of what happened between us. Now it can never happen."

"I am sorry for your loss but, as I said in the basement, you cannot allow it to deter you from what has to be done."

"It won't," Andre said, his voice etched with determination. "When I find the monster I will end him for what he's done."

"And how do you plan to find him?" Nathaniel folded his arms across his broad muscular chest.

"I don't know yet, but I will." He stood, walked around the bed, placed the photo frame in the drawer and closed it.

Nathaniel's cell phone vibrated and he whipped it from his pocket. "What is it?"

"We're on our way to where Dracula is headed. Arianne slipped a tracker into his pocket. I'll let you know when we're at the location so you and Andre can meet us there."

"Very well. I will await your call." He slid his phone back into his pants pocket. "Reece. They are tracking him."

"How?" Andre crossed the room.

"Arianne hid a device on him."

"Let's go." Andre pushed past Nathaniel and headed to the door.

"Reece will call back to let us know the destination when Vlad arrives there."

Andre paced. "I don't want to wait. Let's get in the car and drive."

"We have no idea in which direction." Nathaniel frowned.

"I can't just sit here."

Nathaniel walked up to him and gripped his shoulders. "You need to relax. Take a breath. We will be where he is soon enough."

৪৩৫৪

Reece traveled along Crystal Springs Drive and realized where they were going when the limousine turned onto Los Feliz Boulevard. "He's heading to the observatory." The PI eased on the brake allowing a few seconds between them before continuing his pursuit.

The black sedan made a right onto Hillhurst Avenue and continued toward the domed white building situated above Griffith Park and overlooking Los Angeles city. Reece turned the van onto the Avenue and followed. As it was well after closing time, no one would be around.

The winding drive was unnerving in the dark, the old fashioned style lampposts to their left emitting only a fraction of light onto the road.

"I wonder what he's planning to do up here," Sarah said. "It's obscure enough."

"Yeah, that's what worries me," Reece said, looking at her in the rearview mirror.

"He seems to be always well prepared," Ed added.

"Yeah, he does. I don't know how he knows our plans. It's as if..." Reece let the thought go as he turned off the headlights and stopped the van at the entrance to the observatory car park.

Vlad pulled the limousine into a parking bay close to the walkway and stepped out. He was alone. He stood beside the vehicle scanning the empty lot. Satisfied the group had followed him he disappeared around the building.

Reece eased the van off the road and turned off the engine. "Let's make sure we're prepared *this time*."

"Are you going to call Andre?" Arianne asked.

"No, I'm not."

"We could use Nathaniel's help," she told him.

"Yeah, we could, but it's better if Andre's not here. He's not in a good place right now and I wouldn't want anything to happen to him because he made a stupid move. Would you?"

Arianne averted her eyes from him. "No, I wouldn't."

Everyone climbed out of the van except her.

Reece turned around and gave her a curious frown. "Coming?"

"Yes. Can I have a minute?" She heaved a sigh.

"Ok, but don't take too long. We need everyone in place." Reece caught up to the others.

With no vampire assistance they were on their own. Arianne was well trained but couldn't do any of the things vampires could, like dissolve into the night and be unseen. Reece talked everyone through the plan. They would spread out and encircle Dracula from all sides, above and below to make sure their bases were covered. Had he known they would follow him here? Was it a setup? Definitely. Reece could feel it in his gut.

It would have taken around twenty five minutes to get from LA to Griffith Park, but Nathaniel had chosen to take to the air which got them there in record time. Once on the ground, they made their way to the back of the observatory. Reece, Charlotte and Ed were on the main level, Sarah was above and Arianne below.

Andre and Nathaniel came up behind Reece.

The PI swung around and aimed his Glock at the pair. "What the hell are you doing here?" He lowered his weapon and scowled at Nathaniel.

"I told you I wanted to kill Dracula for what he did to Beth but you were going to leave me out of it."

Reece figured Arianne had called him when she'd needed that minute. Stupid girl. Did she want to get Andre killed? He still wondered if she was working with her father, after all.

"Look, you're not in the right frame of mind to challenge him. Don't do something you'll regret... or make me regret."

"I can take care of myself, Reece. I'm an immortal, remember?"

"Yeah, so what? Dracula is faster, stronger and more powerful than any of us, including you. Don't make the mistake of letting him kill you." Reece was pissed at Arianne for telling his friend where they were.

"I won't," Andre said, turning to Nathaniel. "Come on. Let's find a good place to wait."

Reece gave a heavy sigh.

"I'll talk some sense into him," Ed said, passing Reece.

"No, Chief, leave it." Reece grabbed his ex-boss's arm.

"But..."

"I know. But he has to do what he has to do. We just need to make sure he doesn't get himself killed in the process."

"I can go as backup," Charlotte told him.

"I'll do it." Reece started off then stopped and turned around. "Watch each other's backs, ok?"

"Will do." Ed nodded.

Reece caught up to his friend. "Andre, wait. I'll go with you."

"You don't need to watch out for me. Nathaniel can do that."

"I want to help you get what you want. What we all want."

"Ok, then, let's go."

The trio headed to the upper level where Sarah was situated. It gave them a good view of the walkway around the building. They could see exactly where Dracula was.

They crept along the parapet making their way toward the priest. She saw them coming and stood up, pointing over the edge. "He's right below us," she mouthed.

Andre climbed onto the edge and looked down at the monster. Reece grabbed him and pulled him backwards off the ledge. "Are you insane?" he whispered. "You don't want him to see you, do you?"

"Yes, I do. I want to land on top of him and drain the undead life right out of him." Andre's face contorted with hate.

"This isn't you. Don't be like him because of what happened to Beth." Reece gripped his friend's arm.

Andre shrugged out of his grasp. "This is me. I *am* like him. I always have been only you didn't want to see it."

"I don't believe you. I know you, Andre, and I know you're nothing like him."

Sarah stood at the edge, crossbow in hand and frowned at Andre. He'd changed. It may have been grief or it may have been a shift in his nature. Either way, he was a danger to himself and everyone else. "Andre, please don't do anything to endanger yourself or us," Sarah whispered, her voice cracking. She hated seeing him like this.

Reece stepped away from the group for a moment. "Everyone move into position with caution," he said into his two-way radio. It was time to finish this.

CHAPTER SIXTY SIX

When Reece turned around Andre and Nathaniel were gone. Sarah was lying unconscious on the ground and her crossbow was missing. "Dammit!" Reece stalked along the roofline peering over the edge. He spotted Ed and Charlotte but couldn't find Arianne. *Where is she?* He broke into a run, raced down the stairs and along the arched walkway. When he caught up to the pair he told them what happened. They continued moving cautiously around the rotunda, their backs to the wall.

Somewhere close by a gun went off. Arianne.

Reece pointed for Ed and Charlotte to back around and come in from the other side.

He continued on alone, his Glock raised.

As he reached the place where he thought the gun had been fired, he peered around the circular wall. Dracula had Arianne in a death lock, Andre and Nathaniel standing in front of them, the crossbow lying on the ground near his feet.

Reece remained out of sight.

"Is this a case of déjà vu? Have we not already been in this position?" He pulled back on his daughter's head revealing her throat, his fangs locking into place.

"Don't!" Andre shouted, hurtling himself at the pair and knocking them to ground.

Nathaniel whipped across the concrete, grabbed Arianne and shoved her out of the way then joined Andre in an attempt to subdue the monster.

Dracula was far too strong, even for the both of them. He threw them off like unwanted clothing and drew a sword from under his longline jacket. "Stay back!"

Andre and Nathaniel did as instructed, neither wanting to be pierced by the silver sword Vlad wielded.

"You cannot beat me. No matter what you do." He laughed. "I am invincible." Vlad leapt forward and thrust the weapon at Andre but Arianne jumped in front of him and the sword pierced them both through the heart.

Vlad's haughty expression changed to stunned disbelief. He hadn't anticipated that his daughter would sacrifice herself for the man she loved.

Reece dashed around the wall and by the time he reached Andre his friend had disintegrated into ash. "Nooo!" He turned his furious gaze to the monster but he was gone. The PI fell to his knees beside Arianne. "You're going to be all right." His dazed eyes flashed to Nathaniel. "Call 911," he shrieked, his voice shattering.

"I... tried... to save... him," she gasped, a bloody trail trickling from the corner of her mouth. "I'm sorry." She exhaled her last breath, her eyes staring up at Reece.

"No! No, no, no." He sat on the ground and sobbed.

Ed and Charlotte rounded the building and stopped short when they saw him.

"What happened?" Ed asked, his face ashen, his stomach churning. Did he really want to know?

Reece looked up at him. "He's dead, Chief." A sob stuck in his throat and more tears spilled down his flushed face. "Andre's dead." His tear-filled eyes moved to the young woman lying beside him. "And so is Arianne." His head fell into his hands and he continued sobbing.

"No. It can't be," Ed said, moving closer. The black residue on the ground and Arianne were proof enough. Proof he didn't want to believe. A single tear slid down his cheek, his jowls quivered and he sniffled. "Andre," he whispered, his heart aching.

Charlotte stood and stared at the ash beneath Arianne's body, tears welling in her eyes. Andre and Arianne were gone.

Sarah staggered in from the direction Ed and Charlotte had come from, breathless. "Where's Andre? What happened to Dracula?" She was still dizzy from being knocked out.

Charlotte looked at the priest. "Andre's…" She shook her head vigorously, as if it would change the outcome. "Andre's dead."

"The monster has fled," Nathaniel said, his eyes remaining on the spot where Andre died. Even he couldn't believe what had happened.

Sarah rushed to Ed and he wrapped his arms around her. "It can't be true, Ed. It can't be." Tears stung the backs of her eyes and she let them spill. "Not Andre."

"I wish it wasn't, but it is." He held her close, his eyes welling

Charlotte walked over to Reece and crouched down in front of him. "I – I'm so sorry, Reece." She reached for him, wrapping her arms around his heaving body and burst into tears.

Reece realized this time it wasn't a horrible dream like the one he'd had when they fought Andre's brother, Jacques. It was real. His best friend, whom he loved, the man he'd called his brother was dead. He continued to sob into Charlotte's tight embrace.

CHAPTER SIXTY SEVEN

Ed and Nathaniel carried Arianne's body to the van, set it down in the back and covered it with a gray storage blanket. Sarah and Charlotte climbed into the back seat, along with Ed, and Reece and Nathaniel got into the front. All were still numb from what had occurred. No one could believe Andre was truly gone. Tears continued to slide down Reece's face and he sniffed back the urge to sob again. Nathaniel started the engine, eased the van into a U-turn and headed down the winding slope.

"Do you wish to go back to the night club?" Nathaniel asked.

Reece nodded but didn't speak.

They drove back to Decadent Desire in silence, each trying to come to terms with what had happened to Andre and Arianne. Dracula had eluded them again. How?

Once parked in the alleyway, everyone climbed out of the van and entered the club through the back door. Nathaniel and Reece had carried Arianne's body down to the freezer room next to the cellar and laid it beside her brother. Arrangements would have to be made for the bodies soon.

Nathaniel crossed the large room to the bar, sat five glasses on the countertop and poured whiskey into each. Everyone downed their drinks in one swallow.

"What do we do now?" Ed asked, his face still ashen. *Andre's dead.* He couldn't get his mind around it.

"I think we should try to get some sleep. It'll be daylight soon." Sarah yawned. "And we need our strength to fight and destroy the monster once and for all."

Reece swung his head around. "How, Sarah? How do we fight him when he continues to block our every move? And we have no idea where he is now?"

"He won't give up, Reece. He'll come at us again. And next time we need to be more than ready for him." Sarah slid off the stool. "He'll want to exact revenge for his sons and he won't stop until he does."

"She is right. We need a successful plan that will work," Nathaniel said, swallowing his drink in one hit.

"Do you expect he'll come here?" Charlotte asked, her face anxious.

"Yes, I do. He knows where we are so he'll formulate a scheme to take us out here. He'll have others working for him. Other immortals too, I expect. We have to come up with a way to eliminate his companions and finish him permanently." Sarah wanted to end her search for the monster for good. She wanted him dead. She wanted her quest to be over.

"We have the means to do it here," Nathaniel told them. "The lighting is in place and the silver net. We only need to lure him into the center of the club alone and we can end him."

"He's shrewd though. He seems to be one step ahead of us every time. It's like he knows what we're planning," Ed said, rubbing the back of his head. He climbed off the stool and wandered over to Sarah. "Let's get some shut eye for a couple hours and look at it again when we're rested."

Reece climbed off his stool and rubbed his fists into his red and tired eyes. He knew he wouldn't sleep. How could he? His friend was gone and he'd never see him again. The thought caused his eyes to water and he shoved it from his mind, otherwise he'd start crying again. Something he was sure he'd do once he was alone, anyway. "Yeah, good idea. We need to recoup and discuss it later."

"You are welcome to stay for as long as you need," Nathaniel offered.

"Thanks." Reece took Charlotte's hand and they followed Ed and Sarah across the night club to the spiral staircase. Before climbing them, Reece turned around and looked at Nathaniel. "Will you be ok on your own?"

"Of course. My team is here."

The PI ran his gaze around the dimly lit club but couldn't see anyone, although he knew they would be there ready to fight, when the time came.

Reece woke up coughing to the shrill sound of an alarm blaring through the PA system. He sprang up off the bed when he realized his room was filled with smoke. His eyes smarted as he fumbled for his clothes, threw them on, and staggered to the door. He felt the wood with the palm of his hand to make sure the fire hadn't spread upstairs then flung open the door and rushed along the hall to Charlotte's room. Pounding on the door, he called, "Charlotte, are you in there?"

Ed and Sarah emerged out of the gray smoke, coughing and gasping for air. "She could be downstairs already," Ed said, pulling Sarah along behind him and rushing to the stairs.

Reece shouldered Charlotte's door and it flew open. She wasn't inside. He frowned and stepped out into the corridor.

Nathaniel came up to him. "We need to get outside now. The fire department is on its way."

He and Reece made their way along the smoke hazed corridor and down the spiral staircase. The club was filled with smoke, meaning the fire had started downstairs.

As the pair stepped off the last step, they could see where the fire had begun. Orange flames licked the metal and glass door leading down to the cellar and heavy smoke seeped from underneath it.

"Have you seen Charlotte?"

"No, I have not. Perhaps she is outside."

Both men raced across the night club and out the exit. Sarah and Ed were standing in the alley but Charlotte wasn't with them. Where could she be? Was she still inside?

Reece made a dash for the doorway but Nathaniel grabbed his arm. "You cannot go back in there. It is too dangerous."

"Charlotte could still be inside. I have to go back." He shrugged out of the vampire's grip and disappeared into the smoke.

"Charlotte?" he called out, coughing. "Charlotte, are you in here?" His chest heaved and his lungs felt constricted. He coughed and coughed as he climbed the spiral stairs to the top floor and raced along the hallway to the other rooms and the office. No one. He hurried back along the corridor, his head dizzy. *Why wouldn't Charlotte have woken everyone up if she was the first to realize the club was on fire?* Just as the thought crossed his mind everything went black.

Dracula stood on the rooftop not far from the night club smiling. He had accomplished his task of getting everyone out of their safe haven. He watched the flames lick the sides of the building and burst through the painted windows. Decadent Desire was no more. He turned around and flew over the edge and onto the ground, the black limousine idling nearby, and climbed in.

Charlotte staggered along the alleyway toward her friends coughing, her lungs filled with smoke. A young paramedic who had appeared out of nowhere came up alongside her. "Let me help you," she said, placing a supporting arm around her.

When Reece spotted the women he rushed along the alley and took Charlotte from the young woman's grasp. "Are you ok? Where were you?"

Still coughing, Charlotte attempted to answer him. "I – I was in the bathroom," she coughed, "and by the time I came out everyone was gone. I thought I was going to die."

"How did you get out?"

She continued to cough. "Out of the exit beside the bar."

He held her close. "Thank God you're ok. I didn't know what to think when I couldn't find you."

Charlotte eased out of his comforting embrace. "What do you mean?"

The young paramedic suggested they move out into the street to the awaiting ambulances so Charlotte could receive some much-needed oxygen. Reece wrapped an arm around his fiancée and they followed the paramedic over to the truck.

Reece didn't tell her he had to be rescued by Nathaniel when he went back inside to find her. He didn't want her to feel guilty. She already had enough to deal with.

Sarah and Ed rushed over to Reece. "Where was she?"

"She said she was in the bathroom and when she came out we were all gone."

"Didn't you check the bathroom?" Sarah asked.

"No. The thickening smoke pushed me back. I called but didn't get any answer so I assumed she wasn't in there."

"Lucky for her she made it out ok." Ed moved his gaze to Charlotte sitting in the open doorway of the ambulance, an oxygen mask on her face.

Reece eyes followed his ex-boss's. "Yeah."

"You should be with her," Sarah told him.

"I'm going over there now. You two ok?" He frowned at the pair.

"Yeah, yeah, we're fine. Go on." Ed waved him off.

Reece turned on his heel and marched over to the ambulance. "How're you feeling?"

Charlotte slid the clear plastic mask up over her forehead. "Better. You?"

He gave a heavy sigh. "I'm ok." He stood with his arms folded.

The young paramedic came over to Reece and motioned for him to step away. "Hi, I'm Jo. Charlotte's lucky. It could've been a lot worse if she hadn't got out when she did. She has a minor burn on her right hand and smoke inhalation but other than that she's fine."

Reece eyed the young woman. "No after effects?"

"I shouldn't think so. She just needed some oxygen to clear the smoke from her lungs and I'll monitor her obs over the next fifteen, twenty minutes. Once her breathing is regulated she'll be fine. I've dressed the burn and told her how to manage it so all good." She smiled. "Excuse me. I have to go check on your friends."

The PI watched her walk across the street to Sarah and Ed who were each wrapped in a red blanket."

Nathaniel had made a quick exit to a nearby storage facility to stay out of the daylight. They would meet up with him later to discuss how to end Dracula. Once again, the monster had known their plans. Burning down Decadent Desire was the only way to prevent his death. This time. How had he known?

CHAPTER SIXTY EIGHT

The team would meet up with Nathaniel at St. Joseph's. They'd be safe there because Sarah knew Dracula couldn't step onto consecrated ground. Not like Jacques had been able to. All vampires were different and it had taken years for her to find out Vlad's powers and vulnerabilities. She'd had special weapons created around those weaknesses and planned to use them against him. After losing Dave, then Adrian, it was inconceivable that they had lost Andre and Arianne as well. Too many lives had been forfeited, too much was at stake, and they needed to make sure they ended the monster for good this time.

Nathaniel arrived at the church just after sunset. When he came through the double doors he stood and bowed his head then continued down the carpeted nave to the others.

Sarah was surprised by his mark of respect. She didn't think vampires had any faith.

Whilst waiting for him to arrive they had been discussing what to do to locate Vlad.

Nathaniel stepped around the front pew and took a seat beside Ed. "What plan have you devised to end the monster?"

"Well," Sarah said, standing in front of the group, "first we have to find him."

"I have spoken to someone who can help us. Marcus. He is an informant of sorts and should be able to acquire the information we need. He will be here soon."

Reece stood up and crossed the nave to him. "Is he a…?"

"Yes, he is an immortal." Nathaniel also stood. "And a reliable one."

"Do you pay him for his services?" The PI folded his arms.

"Yes, very handsomely."

"What's to say Dracula doesn't make him a better offer?"

Nathaniel was silent for a moment. "Because he knows the consequences of his betrayal."

"Death?"

He shook his head. "Much worse than death to a vampire. Starvation."

"I thought you didn't believe in doing that."

"Drastic times call for drastic measures. Normally I would not. But we are under siege and require loyal followers."

Reece's left eyebrow rose and he stared at the large black vampire for a long time. Jacques had used the same tactic on one of his own and Nathaniel had been against it. Now he was prepared to do the same thing to help them. The PI wasn't sure he liked the idea of changing Nathaniel's principles to meet their needs. "It's not the way to go, Nathaniel."

"Yes, it is. Otherwise the immortals who work for me will believe I am soft and I cannot allow it."

Reece couldn't argue with that.

"Can we focus, please?" Sarah asked. "I have other weapons I've been keeping safe for my battle with Dracula. They are under here." She led them over to a stone plaque in the floor with a Latin inscription and two knights riding one horse carved into it. "The stone was laid when I first arrived at this church. I didn't think I would ever need to use what's underneath it because I didn't believe I would ever come face to face with Dracula. I hoped I would one day, but I knew it was highly unlikely. And unless I was sent by the church to another location overseas I had no use for them." She gazed around the small group. "Until I met you. And now Dracula is here, of course."

"Can the stone be lifted?" Ed asked, frowning.

Sarah shook her head. "Not by humans." Her eyes moved to Nathaniel. "But I think he can."

"Do you wish for me to open it now?"

"May as well." She gestured for him to attempt to lift it.

Nathaniel bent over and wrapped his fingers around the thick edges, the muscles in his biceps rippled under his clothing as he heaved the solid plaque. It moved a fraction. He tried again. The stone slid away from the opening to reveal a large chest sitting in the cavity beneath.

Sarah kneeled down, took a key from around her neck and slid it into the lock. What she had inside surprised them all. The weaponry was sophisticated and new age. "These were created by the Order of Solomon's Temple, or as they are better known, The Knights Templar. A small number of these holy men were sent back from the future and are among us today."

Everyone stared at her.

"Yes, from the future. Time travel. When the order was disbanded in 1312 by Pope Clement the fifth, many of the knights had been tortured into giving false confessions and burned at the stake, but some managed to escape and was helped by a wizard who sent them a thousand years into the future." She gestured toward the arsenal. "Where would you see anything like this in the past or the present?"

"With everything else we know, I don't doubt it," Reece said. "How do they work?"

"They're powered with ultraviolet light and forged in sanctified silver, the only weapons deadly to immortals. If a vampire attempts to disarm its user they *will* die."

"What year are they from?" Ed asked, his eyes roaming the unique arsenal.

"2312."

"Are they ready to use now?" Reece folded his arms and stared at the array of weapons.

"They are. They're also self-generating. They never run out of power."

"You still have to reload 'em though, right?" Ed frowned.

"Yes, but not as often as regular weapons."

"What about Nathaniel? If we use them he'll be at risk," Reece said.

She smiled. "I have that covered." Nathaniel lifted the tray of weapons out of the chest and Sarah produced a black colored, hooded body suit. "I wasn't sure if I would turn with the blood I've had to inject to keep me alive this long, so they made this for me to wear, just in case."

"It's not gonna fit the big guy," Ed told her, glancing at Nathaniel with a sheepish expression on his face. "I'm not sayin' you're fat or anything."

"I understand."

Sarah stood up. "Yes, it will because it adjusts to the size of its wearer."

"Are you shitting me?" Ed scratched the back of his head. Realizing he'd cursed in a church, he glanced up at the life-sized statue of Jesus on the cross and said, "Sorry."

"Here." She passed the suit to Nathaniel. "Try it on."

The huge vampire raised the garment to eye level and frowned. "You are sure?"

"Go ahead." Sarah motioned for him to try it.

He unzipped it and stepped into the suit. It adjusted to his size, covering him from head to foot.

"Amazing," Charlotte said.

At that moment, the internal doors burst open and six vampires flew into the church.

Sarah threw weapons to each of the team and took up an automatic device which resembled a small, sleek, futuristic jet plane and fired a beam of pure ultraviolet light at one of them. Everyone opened fire, the dim expansive space lighting up like daylight.

Two vampires erupted into flames in the air, their bodies disintegrating, their ashes raining down to the floor like black snow. The other four were super-fast.

Reece aimed at one female and fired. The ultraviolet capsule rocketed toward her and blew a hole in her chest. She shrieked, burst into flames and dissolved into soot.

Ed's device shot small orbs into the air like the large one they'd used in the Vegas tunnel. They spun open, encircling one vampire and emitting enough rays to turn him to ash.

Two remained.

Charlotte fired continuous beams of light at one male. He was fast. Her aim was perfect, although he managed to dodge the slim, bright blue circle. As she aimed and fired again, Reece fired off a shot and both hit the airborne immortal.

The last vampire vanished through the damaged doors in a blur.

Nathaniel took off after him. They couldn't allow him to go back and inform Dracula about the special weapons or what had occurred at the church.

When Reece and his team raced out of St. Joseph's they stopped short. Nathaniel had been captured by four equally as strong vampires and was restrained on the sidewalk. Dracula stood outside the fence line with at least a dozen vampires. More than the team could manage with their small number.

Vlad raised his hand and beckoned. "Come."

Charlotte stepped between Sarah and Ed and descended the stairs.

"Charlotte?" Reece made a move to follow her but Sarah stopped him. "Don't go after her, Reece. He's compelled her."

The PI watched his fiancée walk toward the vampire without hesitation.

"Now we know how he's been able to hinder all of our plans."

"What the fuck?!" Ed's eyes widened and he turned to Sarah. "She got Andre killed?" He shook his head. "Nah, that can't be right."

She motioned to the street. "What more proof do you need? He called her and she went to him. The Charlotte we know wouldn't have even considered it."

Giving the group a self-satisfied smirk, Vlad said, "You are right, *Priest*. I did do as you say and she has proved herself worthy. But now she has served her purpose I have no further need of her." He stared into her eyes and released her.

Charlotte's face paled and she stepped backwards, an agonizing scream escaping her lips. She glanced up at Reece and the others. "I'm sorry. I am so so sorry," then fell to her knees on the sidewalk, sobbing uncontrollably, her mind unable to grasp that she had played a part in Andre's and Arianne's deaths. *Andre. No!* She wrapped her arms about herself and rocked back and forth, the unbearable pain in her heart threatening to destroy her. *And Arianne.* Wracked with guilt, her body shook as she continued to sob with her head in her hands.

Reece's throat constricted, he couldn't breathe. His thoughts felt jumbled, incoherent. His mind teetered on the edge of reality at the realization that the woman he loved had gotten his best friend killed. How could he look at her again? How could he love her now?

Dracula knew he had dealt them a death blow, not by administering actual death, but by reaching into their human emotions with sinister fingers of revenge and ripping out their souls.

He stepped into the idling limousine, pausing to glance over his shoulder at the group surrounded on the stairs. His minions would attack as soon as the car drove away. Whoever remained would be his next target. That is, of course, if anyone survived.

CHAPTER SIXTY NINE

As Dracula's limousine pulled away from the curb, Nathaniel threw off the four holding him down, whipped across the sidewalk, scooped Charlotte into his arms and dashed up the stairs. He dropped her onto her feet on the landing behind the others and took up position in front of the four humans. "Get inside and grab the weapons!"

The group raced into the church, down the nave and collected the weapons from off the right-hand front pew. Nathaniel bolted the exterior doors and hurtled himself down the aisle. Reece, Sarah, Ed and Charlotte were armed. Could they defeat the vampires outside?

Nathaniel covered his face with the hood of the suit he had on. "The doors will not hold them for long."

"Let's spread out so we have a better chance of picking them off," Reece said. "Sarah, how long will these weapons last before they need reloading?"

"We should have plenty to do what we have to." She checked her gun's digital face. She had enough ammunition to take out half of the horde, if she aimed right. "Check the digital read out, it will tell you."

Reece, Ed and Charlotte did as she suggested, they each had enough ultraviolet capsules to take out the dozen vampires. If all went according to plan.

Everyone took up a position at the far end of the pews closest to the entrance, which would allow them to open fire on whoever came through the front doors first.

A heavy thud against the solid doors echoed around the cavernous hall.

Nathaniel flew up to one of the overhead stained glass windows and peered out. The incensed group had ripped a tree from the grounds and was using it to pummel the doors. "They are using a tree as a battering ram." He lowered himself onto the floor and took up a safe position away from the ultraviolet light, but where he could attack from behind.

"Make sure you aim to kill," Reece told his team, swallowing the lump of anxiety wedged in his throat. They didn't have Andre or Arianne to help them now and they were well and truly outnumbered.

The thumping continued to resonate around them. It wouldn't be much longer before the vamps were inside.

Ed joined Reece. "They'll be in here any second."

"Yeah, I know. Let's hope these weapons do their job."

The double red doors burst from their hinges in a spray of splintered debris and the vampires surged inside, some on foot, some in the air.

Everyone sprang from their hiding places and opened fire.

Shrieks and screams erupted around them as one by one the swarming vamps dropped to their deaths. Dracula hadn't planned on them having a means of destroying his horde.

The team fought the remaining members through swirling ash, and ultraviolet beams of light firing at their targets with absolute precision. They had no choice, their lives depended on it.

Sarah strutted along the nave, shooting at anyone who came within a few feet of her. She wished Dracula had stayed to fight. With every fiber of her being she wanted him dead.

A lone vampire swooped in and kicked the weapon from her hand. Sarah lost her balance and fell backwards. Two other vamps whipped down the nave and were about to attack when Reece dashed in front of Sarah and fired at them. Both disintegrated into black ash. He swung around to find the first vampire sinking his fangs into the priest's neck. He fired first, asked questions later. The vamp dissolved into ash all over her.

Reece tugged Sarah to her feet and the pair raced over to where Nathaniel was fist fighting another vampire who had snuck up on him.

Ed charged between the pews and fired continuous rounds at a female about to swoop down and attack Charlotte. "Take that bloodsucker!"

Charlotte rushed up to him. "Thank you," she said, breathless.

"No problem."

Reece and Sarah took off along the nave to the front entrance and scanned the street. No more vampires. Thank God.

"That's it. We got them all," Reece called to the others.

Right at that moment, a vampire lowered himself onto the front landing from above the decimated doorway.

Reece recoiled, raising his weapon, his finger on the trigger.

"Stop!" Nathaniel bellowed, his deep voice booming around the church hall. "He is the informant I told you about."

CHAPTER SEVENTY

Back at Reece's apartment, the group did a debrief of what had occurred at the church and also what the informant had told them. It appeared the monster had fled LA by private jet. He would live to fight another day. Unfortunately.

Charlotte had positioned herself in an armchair by the window away from everyone, not knowing what to say to them or how they felt about her now. She still couldn't believe she'd been feeding Vlad Dracul information about their plans to get rid of him. Only realizing now that, while he'd had her at her most vulnerable, he'd compelled her to betray the people she cared about. She couldn't get her head around the fact that Andre was gone. Really gone.

She glanced across at Reece. He wouldn't even look at her, and she couldn't blame him. The friend he'd loved for over 12 years was never coming back. Could he ever forgive her for her part in Andre's death? A tear slid down her cheek and she discreetly brushed it away and blinked back more threatening to spill. If she were in his shoes she probably wouldn't forgive her either. She had committed the ultimate act of betrayal and people had died because of it.

Sarah stood up and crossed the room to her. "How are you feeling?"

Charlotte glanced up at the priest. "How do you think? I allowed that monster to kill Reece's best friend, how can I live with that?"

Sarah sat down on the footrest beside the armchair. "You had no choice about what you were doing, Charlotte. You were under Dracula's control."

She gave a heavy sigh. "Tell that to Reece. I don't think he'll believe you."

"He'll feel differently once he's had time to think it over. He's grieving and his mind is in another place right now."

Charlotte shook her head. "I know you mean well, Sarah, but I don't think so. And I can't blame him." Another tear slid down her cheek. "What am I going to tell Tommy? He thinks we were married in Vegas. He thinks Reece is going to be his new dad."

Sarah squeezed her hand. "Give it some time. Reece loves you. He's a sensible man, he'll work it out."

"I wish I could believe that."

Reece's serious gaze moved to the women. He could see Sarah was consoling Charlotte. He knew he should have been the one to do it, but he couldn't bring himself to speak to her. Not now. His best friend was dead because of her. Would he ever be able to forgive her? He didn't have an answer. Did he still love her? His heart told him he did, but he wasn't even sure about that.

"Where do you think Drac's gone?" Ed asked.

"I do not know, but if anyone can find out it is Marcus." Nathaniel's eyes moved to the PI. The vampire could sense the turmoil raging inside him. "Reece." His gaze moved to Nathaniel. "You know it is not Charlotte's fault. Once a human is compelled it is as though they were hypnotized. Her subconscious would not allow her to realize what she was doing. And she would not remember it afterward."

"But it still doesn't change the fact that Andre's dead. Does it?" He jerked out of his chair, stalked along the hall to his room and shut the door.

"He'll figure it out. He loves Charlotte." Ed gazed along the hallway. At least he hoped Reece would. Everyone had lost too much already.

Later that evening, Reece, Ed, Nathaniel and Sarah drove to the Double D Investigations office to do a cleanup. Reece needed to keep himself busy, despite grieving for his best friend. They had to locate Dracula and deal with him, and if that meant traveling to another state or even another country that's what they'd do. He couldn't allow the monster to continue his quest to destroy humanity.

Charlotte remained at the apartment alone. She thought it best to give

Reece and the others some space. She felt wholly responsible for what had happened and even though Sarah had reassured her that it wasn't her fault, to her it felt like it was. How could she deny what she had done?

Reece unlocked the office door, swung it back and flicked on the light. He stood at the threshold and gave a heavy sigh. The place was a mess. Smashed computers and chairs, filing cabinets turned upside down and files strewn from one side of the room to the other. It would take some doing to get the office back to working condition. He stepped inside, the others following him in, and closed the door.

Ed gazed around the small space. "Where do you want us to start?"

"Let's each pick a task and work on that until it's finished then move on to the next one as quickly as we can. I'd like to get some kind of sleep tonight, if it's at all possible." The PI wandered over to his upturned desk and picked up the drawers from off the floor.

"Ok. I'll collect up the files. I won't be able to put them together but at least the paperwork will be off the floor," Sarah said.

Nathaniel crossed the room and stood the gray metal filing cabinets on their feet as though they were weightless.

Ed helped Reece turn over his and Andre's desks then set about cleaning up the broken computer components and other objects strewn across the floor.

The four worked systematically for a good three hours and when they stopped for a well-earned break the office looked almost normal again. Reece had ordered pizza from a late-night pizzeria and they were waiting for it to be delivered.

A knock echoed into the room and all heads turned toward the frosted glass and green wood door. "About time," Ed grumbled, wandering across the office.

As he reached the door it flew open and they were confronted by Jacques, Andre's supposed dead brother.

"Shit!" Ed backed away and made a beeline for Reece and the others.

Jacques stood at the threshold, his dark gaze moving from Nathaniel to Ed to Reece and Sarah. "Here you all are. One big happy family."

"I knew you weren't dead." Reece's intense gaze focused on him.

"Well aren't you the clever one. I was quite dead, actually."

Ed frowned. "So how are you here?"

"Why are you here?" Reece moved around his desk and stood next to Nathaniel and Ed.

"One question at a time, if you don't mind." He motioned with his hand. "Aren't you going to invite me in?"

"Whatever you have to say you can say from there." Reece folded his arms and stared at him, incredulous. Now they had this monster to deal with again.

"Very well. I have a proposition for you."

"What could I possibly want from you, Jacques? Haven't you done enough?" The PI glowered at him.

"I think you will want to hear what I have to say."

"So say it."

Jacques smirked at Reece, keeping his dark gaze on him for longer than was necessary. Anticipation hung in the air and the vampire enjoyed the sensation. "I can help you bring my brother back from the dead."

The series continues with the heart-stopping

Book four in the Dark Legacy series

M. A. Anderson

Coming in 2019

Read an excerpt from the first chapter…

CHAPTER ONE

Reece stood with his arms folded and stared at Andre's brother in disbelief. How was he here? Why was he here? It was difficult to get his head around the fact that Jacques was alive, *again*, and his best friend was dead. Being identical twins made it even harder to deal with because looking at him made the gaping hole in his heart hurt like hell. He even sounded more like Andre now because the hint of French accent he once had was gone. The PI's scrutinizing gaze remained on the vampire standing in the doorway. "How can you possibly expect us to believe you? Why should we after everything you've done?"

Jacques reached inside his unbuttoned, calf-length black jacket and produced a glass vial containing a gray powdery substance and held it at eye level. "Because, my dear Detective, this contains some of my brother's ashes," he said, his dark gaze moving from the small bottle in his hand to the four suspicious faces, "and you have a quantity of his blood stored for emergencies. Am I correct?"

"So?" Reece stepped away from the others and stood in the center of the office, his hands on his hips. He wondered how Jacques knew about Andre's blood. How long had he been alive and why had he been keeping tabs on them?

"So that means with both of those elements and a sorcerer's assistance we can bring my brother back from the realm of the dead. That is what you want, isn't it?"

"How do we know what he's tellin' us is true?" Ed remained beside Sarah, arms folded, his disbelieving eyes steadfast on their nemesis.

"Because I am living proof." Jacques spread his arms wide. "How else could I stand here before you now? You saw me die and yet here I am."

Ed glowered at him. "You're a liar and a murderer. Maybe you made us see what you wanted us to see. Maybe you've been alive all this time just waiting for a chance to scheme your way back into our lives. Andre is *dead*."

Sarah gripped his arm and gave him a nervous frown. She didn't think it was a good idea to antagonize Jacques. They had all been on the receiving end of his wrath once before.

"It has been done," Nathaniel said.

Reece's focus moved from Jacques to Nathaniel. "You're sure about that?"

"What I was told came from a reliable source. Someone who has seen the ritual performed." He stepped up beside Reece, his eyes never leaving Jacques for a second. He knew how his former master's mind worked. "Although I have not witnessed it myself, I believe the immortal that provided me with the information told the truth."

A satisfied smirk spread across Jacques' pale, handsome face and his left eyebrow arched. "You see. Now do you believe me?"

The PI swung his head around and scowled at the vampire. "What's in it for you? You wouldn't be here offering help unless it benefited you. So what is it?"

"How shrewd of you, Detective." He returned the vial to the inside pocket of his wool coat and stepped across the threshold. "Yes, there is something I want in return. But I shall leave that for another time." His intense gaze locked onto Reece and he searched the PI's soul. Would he do what he wanted? "Consider my offer carefully. Would you want to pass up the opportunity to have your beloved friend returned to you?"